THE FALCON AND THE OWL

AN ANN KINNEAR SUSPENSE NOVEL

MATTY DALRYMPLE

WILLIAM KINGSFIELD PUBLISHERS

For Wade Walton and Mary Dalrymple, the best cheerleaders an author could hope for.

For my sisters in crime Jane Kelly and Lisa Regan, plot brainstormers extraordinaire.

And to everyone in the general aviation community who is working to keep GA alive and vibrant for the next generation.

'Tis unnatural,
    Even like the deed that's done. On Tuesday last,
    A falcon, towering in her pride of place,
    Was by a mousing owl hawk'd at and kill'd.

Macbeth, William Shakespeare

1

Bryan Calvert straightened from his work, then leaned backwards to ease the kink in his back. The tundra tires on his Cessna 180 had been overdue for replacement and blowing a tire during a landing at the Clinton County field he used as a landing strip would be a rotten way to start his weekend at the cabin.

He glanced at his watch: nine forty-five.

"Eight hours bottle to throttle," he said, and tipped back the last two inches of his second bottle of beer. That put him right for a six o'clock departure the next morning.

He had worked the last of the wing jack legs out of its base when he heard the sound of a vehicle approaching fast, then a spray of gravel hitting the side of the hangar as the vehicle came to a halt. He hefted the heavy metal jack leg in his hand and walked quickly to the hangar's window. There wasn't much violent crime in Avondale Township, Pennsylvania, but there was a first time for everything.

He looked out the window and saw Hal Burridge climbing unsteadily out of his Honda Ridgeline pickup.

"Shit," he muttered under his breath and laid the jack leg on the workbench next to the collection of other tools and equipment he had been using: tire talc, air chuck, pry bar, ratchet wrench.

The hangar door banged open and Hal staggered in. Bryan was struck by the change the last year had wrought in Hal. He had always been thin, but now he was gaunt, his skin stretched too tight over his cheekbones but beginning to hang loose at his neck. When Bryan had first met Hal, he would have guessed his age a decade too low. Now he looked far older than his fifty years.

"What the hell?" Bryan said, exasperated. "If you're going to drive drunk, at least drive slow."

"What do you care?" Hal's words were slurred. He put a hand out and steadied himself on the doorframe.

Bryan tried to swallow down his frustration. "Come on, Hal, we've been friends for a long time. Of course I care what happens to you." He took a step forward and, as he drew closer, he could see tears streaking the older man's cheeks.

Hal choked back a sob. "You weren't so worried about our friendship when you—"

Bryan halted. "When I what?"

"When you … you and Gwen …" Hal swiped his hand across his eyes. "Don't make me say it."

Bryan raised his hands in a conciliatory gesture. "Hal, I don't know what you heard, but if you think Gwen or I were doing anything behind your back, you're wrong."

Now it was Hal's turn to advance across the hangar. "Not you *or* Gwen. You *and* Gwen. I treated you like a son! Let you set up shop at my airport, let you work on Gwen's Extra, on her Lancair. I trusted you with her life!"

He had almost reached Bryan, backing him up against the workbench.

"Hal, I never did anything but take good care of Gwen—" He

stopped and, he couldn't help himself, felt his lips curling up in a smile.

"You *what*?" Hal's voice was almost a shriek. "You son of a bitch!" His bleary eyes scanned the workbench and landed on the jack leg. "You ungrateful bastard!" He grabbed the heavy length of metal.

Hal turned back toward Bryan but lost his balance and almost fell. He caught himself but didn't straighten. He stood hunched over, one hand on a knee, the other holding the jack leg, his eyes on the floor.

"For God's sake, Hal," said Bryan with disgust. "If you have no other reason to sober up, do it so you don't make a fool of yourself in a bar fight."

With a roar, Hal reared back and, as he did, swung the jack leg up blindly.

The movement took Bryan by surprise, and he barely managed to jerk his head back in time to avoid having the metal connect with his jaw. "Goddammit, Hal!"

Hal regained his balance and, in cumbersome slow motion, swung the jack leg back in the other direction.

Bryan grabbed Hal's wrist and twisted, and the weapon fell to the concrete floor with a deafening clang.

Hal slumped back against the workbench.

"Jesus Christ, Hal," said Bryan, breathless from adrenaline, "if you want to hold on to Gwen, get your freakin' act together."

As Bryan bent to pick up the jack leg, he saw Hal's feet turn toward the workbench, his hand move toward its top. He heard the scrape of something moving across its surface.

The pry bar.

Bryan jerked away from Hal and swung the jack leg up to block the attack he anticipated. He barely saw the metal rod connect with the side of Hal's head. He did see the beer bottle that Hal had knocked over roll off the edge of the workbench, the shards scattering in a pretty play of light as it shattered on the concrete floor.

Hal tottered, stiffened, then hit the floor, face down, with a thud.

Bryan staggered back against the workbench, looking wide-eyed at the prone body. His breath was coming fast and his heart was thumping with a jackhammer beat. "Hal?"

There was no movement.

Moving automatically, he picked up the unbroken neck of the beer bottle, then took a step toward the unconscious man. "Hal!"

He was about to bend to check for breath or a pulse when the door of the hangar slammed open and Gwen Burridge stood in the doorway, her auburn hair a tangle, her cheeks flushed.

"What the hell?" She rushed to Hal's side and began to lower herself onto her knees next to him.

"Careful—broken glass," said Bryan.

She glanced at the bottle neck gripped in his hand.

"He attacked me," said Bryan.

She gestured at the bottle neck. "With that?"

"No, with this," he said, lifting the jack leg in his other hand. "I got it away from him. Then I thought he had the pry bar."

"You hit him with the jack leg?"

"Yes."

"Where?"

"In the head."

She bent and tugged at the sleeve of Hal's shirt, trying to roll him over.

"The glass—" began Bryan.

"If you hit him in the head with a wing jack leg," she retorted, "a couple of splinters in his back aren't going to be his biggest worry."

Bryan set the bottle neck and the jack leg on the workbench and helped her roll Hal onto his back.

His eyes were closed, his skin ashen. There was no blood, just a faint red mark at his temple.

Gwen knelt next to him—Bryan could tell from her wince that she had knelt on a sliver of glass—and pressed her fingers to Hal's neck.

"Is he okay?" Bryan asked, his voice tight.

Gwen looked up at Bryan. Her chalk-white face and wide eyes were her only answer.

G wen stood, pulled her phone out of her pocket, and tapped. "Sweep a clear place on either side of him."

Bryan grabbed a whisk broom off the pegboard over the workbench and quickly swept two glass-free areas as Gwen tapped and scrolled.

"Are you calling 911?" he asked.

"Thirty compressions to two breaths," she muttered, then slipped her phone back into her pocket. "Which do you want to do?"

He tossed the whisk broom onto the workbench. "What about 911?"

She knelt next to Hal. "I'll do the breaths."

She tilted Hal's head back, sealed her mouth over his, and blew. She took a quick breath and blew again. "Thirty compressions to two breaths," she said without looking up.

Bryan knelt on Hal's other side, locked his hands together as he recalled being taught back in high school, positioned them over Hal's sternum, and pressed. "One, two, three, four ..." His eye wandered to the large clock over the workbench, and he unconsciously adjusted his rhythm to match the ticks of the second hand. When he reached thirty, Gwen gave two breaths, then he resumed the compressions. "One, two, three, four ..."

After two rounds, Gwen checked for a pulse.

"Nothing." She bent again to Hal's mouth and gave two breaths. "Compressions."

Bryan watched the second hand of the clock over the workbench sweep through five circuits, Gwen's checks for a pulse yielding no sign of life. Finally, he sat back on his heels. "We're not doing any good." He pulled his phone out of his pocket.

"What are you doing?" she asked, her voice rising.

"I'm calling 911."

"What do you think they're going to be able to do for him that we're not doing?"

"We're not experts. They have equipment and meds."

She lowered herself into a sitting position. Her face was flushed, her hair falling in her eyes. "It doesn't matter. He's gone."

"Don't you want to see if he can be saved?"

She scrambled to her feet. "We tried, Bryan! We tried to save him and it was no use!"

He got to his feet as well. "You don't know that for sure."

She put her balled fists on her hips. "Okay, say they came with their equipment and their meds. Say they hooked him up and shot him full of whatever they have that would bring him back to life. How long would that take? What if they actually got his heart going again? How do you think that would work out?"

She glared at him and he glared back.

"I'll tell you how it would work out," she continued. "He'd be a vegetable. And the same would have been true even if we had called as soon as it happened. The nearest ambulance is miles away—they couldn't have gotten here in time, the damage would already have been done." She crossed her arms. "Especially if this happened because you hit him in the head."

"It was an accident. It was self-defense!"

"Well, which was it—an accident or self-defense? Your lawyer's going to want to know."

"He attacked me!"

"A fifty-year-old drunk came after you with a broken beer bottle and you hit him in the head with a jack leg and killed him."

"He tried to kill me with the jack leg first!"

"Which you evidently got away from him, unscathed, as far as I can see."

"Whose side are you on?"

"I'm on your side, Bryan. No one is going to believe that it was self-defense ... especially if they find out about us."

He looked for a long moment at Hal's body, then slowly put the phone back in his pocket.

"How did he find out?" he asked.

She sat heavily on one of the stools next to the workbench. "We had an argument."

"About us?"

"Not at first. It started out about the airport." She glanced toward Hal's body, then at Bryan. "He told me he and Arno are going to sell the property to developers—Turriff Brothers."

Bryan stared at her for a moment, then dropped onto the second workbench stool. "Holy Christ."

"That's right—a whole row of shoddily built McMansions where Runway Two-four is now. They can turn the FBO into the community center."

"What the hell was he thinking?"

She sucked in a deep breath. "He was thinking that he and I could go somewhere else. Get a fresh start."

"You don't need a fresh start. You need to—"

She cut him off with a slash of her hand. "I'm not having that discussion now."

"And tonight was the first time he mentioned selling the airport?"

"He had mentioned it before, but I had talked him out of it—or at least I thought I had. Arno must have worn him down."

"I had heard rumors, but there are always rumors. Even if the rumors were true, I didn't think Hal would cave." He ran his hand down his face. "Who else knows?"

"He said just him and Arno. And me. And now you."

"And they already signed the contract?"

"Evidently Arno signed it earlier today, then Hal brought it home to sign."

Bryan looked back at Hal's body. Gwen turned her gaze toward the darkness-blackened window.

After a moment, he said, "There's only one copy of the contract? Then just tear it up. If it's true that no one knows other than us and Arno, it will just be Arno's word that Hal signed it."

She glared at him. "I would tear it up if I knew where it was. Hal said he had put it somewhere safe—probably because he was afraid I'd do exactly that when he told me what he had done."

"Christ almighty," groaned Bryan.

"No airport, no airplanes, no need for an airplane mechanic," she continued. "You'll be out of a job, and if we report this, that will make this look even more suspicious."

He looked at her, guarded. "What are you suggesting?"

"I'm suggesting that it would be better for you if the police didn't think Hal had died after you and he had a brawl in your hangar."

"And after you and he had an argument about the two of us screwing around."

"I'm not the one who was standing over him holding a wing jack leg and a broken beer bottle!"

"Don't act like you're covering up Hal's death just for me," he shot back. "Your fans wouldn't be too happy if they found out what happened here tonight. Your sponsors wouldn't be too happy either."

She appeared ready to respond, then raised her hand in a tired acknowledgement. "I know, I know. It's better for both of us if no one knows what happened. We have other things to worry about."

He ran his fingers through his hair, then took a deep breath. "How did you get from the Turriff Brothers deal to us?"

"I told him he needed to stop letting Arno order him around. I told him he had a responsibility to the airport community and he better step up to it. He said his responsibility was to me, and I told him he had stopped living up to his responsibility to me a year ago."

"Including certain husbandly responsibilities?"

"That's evidently what he thought I meant. I told him not to be silly, that I was talking about the airport, but I guess I don't have much of a poker face. Plus, by that time, I was trying to make a point. I would never have cheated on him before he became a drunk."

"Gee, thanks."

"Don't act like it was more than it was."

Bryan glanced toward the body, then down at his hands. After a moment, he looked up at Gwen again.

"He did what he did because of you."

She stood. "Nobody becomes a drunk because of someone else. They become a drunk because they can't stand themselves."

Bryan pushed himself off the stool, walked to the Cessna, and gripped the edge of the wing. "Shit. Just ... shit. All I ever wanted was to be able to tinker with planes, go flying, go fishing, and be left alone."

"That life is out the window if anyone finds out about this.

Then you can kiss fishing and flying goodbye. And a pretty boy like you isn't likely to be left alone in prison."

He glared at her. "I put my phone away, didn't I? My cousin was in Graterford. He never got out—he died of blood poisoning —but I heard the stories about what happened to him in there. You don't need to keep trying to convince me."

She clamped her lips together. After a moment, she gave a curt nod. "Fine."

Bryan dropped his eyes to the ground, drew a deep breath, then turned an exhausted gaze toward Gwen. "How much longer do you think you can keep it up?"

She set her shoulders in a posture he had seen many times —before a race, or when faced with anyone who questioned a decision she had made. "I just need to get to White Lake next month. I'm going to fly the air races and then I'll retire."

"Jesus, Gwen, I can't believe you're really going to fly White Lake. It's not like you have the whole sky to yourself—you're a couple of plane lengths from the other racers."

"I'll withdraw if I have to."

He eyed her. "No, you won't. I've never seen you make a plan and not stick with it until the bitter end."

"It's a marked course in broad daylight. I don't need to win, I just need to fly. I won't take any stupid chances."

"The whole thing is a stupid chance."

She waved her hand. "I'm not going to argue with you about that right now. We have other things to worry about. What do we do with ..." She gestured toward Hal. "You were going to the cabin this weekend, right?"

"Tomorrow morning."

"And you've mentioned the trip to some people?"

"Sure, a couple."

"Go up tonight and take him with you. You go up there all the time, so the trip isn't going to make anyone suspicious, and leaving tonight instead of tomorrow morning can be easily explained, if anyone even notices."

Bryan's eyes drifted to the empty beer bottle still standing on the workbench, and then to the remains of the second bottle scattered across the floor.

"You're okay to fly?" she asked.

"Under the circumstances, I guess I have to be."

"I'll get rid of the bottles." She glanced around the hangar and her eyes fell on a plastic grocery bag balled up on the work-bench. "Let's put the broken bottle in that."

He got a dustpan down from the pegboard and they began sweeping up the shards of glass.

"Your cabin's right on the Susquehanna, right?" she asked as they worked. "You could weigh down—" she waved her hand toward the body without looking at it, "—and put it in the river."

"It's not deep enough."

"How about burying it?"

"That would probably be better. There are thousands of acres of state forest and game land up there where no one would find him, even if they think to look for him in Clinton County. They don't call it the Pennsylvania Wilds for nothing." He emptied the last of the glass shards into the bag Gwen was hold-ing, straightened, and glanced toward the window. "What do we do with his pickup?"

"I'll take care of it," she replied. "I rode my bike over from the house, I'll just load it into the back of the truck." She hesitated. "But I don't know what the deal is with security cameras on the airport property. What if there's video showing Hal driving the Ridgeline to the hangar and me driving it away?"

"I helped Hal install the cameras. There are only a couple of them, and they're all pointed at your hangar. Doesn't he usually come in by the back gate?"

"Yes. It's the closest to the house. That's how I came."

"There are no cameras back there. What are you going to do with the truck?"

"The less you know, the better," she said. "You have a vehicle up at the cabin, right?"

"Yeah, I have an old Jeep at the airstrip. It'll be easy to get him from the plane into the Jeep."

He pulled his phone out of his pocket.

"Who are you calling?" she asked, her voice rising.

"Calm down, I need to get George to turn on the lights."

"Who's George? What lights?"

"George is the guy who owns the field where I land. We rigged lights so I can land at night, but I can't turn them on from the air—he needs to turn them on. I'm a good pilot, but not so good that I can land on a homemade airstrip on a moonless night."

"Does George come out to the plane when you land?"

"Are you kidding? He barely comes out of his house. He wouldn't even take my phone calls if I wasn't giving him a couple hundred bucks a month to use the field." As he waited for George to answer, he pointed to the wing jack leg where it lay on the workbench. "Wipe that down."

"Jesus, Bryan, wipe it down yourself."

After Bryan made the arrangements with George, he slipped the phone into his pocket.

Gwen stepped reluctantly over to the body. "You pick him up under his arms. I'll get his legs."

Bryan pushed the body into a sitting position, squatted behind it, and got his arms around Hal's chest. Gwen hooked her arms under Hal's legs, and they hoisted him off the ground.

"This is a lot easier than it would have been a year ago," he said. "When did he get so thin?"

"When all his calories started coming from whiskey."

The fact that Bryan's Cessna had doors on both sides eased

their task somewhat, although the wing strut was a challenge to work around and the cockpit space was as cramped as in any general aviation aircraft. Bryan was glad Gwen wasn't some petite thing—she was almost as tall as he was and, he knew from personal experience, there was plenty of muscle underneath the curves.

When they had the body propped precariously up on the passenger seat, Bryan climbed into the pilot's seat to tug the body into position as Gwen hoisted Hal's legs in.

"Hold his torso up so I can get the seatbelt fastened around him," said Bryan.

Gwen stepped back and wiped a strand of hair out of her eyes with the back of her hand. "He won't care if he bumps his head in turbulence."

"I don't want him falling forward into the yoke."

After a brief hesitation, Gwen stepped back up to the plane and held Hal's torso upright until Brian got the seatbelt fastened, then pressed the passenger-side door closed as Bryan climbed out of the cockpit.

"How long were you planning to stay up at the cabin?" she asked.

"Couple of days."

"Don't change your plans. And don't call me. We don't want there to be a record of a call in case the police get involved."

"The police. Holy Christ." He grabbed the jack leg off the workbench, rubbed it down with a rag, and returned it to its usual place. After a moment's hesitation, he tossed the rag into the plane.

"It'll be fine," she said, her tone resuming its usual briskness. She glanced around the hangar, perhaps for other telltale signs of Hal's presence. "We'll be fine."

"'Fine' is not a word I would use to describe this situation."

She wheeled on him. "You know what I mean. He was my husband, Bryan. I know it's not fine."

He held up his hands. "I get it." He dropped his hands and sighed. "I just thought when we were done with Preston that we were done with all this cloak and dagger shit."

She snatched the intact beer bottle off the workbench and dropped it into the plastic grocery bag. "Let's get through this and then you can have a crisis of conscience."

Gwen helped Bryan put away the remaining tools and equipment, ensuring the hangar was as tidy as Bryan would normally leave it before any trip to his cabin. Then he followed her out of the hangar and helped her lift her bike into the back of Hal's truck.

"You'll be okay ... you know ... at night?" he asked.

"Fine. I'll be fine. I'll see you when you get back."

Without a backward glance, she climbed into the truck, started it up, and rolled slowly away.

3

B ryan checked the needle, ball, and airspeed as he climbed away from Avondale Airport, then he turned northwest.

His regular route to Clinton County would keep him out of controlled airspace and he never got flight following—he didn't need some controller in the Harrisburg tower babysitting him. His stomach twisted with a moment of panic—the plane's transponder would provide a record of the flight—then his insides unclenched. There was no need to keep a secret of the flight, just the flight's cargo.

He replayed what had happened in the hangar. Could he have waited that extra second that would have enabled him to see that Hal had just knocked over the beer bottle, not picked up the pry bar from the bench? Could he have reacted in a way that would have meant that Hal Burridge's body would not now be strapped into the seat beside him, headed for an unmarked grave in the Clinton County forest? He shook his head. If it *had* been the pry bar that Hal had picked up, and if Bryan had waited that extra second, it might have been Bryan who was heading for an unmarked grave.

He scanned the six-pack of instruments in the panel of the Cessna, lit not only by their own luminescence but also by the red light that suffused the interior, providing illumination without degrading his night vision. Airspeed indicator, altimeter, vertical speed indicator, attitude indicator, heading indicator, and turn coordinator. None of that fancy glass-panel flying for him. That wasn't real flying, that was just playing a video game in the air.

If Hal had managed to catch him with a lucky swing of the wing jack leg, would he have been on the phone to 911 the next minute, undeterred by the thought of the consequences to himself? A year ago, Hal would have made that call to 911. But, thought Bryan, a year ago Hal wouldn't have had any reason to be swinging a wing jack leg at his wife's mechanic's head.

He ran through what he would do when he landed. He didn't have to worry about George—he didn't even interact with him to give him the monthly check, just left it in a battered mailbox the old man had set up next to the Cessna's tie-down. Even if George spied on Bryan from his house, there was no problem. Bryan parked the plane on the opposite end of the airstrip from George's house, the night was moonless, and not even the airstrip lights would illuminate his activities. He was usually barely on the ground before George flipped off the lights—"No need to waste the electric," as he said.

It was lucky he had the Jeep at the airstrip. He would pull the Jeep up to the plane, his usual practice if he had any gear to unload, and transfer the body to the back of the vehicle. He'd wait until the morning to bury it since, if he lit a lantern to illuminate his work while it was still dark, he might attract the attention of a camper or game warden. He'd cover the body with a tarp, drive to the cabin, and when the sun rose, he would follow one of the logging roads into the woods and pick out Hal's final resting place.

He scanned the instruments, adjusted his directional gyro, and thought back to the trip he had made to Clinton County with Hal two years before.

~

HAL HAD APPEARED in the door of Bryan's hangar, canvas duffle bag slung over his shoulder, a cooler in his arms. The sun was just peeking over the low fringe of trees on the far side of the runway, behind the chain link fence that separated the airport from the quarry property. Its beam cut through the hangar, illuminating motes of dust that hung in the warm August air.

"Nice flying weather," said Hal.

"Yup," said Bryan. "Perfect." He nodded toward the cooler. "Want me to load that up?"

"Sure." Hal handed over the cooler.

"Jesus," said Bryan, "what have you got in here?"

"Couple of six-packs from Kennett Brewing Company, couple of bottles of Cab, and a couple of ribeyes I picked up at the market." Hal suddenly looked abashed. "Hope that's okay."

Bryan laughed. "It's okay by me—I'm used to the guys'-weekend-away contribution being a case of Bud in cans."

Hal followed Bryan to the plane, where Bryan loaded the cooler into the back. "I appreciate you inviting me along to the cabin. I know you like your private time."

"No problem. Just as long as you don't expect a crazy bachelor weekend away."

Hal laughed. "Not really my style. I wish I could offer to take us up in the Lance, but off-airport landings are not exactly my area of expertise. A runway leading to a terminal serving a good burger is more my speed."

"I don't mind taking the Cessna," Bryan replied. "The tundra tires make it easy."

Hal tossed his duffel bag into the back of the Cessna, then helped Bryan pull the plane out of the hangar.

It had been a long time since Bryan had taken anyone with him to his cabin up in Clinton County. There was the occasional girlfriend—usually never more than once or twice—and once a buddy from high school, but Hal was correct in his under-standing that Bryan had bought the cabin as his place to be alone. Some might have considered his life back in Chester County—the maintenance shop that he ran at Avondale Airport, his small apartment in nearby West Grove—to be sufficiently solitary, but there were always people around. The owners of the airplanes he worked on would stop by the shop to check on the status of maintenance or a repair and expect to engage in a little hangar flying with him while they were there—recounting their latest close call, or the misfortunes of a fellow pilot. The people he encountered in the Chester County bars and brew pubs in his quest for live music always seemed eager to compare notes on bands and venues with fellow fans. He didn't mind so much, but he would have been just as happy working on the planes or listening to the music undisturbed.

But when Hal had visited the hangar while Bryan was finishing up the inspection on his Lance, he had noticed the photos tacked up above the workbench. They were just cell phone shots, but they pleased Bryan and he had gotten prints made: the cabin against a vivid orange-and-red backdrop of autumn leaves. A creek, cool under the dappled shade of over-hanging trees, bubbling over rounded rocks, a slice of blue sky visible through the branches. And the one he was most pleased with: a shot from an overlook at Hyner View State Park capturing a hang glider in flight, the graceful curve of Highway 120 cutting through the tree-covered mountains, a muddy Susquehanna wending its way through the scene.

"This your cabin?" Hal asked, pointing to the log structure.

Bryan stepped up beside him, wiping oil off his hands with a rag. "Yeah."

"Hunting camp?"

"Probably was originally built as that, but I'm not a hunter myself. Fishing's my thing."

Hal looked over the other photos. "Nice pictures. You have a good eye."

Hal was too polite to invite himself to the cabin, but he lingered at the workbench, gazing at the photos.

"Any news from Gwen about the flight to White Lake?"

"She was concerned that the spare engine might not arrive in time, but the truck showed up with it this morning."

"That'll make the trip back a little more relaxing."

"Yeah, I wouldn't want to be flying a plane powered by an engine that just took that beating in the races."

"You going out for the races?" asked Bryan.

"Yeah, I'm leaving on Wednesday. I have some Scanridge Transport meetings I need to be here for early in the week. Arno has some good ideas—extending our routes further west, adding some residential delivery services that most of the other trucking companies aren't offering yet—but it's going to be pricey." He smiled. "Have to stay around to make sure he doesn't get ahead of himself. How about you?"

"Leaving Monday."

"Taking the Cessna?"

"No, I can't take the time—I'm flying commercial." He glanced toward the row of photos. "I'm going up to the cabin this weekend—want to come along?"

Hal raised his eyebrows, evidently as surprised by the offer as Bryan was.

"If it wouldn't cramp your style ..."

"Not much 'styling' going on in Clinton County," said Bryan.

"Not much of anything going on, in fact, but you're welcome to come along if you'd just like a weekend away."

"Sure, sure, that would be great," said Hal, clearly cheered by the idea.

After they took off from Avondale into a morning of "severe clear," Bryan gave Hal a turn at the controls, prompting him through the ways in which the Cessna, with its minimal instrumentation, differed from Hal's glass-paneled Lance. Hal might have poked fun at his own flying as nothing more than a quest for the canonical hundred-dollar hamburger, but he had a sure touch at the controls, even in the unfamiliar aircraft. Bryan was also relieved to find that he wasn't the type of passenger who felt the need to fill the quiet of the flight with conversation.

Bryan took the controls again for the landing, angling the plane down between the tree-covered ridges. Hal helped unload the fishing equipment from the plane into the Jeep, whistling an almost inaudible rendition of something that sounded operatic, pointing out a deer watching them at the verge between the mowed field and the woods. Bryan hadn't seen him this upbeat since Gwen had left for White Lake.

By the time they reached the cabin, Bryan was anxious to get to the creek for some fishing.

"Want to come?" he asked Hal, not as reluctant as he usually was about inviting someone along. "I have extra gear you can use."

"No, thanks—if it's okay with you I think I'll take a run, loosen up after the flight."

"Sure, no problem."

When Bryan returned a few hours later, he found Hal sitting on the porch paging through a copy of a magazine called *Logistics Management*. Bryan pulled a worn copy of *Trout Madness* out of the shelf in the cabin and that's what they did that evening, moving from the porch into the cabin as the temperature dipped after the sun went down. When they got hungry, Bryan cooked up the fish he had caught—they had decided to have a steak-and-eggs breakfast with the ribeyes—along with a few ears of corn. Bryan had a couple of beers, and Hal opened one of the bottles of Cabernet.

Saturday was much the same, Bryan going fishing while Hal was content to hang out at the cabin, reading and taking periodic hikes through the surrounding fields and woods.

On Saturday evening, they went into Lock Haven for dinner at Bryan's regular hangout, the West Branch Bar and Grill, which in Bryan's opinion served the best burgers in Clinton County. An interview with Gwen from the White Lake Air Races was scheduled to air at eight o'clock, and Hal called ahead to make sure that they could watch it in the bar.

The bartender brought them a pair of Yuenglings and, at Hal's request, switched the channel on the big-screen TV from a stock car race to the sports channel that would carry Gwen's interview. Fortunately, the other patrons seemed happy to watch any sports-themed channel. The burgers when they arrived were as good as ever—each bite necessitating a lean over the plate to catch escaping dollops of mayo and juice from the ripe tomatoes.

"Any more updates from Gwen?" asked Bryan.

"You know she's loving every minute of it," Hal said with a smile. "Registration, tech inspection, practice, not to mention dinners with the sponsors." He took a sip of his beer. "I wish she'd get a ferry pilot. It makes for a long time away when she flies out there herself."

"I'm guessing she doesn't want anyone else flying the Lancair," said Bryan, taking a swallow of beer.

"Yeah, especially after the race. She wants to baby it home."

"She could have the wings removed—truck it back."

Hal sighed. "I've suggested that, but she's not interested." He looked up at the TV and straightened on his stool. "There she is."

A man with a microphone stood next to Gwen Burridge, who was wearing a body-hugging silver flight suit, her visored helmet held under her arm, extra-dark round sunglasses lending her an air of old Hollywood glamour that was accentuated by the auburn waves that always reminded Bryan of a World War 2 pin-up. The bar was too loud to hear the audio, but Hal gazed raptly at the picture. The reporter appeared transfixed by whatever Gwen was saying as well.

"I could do that," said a slurred voice that cut through the din of the crowded bar.

Bryan looked over Hal's shoulder at the speaker. He was about Bryan's age, with a shaved head that reflected the light from a flickering neon beer sign and a neck that was inked with a snake whose jaws gaped open just behind his ear. The sheared-off sleeves of his denim jacket revealed the kind of muscles that only hours of pumping iron could produce. An empty stool separated him from Hal. The man leered at the screen.

"Check out them tits."

Hal turned slowly on his stool. "That's my wife."

Bryan had thought back to this moment off and on over the intervening years. Hal Burridge in a bar that he didn't know, surrounded by strangers, turning on his stool to face this man two decades younger than he was. Bryan was a regular, but he had no illusions that the bartender would take their side over the locals. His hand tightened around his beer bottle.

The young man and Hal locked eyes for a few long seconds, and Bryan could sense the anticipation that rippled through the few people close enough to overhear the exchange. Then the young man lifted his beer to Hal.

"Lucky man."

Hal lifted his own beer. "I am."

THE JOSTLE of a pocket of turbulence brought Bryan back to the gruesome task at hand. He glanced over at Hal's body just as the plane hit another bump. He jumped as Hal's hand, which had been resting on his leg, slid off and dangled at his side.

"Goddamn, Hal, keep still over there," he said with a nervous laugh. He slowed the plane a bit in view of the turbulence. "Wish I could have seen whatever that guy in the bar saw in your face," he murmured. "That took balls." He laughed softly. "But then is there anything you wouldn't have done for Gwen?"

There were plenty of men who had fallen under Gwen Burridge's spell. Hal. Himself, he thought with a grim smile. Preston Gilman.

Preston had been another of Gwen's admirers, although nothing like Hal: short, chubby, bespectacled ... sober. Although none too careful with his pre-flight checks. The final NTSB report had deemed the cause of Gilman's crash to be fuel depletion caused by a loose fuel line. Bryan glanced at his own fuel gauge and switched from the right tank to the left.

"The Falcon sure casts a spell, doesn't she? Hope things turn out better for me than they did for you and Preston. But Jesus, Hal, selling the airport? What the hell were you thinking?"

Bryan's A&P business at Avondale was sweet—he wouldn't be likely to find another position as good, if he could find one at all. He could keep working on Gwen's Extra and her Lancair, but that wouldn't bring in enough money to maintain even his modest lifestyle. In any case, the Peregrine Falcon claimed she was going to retire after the White Lake Air Races in August, just a month away. Assuming she stuck with that plan, his comfortable life was about to come to an end one way or the other.

His thoughts drifted to who else might know about his affair with Gwen. "It hardly counted as an *affair*," he muttered. "We were just having some fun." He shot a glance at the body in the seat beside his, then returned his gaze to the instruments. "It started the week you were attending that trucking conference in Las Vegas—but how much of that conference did you really attend ... and of the parts you did attend, how much do you remember? You were so out of it, it seemed like a safe bet that you wouldn't figure out what was going on. I certainly didn't brag to anyone—no one's business but mine and Gwen's. But you wouldn't have told anyone else even if you knew, right, Hal? Too proud to let word get out that the love of your life had been unfaithful to you."

Would Gwen stay faithful to her agreement with Bryan to keep the circumstances of Hal's death secret? Bryan snorted out a bitter laugh. "I don't fool myself that I'm anything but a means to an end for her," he said. "The ends being a well-maintained airplane or a well-serviced libido. If things go tango uniform, she'll throw me to the wolves in a minute to save herself and her career. Am I right, Hal?" He scanned the instruments again. "But I have some ammunition of my own, if I need it."

But he had no desire to end the Falcon's career prematurely. He drew a deep breath. Look what had already been done in the name of her career.

4

Gwen pulled the Ridgeline carefully into the driveway of a handsome but modestly sized house built in the mid-century modern style. She hadn't bothered with gloves or some cobbled-together alternative since she often drove Hal's truck during the day. If the police felt the need to dust for fingerprints, they shouldn't be surprised to find hers on the wheel.

The house had been Hal's before he had met her. When they got together, he had offered to buy something larger and grander, but she was happy with this—especially the location, just a few miles from the airport. For her it was mainly a place to sleep. If she was awake, she was at the airport. If there was money to be spent, she spent it on planes or equipment, especially now that she had product sponsorships and it was her own money and not Hal's that she was spending.

Taking the plastic grocery bag containing the beer bottle and glass shards with her, she followed the path from the driveway to the back door, which led to the sunroom and kitchen. She put the bag on the kitchen counter, acutely aware of the window-lined space that turned the illuminated interior into a spot-lit stage for anyone outside, then continued on to Hal's office. She started for the bar cabinet, then paused. It was likely Arno had the contract, but not out of the question that Hal had brought it home. She detoured to his desk.

The top was covered with the detritus of a distracted mind. A coffee-ring-stained copy of *IFR Magazine* lay next to a few crumpled paper towels. One of a jumble of felt-tipped pens had lodged its uncapped end against a pile of unpaid bills, leaching its red ink like blood into the fibers of the paper. It was not a desk she would have associated with the fastidious man she had married five years before.

She shuffled through the papers on the blotter, then eyed the precarious stacks that formed a parapet at the edges of the desk. A not-so-fine coating of dust suggested that they hadn't been touched in months, but she would look through them if the contract didn't turn up elsewhere first.

Leaving the desk, she went to a Frederick Wagner pastel of the Philadelphia skyline and swung it to one side, revealing a wall safe. She stood gazing at the dial for a moment. Hal had told her what the combination was years ago, but she never thought she'd need to know it. She tried the day, month, and year of their wedding. The safe stayed locked. She tried other variations—year, month, day—and other dates—his birthday, her birthday—but none worked. With a frustrated sigh, she swung the painting back into place and, grabbing one of the paper towels from the desk, turned back to her original destination.

The bar cabinet held a half-full bottle of Johnnie Walker Gold Label, with a few full bottles in reserve behind it. Using the paper towel, she gingerly picked up the bottle. Her fingerprints here would be harder to explain, and she needed to preserve the evidence of Hal's handling of the bottle. She went to the kitchen and, after carefully working the cap out of the bottle, poured its contents down the drain. Setting the empty Scotch bottle aside, she turned her attention to the beer bottles.

She had thought about just tossing them out during the drive to the house, but if the police got involved and somehow found them on the relatively litter-free road between the airport and the Burridges' home, it wouldn't look good, and she was loathe to extend the drive just to find another place to dispose of them. She also realized she didn't have a clear sense of how the broken bottle had factored into the altercation between Bryan and Hal. It had Bryan's fingerprints on it—and perhaps some evidence that would link it to Hal as well—and it would be tricky to wipe the shards clean. She'd make sure that the bottles ended up in a place—and in a condition—that would make any analysis problematic.

She went to the pantry and got a cardboard carrier six-pack of HopDevil, the same type of beer Bryan had been drinking in the hangar. Thank God Hal and Bryan had similar tastes in beer. She put two of the bottles in the refrigerator, then poured out the contents of the remaining four bottles. She replaced the four empty bottles, plus the intact bottle from Bryan's hangar, in the cardboard carrier, and placed that in the plastic grocery bag, which still contained the swept-up shards of the broken bottle.

Carefully gathering up the bag and using the paper towel to pick up the empty Johnnie Walker bottle, she returned to the pickup and ventured again onto the nearly deserted roads, heading back in the direction of the airport.

A few minutes later, she pulled onto a dirt road that led to the back of the quarry whose property adjoined the airport. The quarry was surrounded by a chain link fence, the road into it blocked by a gate. She got a key out of the cupholder, climbed out of the truck, and unlocked the padlock on the chain securing the gate.

Years before, when the builders had needed to get rid of the dirt that was excavated to pour the slab for Gwen's hangar, the quarry's owner had given Hal the okay to dump it on the property and had given him a key to the back gate. The owner had never asked for the key back.

Before Preston, Hal had enjoyed taking his dog, Rosie, for runs there. After Preston, and after Rosie had succumbed to old age, Hal had gone to the quarry to drink. More than once in the last year, Gwen had gotten a phone call from one of the quarry employees asking that she come get her husband, passed out in the bed of his pickup. She credited the character of the man she had first met at Avondale Airport—the character that had made it easy for Hal to talk the quarry owner into giving him a key to the property—with the fact that they called her and not the police.

If anyone called her this time, it would be to report that they had found the pickup but not the driver.

She dropped the key back in the cupholder and maneuvered the truck carefully over the rutted track of the dirt road that led through the wooded portion of the property. After a short distance, the branches arching over the road gave way to a starry sky, and the headlights illuminated a packed dirt-and-gravel parking area, then scrubby grass that stretched away into the darkness. She had almost come to a halt when she heard a thump on the bumper.

"Dammit!"

She knew what she had hit—she had just misjudged its location.

She backed up a few feet and killed the engine, then got a flashlight out of the glove compartment and climbed out. She wasn't overly worried about the light being seen—the pit on this side of the quarry was no longer used, and the active pits were several hundred yards away, beyond a stand of trees.

This was where Hal had always parked. In fact, he had come

here so often that he built a bench for himself, and erected a lower bench for Rosie, a now-rotting blanket tacked to its top. It was Rosie's bench that Gwen had bumped. There wasn't much damage to it—just a small tear in the blanket where the material had caught on the truck's bumper.

She supposed a scratch on the bumper would make it look even more as if her drunkard husband had been the driver.

She retrieved the plastic grocery bag from the truck. Then, following the flashlight's puddle of illumination, she made her way carefully across the grassy field, which pitched down in a gentle slope. When she reached the area where a few boulders shouldered their way up through the rocky soil, she knew she was nearing the pit and slowed her pace even further. After a few more steps, she stopped and shone the flashlight forward.

The beam of light disappeared into the darkness, not strong enough to reach the other side of the pit, and likely not strong enough to reach its bottom, although Gwen didn't intend to get close enough to the edge to find out. Swinging her arm a few times to judge the weight of the bag, she let go on a forward swing, sending the bag sailing into the pit. A few seconds later, she heard the splash as it hit the water—hopefully now six broken bottles, not just one. Even if they pulled up the bag during the search for Hal's body, she couldn't imagine that it would raise any eyebrows. The quarry seemed like the kind of place where surreptitious beer-drinking might take place, and she had no doubt other six-packs had been disposed of in this way.

When she got back to the pickup, she replaced the flashlight in the glove compartment, and, leaving the empty Johnnie Walker bottle on the passenger seat, pulled her bike from the back. She flicked on the bike's headlight, but even so, it wasn't long before she hit a rut hidden in the shadows dancing in its beam and went sprawling off the bike. Swearing, she climbed to her feet. She hated that kind of clumsiness. Scrapes on her hands sent out a sting of remonstrance. She wouldn't be pushing the goddamned bike through the goddamned quarry in the dead of night if her goddamned husband hadn't decided to sell the airport out from under her.

Jerking the bike upright, she pushed it up the dirt road.

She didn't fool herself that the scene she had staged would be enough to convince the police that Hal had thrown himself into the water-filled pit, but they would certainly spend time pursuing that possibility, and she guessed that the more time that passed with no sign of Hal, the better it would be for her. And for Bryan, of course.

She knew she would have to contact the police. No matter how erratic Hal's behavior had been over the last year, it would undoubtedly generate suspicion if she didn't. However, for a day or so, it would be perfectly reasonable for her—and the police— to assume that her husband was just on another bender. They had gotten their fair share of calls about Hal Burridge—calls from people less sympathetic than the quarry employees—to make it an obvious assumption.

She was supposed to fly to Dover, Delaware, in the morning for an aerobatic demonstration in the afternoon and a dinner in her honor in the evening, returning home the following morning. She would contact the police when she returned from Dover.

With each step of a plan thought through and decided upon, her emotions were minutely soothed.

But she couldn't plan for everything, and she certainly hadn't planned for this. She was sure Arno was preparing to gloat over his victory next time he saw her, although his gloating might be moderated by the disappearance of his friend and partner, Hal Burridge.

As she neared the road, she strained her ears for the sound

of an approaching vehicle. Anyone passing would certainly take notice of a light in the normally deserted quarry property. She experimentally turned the bike's light off, but the darkness was absolute. She switched the light back on.

She had just pulled the gate open and was pushing the bike through when she heard the thrum of an approaching engine. She flicked off the bike's light and could see a pair of headlights approaching.

She hauled the gate closed but didn't have time to fasten the padlock. She shoved the bike into the drainage ditch that ran next to the road, then threw herself in behind it. She could feel mud sucking at her shoes and oozing up between her fingers as the car approached. It slowed, and she could hear the voices of its passengers through windows open to the warm July night. Then it turned onto the road leading to the gate.

She lowered her head almost to mud level and wished she were wearing mud-colored clothes. Her brain spun through and discarded various explanations. She decided that if they saw her, she would claim she had crashed her bike into the ditch and must have been temporarily knocked unconscious.

She heard the car door open, then the crunch of gravel as the driver stepped out. A few steps approached the gate, then stopped.

"It's unlocked." A male voice. Young.

"Does someone else know about this place?" Young and female.

"Maybe." Uncertain, then, with more assurance. "Maybe someone was here and just forgot to lock up. If there's someone at the overlook, we'll find somewhere else to go."

Overlook? Like they planned to do any sightseeing at this time of night.

"Let's just go somewhere else, Jamie. It's creepy."

"Probably just that old guy who comes here to drink."

Gwen's heart hammered in her chest. She dug her fingers into the mud and felt a nail bend and break.

"That's even creepier. Come on, let's go somewhere else. Allison's family is away at the Shore, and she told me the motion sensor lights on the back deck aren't working ..."

Jamie gave a theatrical sigh. "Okay, if you want." The steps backtracked, the door thumped shut, and the car reversed out of the road and headed off in the direction from which it had come.

When Gwen could no longer hear the car's engine, she climbed out of the ditch, hauling her bike out behind her. When she flicked on the bike's light, she saw that the tires and her feet had left streaks and splotches of mud on the road. She consoled herself with the fact that they probably looked no different than they would if a biker had, in fact, gone into the ditch by accident. As long as the mud trail didn't lead to her house, she couldn't imagine there would be a way the mess could be connected to her.

She climbed onto the bike and turned it in the opposite direction from the house, stopping occasionally to turn the bike's light to check the pavement behind her. When she could no longer see a residue of mud, she reversed direction and headed for home. When she got to the house, she'd hose off the bike—and herself—in the yard.

But this time, having another step in her plan didn't quiet the thud of her heart or loosen the knot in her stomach.

5

B ryan glanced down at the GPS on the iPad attached to the yoke. This was the trickiest part of the flight, as he descended into the mountains and toward his cabin. At least the turbulence had abated.

Bryan glanced over at Hal's body as he began to think through the process of getting him out of the plane and into the Jeep. He turned his attention back to the instruments, then did a double take. Hal's hand was resting on his leg.

Had Bryan returned Hal's hand to its original position after it had slid off his leg when they hit the turbulence? He wouldn't have forgotten a thing like that—touching the hand of a dead man.

Because Hal was dead.

Wasn't he?

Trying to divide his attention between the instruments and the body next to him, he reached his hand toward Hal's—then let out a strangled yell as Hal's fingers shot out and clamped over his own. Hal's head rolled backwards, and in the eerie red light, Bryan could see that Hal's eyes were open ... and were returning his gaze.

"Jesus Christ!" Bryan jerked his hand away and at the same time pulled back on the yoke—he couldn't keep track of mountain ridges with this shit happening in the cockpit. He'd climb, then circle back to land once things were under control. The mnemonic used by pilots to prioritize their tasks in an emergency drifted through his consciousness: aviate, navigate, communicate. Fortunately, he didn't have to worry about the last —communicating his predicament was the last thing he needed to do. He checked his altitude and rate of climb, adjusted his ascent rate, then looked back toward the form in the passenger seat.

Hal's eyes were closed again, his hand again hung by his side. But his lips were moving, although what he might be saying was lost in the noise of the cockpit.

Bryan couldn't hear Hal, but could Hal have heard what Bryan was saying during the flight? Bryan played back his one-sided conversation—but had it been one-sided? Maybe Hal had been conscious all along. If he had actually heard and understood what Bryan was saying, Bryan was screwed. His stomach twisted. He was screwed even if Hal hadn't heard or understood what he was saying.

At that moment, Hal's hand reached out again and grabbed the passenger-side yoke. He hauled back and the Cessna obediently reared up. Bryan felt the telltale buffet in the yoke and the rudder pedals as the reassuring sound of wind slipping past the fuselage dropped to almost nothing. Straight up was as bad as straight down at this altitude—there was no space to recover from a stall.

Bryan jammed the yoke forward and at the same time slashed his hand sideways into Hal's throat in the move that every pilot learns as the fastest way of getting a panicked—or murderous—passenger's hands off the controls. Hal's eyes rolled up in his head and his hands fell from the yoke.

Bryan took a deep, trembling breath. What would happen if he landed not with a dead body but with an injured and angry man? Would his attempt at a cover-up be foiled not by the police but by the victim?

But that wasn't his biggest cause for alarm. If Hal was trying to cause the plane to crash, he evidently didn't mind sending himself to his death as long as he took Bryan with him.

Hal's hand twitched.

Bryan scanned the objects within reach in the tight confines of the cockpit and, after a brief hesitation, pulled out a heavy flashlight tucked into a holder in the footwell. Hefting the flashlight in his hand, he looked over at Hal.

Hal's body was twisted in the seat and his head had dropped onto his shoulder, but his eyes were open again and he glared up at Bryan from under brows that until a year ago had been dark brown but that were now shot with gray. He mouthed a word, and Bryan didn't need Hal to be wearing a headset to know what he had said.

Bastard.

Bryan pulled his arm back and swung the flashlight toward Hal.

With the seats only inches apart, it was hard to aim, and the heavy metal handle connected with Hal's nose. His head snapped back onto the headrest.

"Jesus, please let that be it, please let that be it," Bryan said through gritted teeth.

But it wasn't it.

Hal's hand reached again for the yoke, and Bryan pulled the flashlight back again and swung it again.

This time he connected with the side of Hal's head.

Hal shuddered, then slumped to the left, his head landing on Bryan's shoulder. Bryan let out another yell and pushed away the dead weight of the body. Hal's body flopped back against the passenger-side door, his head wedged between the headrest and the window.

His hands shaking, Bryan dropped the flashlight to the floor and scanned the instruments. They were still gaining altitude. He leveled the plane and took a deep breath.

Then he heard Hal's voice in the headset.

"You should never have done it, Bryan."

"Mother of God ..." groaned Bryan. He forced his eyes back to the body in the seat beside his.

The voice continued, although Hal's lips didn't move. "I can understand why Gwen did what she did. I know what's happened to me in the last year."

The light in the cockpit was dim. Maybe Hal's lips were in fact moving. Bryan groped on the floor for the flashlight, then flicked it on and aimed the light at Hal's head. He wasn't sure which outcome would be less horrible—learning that Hal was still alive despite the blow to the head or that he was dead.

Hal's voice in the headset continued. "I know Gwen deserves better than me. But she sure as hell deserves better than you."

Bryan flinched and the flashlight went tumbling back to the floor, casting writhing shadows in the cockpit as it rolled back and forth in the footwell.

"Hal, what happened at the hangar was an accident," Bryan said, his voice trembling. "I thought you were coming for me with the pry bar."

"And you were worried? I thought I couldn't handle myself in a bar fight."

Bryan was silent, his brain groping in vain for the right response to this horrific scenario.

"And when I come to," continued Hal, "where do I find myself? Not in an ambulance headed for Mercy Hospital. I find myself in your plane, headed, as far as I can tell, for Clinton County."

"I thought you were dead. There was no breath, no pulse." Bryan's voice was spiraling upward, and he swallowed, trying to get it under control. "It would have taken too long for the ambulance to arrive. You couldn't have recovered. You would have been a vegetable. You wouldn't have wanted that." He paused, hoping that Gwen had been right about what her husband would and wouldn't have wanted. "Right?" he asked desperately.

There was silence over the headset. One minute ticked by, then another. Was this gruesome conversation finished?

The pounding of his heart eased fractionally. He tore his eyes away from the instruments and looked over at where Hal— Hal's body—still lay slumped against the door. "Hal, what ... how ...?"

"What am I doing? And how am I doing it? Damned if I know the *how*, but here's the *what*."

The voice went silent again. What did that mean? Bryan couldn't sense any difference in Hal, himself, the plane, or the flight. He glanced down at the panel to get his bearings.

Something was obscuring the reading of the airspeed indicator, fingers of whitish gray creeping across the instrument's glass. He wiped at it to no effect. It was too warm for frost, and condensation would never collect that quickly.

"Hal ...?"

He glanced at the altimeter and saw that the same phenomenon was happening to it—the glass clouding until it was an opaque circle.

"Hal, are you doing this?" he asked, trying to keep his voice steady.

One by one the readings on the other instruments—vertical speed indicator, attitude indicator, heading indicator, and turn coordinator—disappeared. He grabbed the rag that he had used to wipe down the wing jack leg and scrubbed the glass, but with no more effect than he had had on the airspeed indicator.

"Goddammit, Hal—are you doing this?"

He looked wildly out the windscreen. The darkness was total, although he knew that the mountains loomed out there somewhere.

"Hal, come on, I'm blind up here!"

"How does it feel, Bryan, to have your actions come back to *haunt* you?" He heard a low, deranged laugh in the headset.

Bryan tried to calm the thundering of his heart, tried to will himself to be able to sense what was up and what was down, but he couldn't.

A movement to one side of the plane caught his eye and he turned just in time to see the breath-halting sight of a treetop flash by.

He hauled back on the yoke to gain altitude and the treetops disappeared, but as they did, he lost the only visual reference he had.

He felt the plane shudder in a stall, and pushed the nose down, despite every nerve in his body screaming to climb.

"Hal, it was an accident—you know that, right? I didn't mean to hit you in the head—I thought you were coming after me with the pry bar!"

"I don't blame you for killing me, Bryan. I blame you for stealing my wife."

The plane shuddered again. He couldn't be stalling again, could he? As far as he could tell, he was flying level. He goosed the throttle and the engine roared.

"Don't ask me how I know this," he heard Hal's calm voice in the headset, "but you're headed right for one of the ridges."

Bryan jerked the yoke back again, and the plane reared, seemed to stand on its tail for a moment, then tipped with maddening slowness—to the right or to the left, Bryan couldn't even tell.

"We all pay for our actions in the end, Bryan."

The plane's landing lights flicked on, and Bryan screamed as he saw the trees rush up to meet him.

6

"High or low, fast or slow?" asked Russo from the right seat.

Ann glanced at the altimeter and airspeed indicator. "Crap. High and slow."

"That should be easy to fix," said Russo.

Ann edged the yoke forward and the plane sank and sped up.

"Keep the numbers steady in the windscreen," he said.

Ann made a slight adjustment to the approach angle.

"Crab for the wind."

Ann pointed the Piper Warrior's nose slightly off-center to keep the plane on the centerline of the runway.

"Once you're in ground effect, relax!" said Russo. "Enjoy yourself! This baby's a land-o-matic. Just look down the runway and let her settle on her own."

The plane's tires touched the runway with a satisfying squeak.

"Run that centerline right up the outside of your right leg."

Ann tapped the rudder pedals to stay on the centerline as the plane slowed.

Russo glanced at his watch. "That's the last one of the day."

Ann puffed out a breath. "Thank God." She looked over at him. "That was pretty good, right?"

"Not bad," he said. "But now you have to make it look easy."

With a sigh, she turned off at the taxiway and headed toward the flight school's ramp space.

She maneuvered the Warrior into its tie-down and ran through the shutdown procedure under Russo's watchful eye. Then he popped open the right-side door and climbed out of the plane, Ann clambering out after him into the sunny July day. Although the temperature was not as hot as it was forecast to get later in the day, her shirt was soaked with sweat and her reddish blonde hair, despite being corralled in its usual ponytail, was a frizzy mess. Russo looked as calm, cool, and collected as he had at the beginning of the flight—in fact, as he always did.

She handed him her logbook and he filled in the details of the flight.

"So, same time in two days?" asked Ann.

"No can do," said Russo. "I have to go to a funeral."

"Oh, I'm sorry to hear that."

He shrugged. "Some great-aunt who I haven't seen since I was a kid, but all the cousins are going to be there. Should be interesting—they're all arguing about her will, and who's responsible for dealing with her priceless Hummel collection." He perked up. "Hey, I should bring you along."

"Why?"

"Open casket funeral. I could sneak you up to the front of the line and you could get her take on the situation." Russo was obviously working hard to hold back his laughter.

Ann rolled her eyes. "Very funny."

Russo wiggled his fingers at her and made ghostly noises.

After Russo headed off to locate his next victim, Ann stopped at the FBO—the fixed base operator—to pay for the lesson and schedule another for the following day. She was wiped out, as she always was after a lesson, and looking forward to a nap when she got back to Mike and Scott's townhouse.

She had just reached the parking lot and was unlocking her Forester when her phone buzzed. She saw a name on the Caller ID that she hadn't seen in some time: Corey Duff. She hit *Accept*.

"Hey, Corey."

"Hi, Ann—long time no see."

Corey Duff had produced a documentary Ann had appeared in several years earlier called *The Sense of Death*. In it, Corey had put to the test the skills of Ann and two other sensers—Ann's sometimes-competitor, sometimes-mentor Garrick Masser and a woman from New Mexico. It had been Ann's first exposure beyond southeastern Pennsylvania, where she and Mike had grown up and where Mike still lived. That exposure had enabled her to make spirit sensing her full-time profession.

She crossed to a bench where visitors sat to watch the planes come and go. "How are you doing?"

"Doing great," he said with his characteristic enthusiasm. "Life is good."

"I hear you moved to Los Angeles," she said. "The big time."

He laughed. "Yeah. I still get home to Pittsburgh pretty often but I'm spending most of my time out here on the Left Coast. How are you doing?"

"I'm temporarily renting out my place in the Adirondacks. I'm staying with Mike and Scott in West Chester."

"It's beautiful in Pennsylvania in July, but I'll bet by August you'll be wanting to get back to the mountains."

She forced a laugh. "Yeah, maybe by August I'll be ready to go back, although it's already pretty hot here. I'm taking flying lessons," she added, mainly to move the topic along.

"No kidding, that's great! I'd love to learn to fly but I never

seem to find the time. Going to be flying yourself to engagements now?"

Her laugh was easier this time. "I have a lot of work to do
before I can do that—I haven't even soloed yet. But I'm trying to
fast track things since I don't know how long I'll be in West
Chester. I don't want to have to start over with a new instructor if
I head back to the Adirondacks."

"I see you're still finding time for *Ann Kinnear Sensing*."

"Yeah. It's booming."

"You don't sound so excited about it."

"It's okay."

There was a pause, Corey likely waiting to see if Ann would
elaborate, then he said, "I'll bet Garrick's business is booming,
too."

"Yeah, he's doing well."

"You keep in touch with him?"

"Of course."

"He's a piece of work," he said with a laugh.

She smiled. "Yeah, he's one of a kind, all right."

"There are some folks here in L.A. who think you're both one
of a kind. Well, two of a kind."

"Three of a kind, if you count the woman from New Mexico."

"Right, right. But there are people who are specifically interested in you and Masser."

"What do you mean, folks are interested?"

"You guys have a unique story—and the video that girl took
of you two in Maine has over a hundred thousand views. The
other videos on your YouTube channel aren't far behind."

"I don't have a YouTube channel."

"Au contraire, Ms. Kinnear. Stand by ..."

A moment later her phone pinged with a text containing a
link. She clicked on it and found herself on the *Unofficial Ann
Kinnear* channel, curated by a person identified only as AnnFan.

"Oh, man," she groaned.

"You really didn't know about it?"

"No."

"I thought your brother might be behind it."

"No. He asked about setting up a channel a while ago, but I vetoed it."

"Ann, you can't let other people take control of the message you're putting out there, especially in video. This person appears to be a supporter, but he or she could just as easily have it out for you. You need to own your social media presence, own your online brand. You should send this AnnFan person a takedown notice and put up your own channel. Have a nastygram ready from a lawyer in case they ignore you."

"Jesus, you make it sound like I need a PR firm *and* a lawyer."

"That's not a bad idea, but I have a cheaper alternative."

"Oh?"

"A follow-up to *The Sense of Death*." She could imagine him sitting forward, the phone pressed to his ear, or maybe pacing the floor, earbuds in place. "Just you and Masser."

"What's the idea?"

"The two of you solving a mystery that only a dead person holds the key to—an unsolved murder, a missing person, a missing treasure."

"Have you talked with Garrick about it?"

"He's excited about it."

"Excited?" she asked, her skepticism clear.

Corey laughed. "Okay, maybe not excited, but willing to do it. But of course it's a package deal—it needs to be both of you for the premise to work."

She sighed. "I don't know, Corey. We're getting plenty of business as it is, we don't really need promotion opportunities."

"It's not just a way of drumming up business. It's a way to

show people you can do what you can do—to convince the disbelievers."

"Why do I want to convince the disbelievers?"

"So they won't think you're a fraud."

"I'm not a fraud," she shot back.

"You and I know that. Let's prove it."

From across the ramp, she could see that Russo's next student had climbed into the plane without having unfastened the tie-down ropes. This should be interesting.

"Let me think about it," she said.

"I can tell I haven't convinced you. Let me come out there, take you and Mike and Scott out to dinner, lay it all out for you."

"Corey, I'm tired from my flying lesson. Now's not the best time for me to be hearing a pitch about a project I'm inclined to say no to. Just let me think about it and I'll get back to you."

"Okay. But don't say no without giving me a chance to convince you in person."

"Fine. I'll have my people call your people."

As she put away her phone, the flight school plane fired up —it was like Russo to let the poor slob go blithely ahead—and then jerked to a halt when the tie-down ropes snapped taut. The engine spun down and Russo climbed out of the plane, followed by the mortified student.

Ann glanced around and saw that she wasn't the only person who had witnessed the student's humiliation. Two pilots stood in an open hangar door, enjoying the show, and she could see Dottie, who ran the office, looking out the window of the FBO.

There it was: a perfect metaphor for what awaited her if she managed to make a fool of herself in Corey's documentary.

7

The master of ceremonies' voice boomed through the ballroom's PA system.

"Our guest of honor has worked tirelessly not only to entertain airshow attendees with her amazing feats of aerobatic skill, which we got to enjoy this afternoon ... not only to thrill spectators at White Lake with her astounding performances at the air races ... but also to introduce flying to the next generation of pilots. As a frequent participant in the Young Eagles flight program, she has taken many boys and girls up for what is often their first flight—although not, I'm afraid, in her Extra 330 or her Lancair Legacy." The MC smiled expectantly, and polite laughter rippled through the audience. "She has traveled to schools to talk about the importance of a solid science education. She has hosted visits to her hangar at Avondale Airport so that aviation enthusiasts—many of them youngsters—can learn more about her wonderful planes. Perhaps most importantly, she has provided an exemplary model, both as a pilot and as a member of the flying community, to young people, and especially young ladies, across the country. And she has achieved all this by an age when most of us were still working to keep our nose wheel on the centerline during landings." More polite laughter. "And so, without further ado, please join me and all the members of the Dover Aero Club in welcoming our guest of honor, the Peregrine Falcon herself, Gwen Burridge."

The applause from the mostly male audience, seated at round tables over dessert and coffee, was enthusiastic.

Gwen rose from her place at the table on the low podium. Her auburn hair was pulled back in a chignon and she wore a simply cut dark bluish-gray dress with bands of white across the bodice and a string of gold beads around her neck. The peregrine falcon in elegant human form.

She stepped to the lectern and, since she was considerably taller than the MC, adjusted the microphone upward. The ballroom lights glinted off the four diamonds at the four compass points of the watch she wore: blue-gray metal with the face circled by a thin band of gold. She smoothed the paper containing her notes on the lectern, then looked up and gave the audience a dazzling smile.

"I couldn't be more thrilled to receive this recognition from an organization as well-established and respected as the Dover Aero Club. And I am especially honored that you have chosen to establish a scholarship in my name for a young woman who is planning to pursue a career in aviation. It demonstrates our shared belief that the future of general aviation depends on keeping the rosters full with the next generation of pilots.

"I grew up in a ramshackle rancher a few miles from Avondale Airport, the daughter of a trucker father who was rarely home and a well-meaning mother who had other things on her mind. I remember the first time I went to the airport, to their first Community Day event. I was ten years old. I had never seen airplanes up close, had never heard people talking about flying, and it was the most magical thing I could imagine. I fell under the airport's spell.

Coffees and desserts sat ignored on the tables. She could see a few nods among the audience members.

"Avondale Airport was the central force in my life then, as it is now. The couple who owned the airport back then gave me a couple of dollars to sweep out hangars, and the pilots took me up for rides. I didn't realize until years later how lucky I was that none of those pilots tried to take advantage—" She gave the room a sly smile. "—at least not until I was old enough, and strong enough, to let them know in no uncertain terms that a plane ride was all I wanted, and an enthusiastic passenger was all they were going to get."

Sheepish laughter greeted this.

"I remember like it was yesterday the first time I was allowed to take the controls of a plane. I was twelve years old, it was a beautiful blue-and-white Tri-Pacer, and the pilot who owned the plane was Archie Castro."

She smiled down at a gnome-like man seated at the nearest table, wild white hair a halo around his liver-spotted head.

Archie cackled and waved at Gwen, then turned in his seat and said in a surprisingly robust voice, "What a natural! What a touch she had!" He drew bushy white eyebrows down in a parody of a scowl. "And don't any of you gents take that the wrong way."

The men at the other tables laughed, and Archie settled back in his chair, pleased at the response his joke had gotten.

"Mr. Castro was kind enough to give me good references to the other pilots at Avondale," Gwen continued, "and they let me fly their planes, too. A Cub. A Bonanza. A Luscombe." She held up her finger. "No take-offs or landings, though."

Another round of laughter.

"If it hadn't been for my husband, Hal Burridge, who, with a partner, bought the airport when I was eighteen, I would still be hitching rides in other people's planes, waiting to hear that magical phrase, 'You have the flight controls' ..." She held her hand out expectantly to the audience.

"'I have the flight controls,'" they chanted.

She smiled. "'You have the flight controls.'" She glanced down at her notes, then put them aside. "But nurturing a love of aviation among the next generation of pilots is not enough to guarantee the future of general aviation. A robust GA infrastructure is vital to that goal as well. No young person is going to fall in love with flight at Philadelphia International or BWI. We must ensure that any young person who is fascinated with flying has the opportunity to utter that phrase, 'I have the controls.' We must ensure that there is never a time when we're talking to our children or grandchildren or great-grandchildren and have to explain that there was a time in the past when the average man or woman—or boy or girl—could take to the air in a plane of their own, or in one they rented at their local general aviation airport."

More enthusiastic applause.

"As the members of Dover Aero Club recognize better than anyone, it is the GA airports as much as the GA pilots we must protect. We must guard against airport owners who put the opportunity for a big payday from a developer ahead of the best interests of the flying community they should be supporting."

There were a few good-natured boos from the audience.

"Airports are open one day and closed the next—airport like Meigs Field in Chicago—"

The boos were more heartfelt this time.

"—and, near my own home base, Shannon, Oxford, Willow Grove. I'm sure you have your own list."

Calls came from the audience: "Dover Airpark!" "Biggs!" "Dupont!"

She gestured to a plaque with her name on it that stood on a stand next to the lectern. "This recognition and the scholarship you have funded are just two pieces of evidence among many of the value Dover Aero Club places on general aviation and on the young men and women who will ensure its successful future."

The audience applauded and whooped their appreciation.

She smiled grimly. At least it would be clear whose side she was on when news of the sale of Avondale Airport hit the aviation grapevine.

"My only regret this evening is that my husband, Hal, could not be here. When I met Hal twelve years ago at Avondale Airport, I was a young woman with a huge dream and very few resources with which to pursue it. I was so fortunate that a man as generous of spirit as Hal Burridge, a skilled pilot himself, saw some potential in that young pilot. And that a man as generous with his money as Hal"—she arched her eyebrows and the audience laughed—"was willing to train and equip me to fulfill my greatest dream: to become an aerobatic and air racing pilot."

More applause, and a few surreptitious eye wipes.

"I'm happy to say that, since that time, sponsors like Jura Bernois Watches have stepped in to provide the financial support needed for me to fund those activities, but I would never have reached that point without Hal's support. This recognition is as much his as it is mine." She raised the plaque. "Thank you, sweetheart."

8

"Cocktails are served," said Mike as he entered the living room with a tray.

A casual visitor to the townhouse might not have realized that he was Ann's brother based on their appearance. Ann's slender build, fair skin, and reddish-blonde hair was more like their mother, Mike's stockier frame and darker hair and complexion more like their father.

Ann looked up from her homework—a calculation of fuel consumption in the Piper Warrior from Avondale to Deck and back assuming a wind from the southwest at eight knots. "Thank God. I need a drink to deal with this." She glanced down at her jottings. "One-hundred-and-fifteen gallons. That can't be right, can it?"

"Seems like a lot," said Scott. He pulled off his chunky black-framed glasses, revealing pale blue eyes in a face framed by clipped blond hair. He set aside the gardening book he had been reading and lifted a small black dachshund out of his lap. "You need to be on the floor, sweetie. We're having cocktail hour."

The dog jumped back onto Scott's lap.

"All right. But you have to behave yourself."

Ann had arrived in West Chester with the dachshund she had befriended—or, more accurately, who had befriended her —at her Adirondack cabin. Scott was so smitten with the dog that Ann now thought of Ursula as more his pet than hers. She corrected herself again: Scott had replaced Ann as Ursula's primary staff.

"What are we having today?" Scott asked as Mike passed out three glasses and three small plates of hors d'oeuvres.

"Gin and tonics with cucumber and shrimp crackers."

Mike had discovered a website that featured cocktail and hors d'oeuvres pairings and was working his way through them.

Scott took a sip of his drink. "This is fabulous. You should go into the catering business, sweetie."

Mike lowered himself into a chair. "I just like doing it for the three of us."

"How are the lessons going?" Scott asked Ann.

"Fun. Exhausting."

Ann's phone buzzed. She pulled it out, glanced at it, and slipped it back into her pocket.

"Who was that?" asked Mike.

"Corey."

"Corey Duff?"

"Yeah."

"Why's he calling?"

Ann shrugged.

"You can take his call if you want," Mike said hopefully. "I won't be offended."

"I already talked to him once today."

"Oh, yeah? About what?"

"You're so nosy."

Mike held up the hand not holding his G&T. "Just expressing interest."

Ann took a sip of her drink. "He wants to do another documentary featuring Garrick and me."

Scott sat forward, causing an annoyed Ursula to jump off his lap. "You and Garrick Masser? That's very exciting!"

Ursula immediately popped into the begging position next to Scott's chair. She could hold that position through an entire meal, although she rarely had to. Scott was an easy touch for hand-outs.

"I didn't say I'd do it," said Ann.

"Why not?" asked Mike.

"Don't we have a backlog of people wanting to hire me?"

"Sure, but—"

"Then why do I need to worry about getting on some documentary with Garrick?"

"You can't pay for that kind of exposure," said Mike.

"Exposure," Ann muttered. "It sounds like something you get from staying out in the cold too long."

"Is Masser doing it?" Mike asked.

"Corey says he's willing," said Ann.

"But Masser isn't giving Corey a firm commitment? Figures." Mike took a sip of his drink. "I wonder in what order they'd bill you. If they did it alphabetically by last name, that would put you first. Even if they did it alphabetically by first name, that would still put you first."

"I'm sure Garrick would be billed first, he's way more established and well-known that I am."

"He's going to keep being more established and well-known if you keep deferring to him."

"I should defer to him—he's helped me out a lot."

"I'd say you've helped him out more."

"Actually, Scott was the one who really helped him out," said Ann, sensing an opportunity to distract Mike from the subject of the documentary. "Garrick loves Scott."

"Everyone loves Scott," said Mike. "He's the only person I can imagine Masser warming up to."

Ann turned to Scott. "If you ever decided to move to Maine, you could get a job as Garrick's personal assistant in a heartbeat."

Mike snorted. "Over my dead body."

"The moving to Maine part," asked Scott, "or the personal assistant part?"

"Both," said Mike. "Maine's too cold, and Masser's ... also too cold."

Ann raised an eyebrow. "Clever."

"A documentary about the two of you would highlight the differences in your approach," said Mike, not to be distracted from the topic. "Viewers who are looking for a senser might well decide to divert their business to someone with a better bedside manner."

"And that would be me?" asked Ann.

"That would be most of the population."

"Hey!" she protested.

"You know what I mean," said Mike, unapologetic. "Sometimes people prefer that the people they hire don't treat them like they're a piece of dog shit on the cosmic shoe of humanity."

"Jeez, Mike," said Ann, laughing. "Where do you come up with this stuff?"

9

The next day, Gwen delayed her departure from Dover, accepting a lunch invitation from the obviously delighted officers of the Aero Club. She didn't want to have to walk past Bryan's hangar. She didn't want to run into Arno. And she didn't want to go back to the house that she still thought of as Hal's.

When she couldn't reasonably postpone her departure anymore, she loaded the Extra. Helmet, flight suit, parachute, Go-Pros, camera mounts, the outfit she had worn to the dinner, and a small bag of toiletries took up her only convenient stowage space in the Extra: the second seat. The plane often felt less like something one entered and more like something one put on.

As she climbed away from Dover, rather than heading directly for Avondale, she turned southeast across the Delaware Bay to Cape May, circled the lighthouse, and flew up the Jersey coast at two hundred feet, waggling her wings at the sunbathers waving from the beach. She passed Millville, overflew the Salem cooling towers and Fort Mifflin, slipped under the Philly Bravo airspace but over the Wilmington Class D, and finally, with a sigh, turned toward Avondale.

Her part in dealing with Hal's unexpected demise should be easy. All she had to do was tell the police that Hal had disappeared again, adopting the worried but also vaguely annoyed demeanor of a woman who had been through this several times before, times that always ended with her husband discovered drunk but safe.

It was fortunate that Bryan had already had a trip to his cabin planned. She had never been to the cabin—had never, as far as she could remember, been to Clinton County—but Hal had gone there with Bryan and she recalled the photos he had shown her: views from a Pennsylvania mountaintop showing trees to the horizon. If Bryan was careful, it should be hard for the police to find a body buried there. She had to believe that the lack of a body would throw a wrench into any investigation of a suspected murder.

She wished she and Bryan had had more time to talk about the details of burying the body. Would the road he took into the woods be muddy? Would traces left on his tires lead the police to a certain part of the forest? Would he leave the shovel behind or bring it back to the cabin with him?

At least he wasn't one to get easily unnerved. She remembered the time when he had offered to fly her to pick up the Extra after a radio repair at the avionics shop in Lancaster. They had been climbing out of three hundred feet in the Cessna when she caught a glimpse of a small shape headed for the plane.

"Bird—" was all she got out before the windscreen disappeared with an ear-shattering bang and a form shot between her head and Bryan's and into the back of the plane.

She looked through a whirl of feathers at Bryan. His headset had been torn off and a deep scratch on his cheek was oozing blood, but he was already turning the plane in a smooth arc back toward the airport.

Her headset was still in place and she keyed the mic.

"Avondale, white Cessna 180 a mile southwest of the airport declaring an emergency. Bird strike." The wind in the cockpit was so loud that she could barely hear her own voice, and certainly wouldn't be able to hear any radio responses. "Returning to the airport, Runway Two-four." She glanced again at Bryan. His expression was grim but focused, with no signs of panic. She scanned the instruments—all seemed normal. She pointed to the panel, then gave a thumbs up. Bryan nodded. She keyed the radio mic again. "Windscreen is gone and visibility is reduced. Any planes in the area, give us a wide berth."

They landed without incident, although she was pretty sure Bryan had had more than two beers once the Cessna was back in the hangar.

She had never been able to get the bird mess out of her shirt.

She sighed. She was holding up her part of the plan, she had to trust him to hold up his part. He had the incentive of protecting the circumscribed world he had built for himself— she didn't fool herself into thinking he was doing it out of any motivation but a selfish one.

As she approached Avondale, she suddenly regretted the detour she had taken. If the airport was going to be plowed under to be replaced by postage stamp lots surrounding cheaply made houses with five bedrooms and five-and-a-half baths, she should take advantage of whatever time she had left to spend there.

She glanced toward the quarry, but the field where Hal's pickup was parked was hidden from view.

She landed, taxied the Extra to her hangar, and shut down. She had climbed out of the plane and raised the hangar door when she saw Russo approaching the hangar followed by two men in uniform—one middle-aged, one in his mid-twenties.

Maybe she wouldn't have to report Hal missing after all.

"Hello, Russo," she said, greeting him with a nod. "What can I do for you gentlemen?"

"Gwen, this is Sergeant Cromar," Russo indicated the older man, "and this," he indicated the younger one, "is Officer Morelli. Gentleman, this is Gwen Burridge. Bryan Calvert worked on her plane."

She noticed that the normally unflappable flight instructor wouldn't meet her eyes. "What's wrong?" she asked sharply.

"Do you know where Bryan is?" Russo asked.

"I think he was going up to his cabin this weekend. Why?"

"There was a plane crash in Clinton County last night," he said. "It was Bryan's plane."

She was glad that the extra-dark round sunglasses she always wore when outside provided some camouflage to her emotions. Bryan's plane had crashed? As fouled up as Hal's life had been for the last year, seeing it end tragically had somehow not been surprising, although she would have never foreseen that particular tragedy. But Bryan crashing his plane? She felt the blood drain from her face and fought the urge to reach a steadying hand for the Extra's wing.

"Would you like to sit down, ma'am?" asked Cromar, stepping forward and extending a hand toward her arm.

"No, I'm fine," she said, taking a step back.

She thought of the empty beer bottles in the hangar. Had he been more impaired than he seemed? She herself rarely drank, but two beers didn't seem like much. Could someone who had dealt with a bird strike with such cool competence have been undone by the darkness during a flight he had made at night dozens if not hundreds of times? She couldn't imagine it.

Cromar was talking. "We're trying to confirm if Mr. Calvert

was in the plane. Is there anyone else who might have been using Mr. Calvert's plane?"

"No, no one else flew his plane."

After a moment, Cromar continued. "Ma'am, you can imagine that we're anxious to confirm the identity of the pilot so that we can notify his next of kin before details of the accident start showing up on the news. We've tried calling Mr. Calvert's cell phone, but it goes to voicemail. However, I understand that the cell service in that part of the state is spotty and, if he wasn't in the plane, it's possible he's somewhere the calls can't go through." He cleared his throat. "The victim was wearing a belt buckle with *White Lake* engraved on it over a design of an airplane." He nodded toward the Lancair in the hangar. "A plane that looked a lot like that one. Do you know if that's Bryan Calvert's belt buckle?"

"Yes. I—" Her voice caught, and she began again. "I gave my team those belt buckles after the White Lake Air Races last year."

"We'll make a positive ID based on dental records, but I believe we should assume for now that Mr. Calvert was in the plane that crashed. I'm very sorry, ma'am."

Her stomach flipped. Jesus—dental records. She didn't need to be told why authorities would have to rely on those for identification. She walked deliberately to the Extra and sank down on the wing. "Thank you," she said dully.

"Do you know how we can get in touch with his next of kin?"

"No. He was estranged from his parents and didn't have any sisters or brothers." She gave a bitter laugh. "Bryan was a lone wolf." She closed her eyes and took a deep breath.

Russo cleared his throat and took a step toward her.

"Gwen, there was someone in the plane with Bryan."

She looked up. "Who?"

"We think it might have been Hal."

She said nothing, weighing what she felt against what the police and Russo would expect. "What makes you think it was Hal?"

"Do you know if your husband planned to accompany Mr. Calvert on his weekend trip?" asked Cromar.

"Not that I know of, but it's possible."

"When is the last time you saw Mr. Burridge, ma'am? I'm just asking because, as with Mr. Calvert, I don't want to jump to conclusions."

"I saw him the evening before last."

"Not since then?"

"No, I've been away since yesterday morning."

She was afraid he was going to press her on her loose sense of her husband's whereabouts. Instead, he shifted uncomfortably. "Ma'am, the other occupant of the plane had an unusual key fob—may I describe it to you?"

"Yes."

"It was brass. Oval-shaped. It had an old-looking plane engraved on one side and some lettering on the other side. It had melted a bit and was difficult to read, but it might have said—"

"Avondale Airport. Burridge and Scanlan."

"Yes, ma'am, I believe so."

"That's Hal's. He and Arno got those made when they bought the airport."

"I'm very sorry, ma'am."

She stood up, then, trying to calculate the appropriate reaction of a woman surprised by the news of her husband's death, sat down again. She twisted her fingers in her lap. "Do you know what caused the crash?" she asked.

"Not yet. The NTSB will be conducting an investigation." Cromar pulled a small notepad out of his pocket and opened it to the first page. "The victims' bodies have been taken to a hospital in Clinton County. Autopsies will be performed and then the bodies can be transported back here." He paused. "Although if Mr. Calvert doesn't have any family in the area ..."

"Bring them both back. I'll take care of Bryan."

"Thank you, ma'am. That's very generous of you." He flipped the notepad closed and slipped it back into his pocket.

"Is there anyone we can contact for you? Family living in the area?"

"I'll contact Hal's family."

"How about your own family. Is there anyone you'd like to have with you?"

"My mother's dead. My father moved to Florida. We haven't stayed in touch."

"Friends?"

"No. I'm fine." She drew another deep breath and stood. "I need to get up to Clinton County."

"It's not necessary for you to go there, but if you would like to, we could provide any assistance in arranging transportation—"

"No, thank you, I can fly myself up there."

He knit his brows. "Do you think that's wise—?"

"I'm certainly not going to sit in a car for however many hours it would take to drive up there," she snapped, "and I'm not sitting in the back of some commercial plane that's going to land me a hour from where I need to be."

He nodded. "Yes, ma'am." He pulled a business card from his shirt pocket. "Here's my contact information, and on the back is the contact information for the police in Clinton County and the hospital where the victims were taken. Please give us a call if we can help in any way. And our condolences on your loss, ma'am. Your losses."

"Yes, condolences," murmured Morelli.

The two officers walked across the pavement to where she now saw two cruisers parked next to the FBO.

"Gwen, I'm so sorry," said Russo. "Anything I can do?"

She drew a deep breath. "Can you let Arno know?"

"Of course."

"And Dottie. Tell her she should take the rest of the day off."

"Will do."

"You can take the rest of the day off, too. Ask Dottie to call any students you have lessons with and reschedule them before she goes."

"I think I'll stick around here."

She looked toward the FBO. "People will have seen the police cars. They'll wonder what happened."

"What do you want me to tell them?"

She drew a deep breath. "Tell them what happened, I suppose."

"Roger."

"Thank you, Russo."

She thought for a moment that he was going to say something else, but then he nodded, turned, and followed the officers.

She felt the men's eyes on her as she pushed the Extra into the hangar. Let them think what they wanted—she wasn't going to leave her plane out on the ramp.

She had to get Hal's truck away from the quarry. There was no sense having a suicide scene staged for a man whose body had been found in a wrecked plane in Clinton County.

10

Ann pulled into the parking lot of Avondale Airport. She was still tired, mentally and physically, from the previous day's lesson—her normal every-other-day schedule would have given her an extra day to recover. However, with the schedule disrupted by Russo's great-aunt's funeral, Dottie had slotted her in a day early.

She was surprised to see two police cars in the parking lot. As she parked the Forester, one of the cars pulled out and headed away from the airport, while the other one relocated to the rectangle of shade cast by the FBO building.

Just as she reached the FBO, Russo emerged. When he saw her, he smacked his forehead. "Crap. I forgot you had a lesson today."

"I saw police in the parking lot. Is everything okay?"

"Yes. Actually, no. There's some stuff going on, is it okay if we reschedule?"

"Sure, no problem."

They went into the FBO, passing a teary Dottie on her way out, her purse hooked over her arm.

"Russo, what's up?" Ann asked.

"Plane crash. Not," he added hastily, "that small plane crashes are common, especially if the pilot is exercising reasonable precautions—"

"Don't worry about that," she said. "Was it someone you knew?"

"Yes. Someone from the airport."

"Oh, man. I'm really sorry to hear that, Russo."

"Yeah. Me too."

Russo booked Ann into a new slot and gave her some extra homework to fill the time: reviewing the emergency procedures and checklists in the *Pilot's Operating Handbook*.

Ann returned to the parking lot and climbed into the Forester. As she did so, a woman emerged from the freestanding hangar on the other side of the ramp, disappeared around the back of the hangar, and then appeared again, headed toward the airport's back entrance. Ann thought she recognized her as the woman who owned the plane she had once seen doing aerobatics near Octoraro Lake, two dozen miles to the west of Avondale.

She pulled out her phone and had just keyed *avondale airport plane crash* into the browser when her phone buzzed with an incoming call: *Corey Duff*. After a brief hesitation, she tapped *Decline*.

Ann had enjoyed working with Corey on the earlier documentary. He had never treated her ability to sense spirits and communicate with spirits in anything other than a matter-of-fact manner. The tests he had set for her, Garrick, and the spirit senser from New Mexico had had a bit of an *Unsolved Mysteries* flavor to them, but he had handled the scenarios respectfully. She knew, though, that Garrick had not enjoyed the experience —or at least had pretended not to. She gazed out across the airport grounds for a moment, then got out her phone, opened her contacts, and tapped *Garrick Masser*.

"Yes," came the answer. She could picture him seated at his large antique desk, which held, as far as she knew, his only phone and whatever book he was reading at the moment. The thinness of his frame would be somewhat disguised by his shapeless black clothing but would be apparent in the jutting cheekbones and deep-set black eyes. If he stood, even his stooped posture would not disguise his height.

"Hi, Garrick, it's Ann."

There was silence.

"Kinnear," she added.

"Yes, I suspected as much," he rumbled.

"Corey called you about the documentary?" An advantage of talking with Garrick was that one could dispense with introductory pleasantries.

"Yes."

"And ...?"

"He told me he was going to talk to you as well."

"Yes. He told me we're a package deal."

"What an odious turn of phrase."

"Are you going to do it?"

"Are you?"

"What is this, a game of chicken?"

He sighed theatrically. "I have plenty of pending engagements. Participating in a documentary would involve some inconvenient rescheduling."

"Yeah, me too."

"So you plan to decline?"

She hesitated. "My brother wants me to do it."

"Oh, by all means, if Mike Kinnear wants you to do it, you can hardly say no," said Garrick sourly.

Ignoring his tone—it was hardly news to her that there was no love lost between Mike and Garrick—she plowed ahead. "It would be a good opportunity to prove that we can do what we claim we can do."

"I don't feel the need to prove myself to disbelievers."

"Still ..."

"If you feel the need to provide such proof, then you should agree to participate."

"But it's an invitation to all the trolls out there to weigh in."

There was silence for a moment, then Garrick, sounding uncharacteristically uncertain, said, "Trolls?"

"On social media."

"Ah, yes," he said, his usual briskness returning. "I don't determine my course of action based on opinions voiced on social media, but if you do, then by all means decline."

"You're no help."

"On the contrary. I stand ready to accept or decline the offer, dependent only on your decision."

"Fine."

"Have you come to a conclusion?"

"Not yet."

"I shall await your decision with bated breath."

She heard the click of a handset being replaced in its cradle.

She tapped the phone on the steering wheel, gazing out the window at the windsock swinging lazily in the breeze, then opened her text messages and, somewhat reluctantly, opened the link that Corey had sent her to the *Unauthorized Ann Kinnear* YouTube channel.

She was always torn between curiosity about what people might be saying about her and fear that what she found would be upsetting.

However, the curator of *Unauthorized Ann Kinnear* was evidently a fan—was, in fact, *AnnFan*—and had done nothing more ominous than collect videos related to her work. There was the news report covering the first time her sensing ability had garnered public attention: when as a teenager she had found a neighbor's body in a cave in Central Pennsylvania. There was coverage of the Philadelphia socialite murder. And, of course, there was the video of her recent experience with Garrick in Maine—the video that had made the two of them household names for a crazy week before their story was displaced by the next tabloid sensation.

Would a documentary focused solely on the two of them cement the idea in the minds of the public that they were partners? *Odious* seemed an overstatement, but, much as she liked and respected Garrick, she had no desire for her future to be tied to his as a *package deal*. She liked her independence. Even Mike, as her business manager, knew he could only push or cajole her so far, and desisted if she dug in her heels.

She tossed the phone onto the passenger seat. She had specifically asked Mike to schedule a break between engagements so that she could focus on her flying lessons. However, even that might be up in the air—or, more accurately, grounded —if Russo continued to be distracted by the crash that had brought the police to Avondale Airport.

11

Gwen looked out of the hangar window toward the FBO. The police cars were no longer in evidence, and it looked like Russo was sending one of his students home. When the ramp was clear, she stepped out of the hangar, locked the door behind her, and then headed for the drive that accessed the airport's back entrance and the road that led to the quarry's back gate. Her Corvette was at the hangar, but if she drove to the quarry and moved Hal's pickup to the house, she'd just have to bike back for the 'vette.

As she walked, her mind ticked numbly through what she needed to do. She'd have to call Hal's parents, a blandly pleasant couple who lived in a leafy neighborhood of stately brick homes on the Main Line. She hoped they would volunteer to call Hal's brother and two sisters.

And what would she need to do for Bryan? She wondered distractedly if he would have wanted to be buried or cremated, then gave an involuntary shudder. The fact that identification would have to be done through dental records and that, according to Officer Cromar, Hal's brass key fob had partially melted suggested that Bryan's body might be part way to

cremated already. Her stomach lurched as she realized the same
would be true of her husband's body. No question of an open
casket funeral, in any case.

As she reached the road, she realized that if someone had
found the quarry gate unlocked after her departure the night
before last, they would have relocked it, and the key to the
padlock was in the Ridgeline, parked next to the abandoned pit.
Even worse, someone noticing that the gate was unlocked might
have entered the quarry property to investigate and found an
unoccupied Honda Ridgeline with an empty bottle of Johnnie
Walker on the passenger seat. She racked her brain for a plau-
sible explanation of how Hal's truck could have gotten there,
when Hal's burned body in Clinton County proved pretty defini-
tively that he had not been drinking in a quarry in Chester
County.

She puffed out a relieved breath when she saw that the gate
was as she had left it. She was also relieved to see that the
muddy footprints and tire tracks she had left that night had
been worn away. She slid the gate open, slipped through, and
pulled it closed behind her.

Her mind continued to churn on what could possibly have
gone wrong on the flight. Had there been a mechanical failure?
The Cessna was a fifty-year old plane, and things could go
wrong that even the most diligent inspection could miss.

When she reached the truck, she recalled her encounter
with the smaller bench. She bent to examine the front bumper
and saw that there was, in fact, a small piece of the blanket from
Rosie's bench stuck to its edge. She plucked it out and stroked it
with her thumb, her thoughts turning to the first time she had
come to the quarry, five years earlier.

∼

"LET'S HAVE A PICNIC," Hal said. "I know a good place."

Gwen was sitting in the sunroom at the back of their house, cup of coffee in one hand, a copy of *Aviation Safety* in the other. She looked up from the magazine. "I have a show coming up I need to practice for. I was going over to the airport in a few minutes."

"I saw you practicing yesterday—you're already perfect."

"Not perfect enough."

He smiled. "Trust me, I'll make it worth your while to postpone one practice. Plus," he added, "it'll give Rosie a chance for a run."

Rosie was a sleek silver greyhound. The dog's previous owner, a racing enthusiast, had planned to euthanize her when he learned that she had a heart murmur. Hal had heard about Rosie's plight and offered to take the dog off the trainer's hands. Hal's buddies sometimes teased him that he had chosen the canine equivalent of the Peregrine Falcon as his companion animal. Gwen had seen the dog run. She didn't mind the comparison.

Hal whistled up Rosie and the greyhound leapt into the back seat of the Ridgeline. Gwen and Hal climbed into the truck and they headed off in the general direction of the airport. Maybe, thought Gwen, the picnic location was at the airport, in which case she could get in a practice afterwards.

However, when they were still about a quarter mile from the airport entrance, Hal turned onto a dirt road barred by a gate in a chain link fence.

"We're picnicking at the quarry?" she asked. She knew he took Rosie there to run but she had never been there herself.

"Trust me."

He got a key out of the cupholder and unlocked the padlock on the gate. He drove through, then closed and relocked the gate. He returned to the truck and opened the back passenger door.

"Okay, Rosie," he said, and the dog shot out of the truck and streaked down the road. As far as Gwen could see, the heart murmur wasn't slowing Rosie down much.

Hal climbed back into the driver's seat and dropped the key back into the cupholder. They rolled forward through a lightly wooded area, then the trees opened up into a grassy field that sloped down to the quarry pit. On the other side of the pit, the branches of another fringe of trees swayed in a light breeze.

Gwen climbed out of the truck and looked around. It was prettier than she would have expected.

Hal pulled two collapsible chairs out of the back of the truck and set them up overlooking the view, then added a small collapsible table. Rosie, who had been sniffing around the field, trotted over and flopped down under the table.

"We forgot to bring picnic food," said Gwen.

"I didn't forget," said Hal, and lifted a wicker hamper out of the back.

He removed two lobster rolls overflowing with creamy lobster meat, each cling-wrapped onto a delicate china plate, and two ears of corn, still warm in their husks.

"Do I sense Dottie's hand in this?" asked Gwen with a smile.

Hal slapped a hand to his heart. "You cut me to the quick—this was all me."

Finally he pulled a bottle of champagne and two flutes from the basket and popped the cork. He poured and handed one of the glasses to Gwen.

"Well, that answers the question about practicing later today," she said, clinking her glass against his. "What are we drinking to?"

"Jura Bernois, among other things," he said. "You should be so proud of yourself for getting such a prestigious sponsorship."

She glanced at the wristwatch that had been her signing bonus. "It is a little more elegant than oxygen systems and oil supplements."

"It shows that they recognize not only your skill but your style as well."

She smiled at him. "And it means you can stop shelling out for my expenses."

He held the back of one of the chairs as she lowered herself onto it, then took the other one. "You know that's not why I'm excited about this, right? I'd be happy to continue to help you, but I know you're happier this way."

She took a sip of champagne. "That's true. I like taking care of things myself."

They ate the lobster rolls and corn—Gwen was grateful that Hal had packed extra napkins—after which Hal produced a miniature chocolate cake that they shared. When they were done, Hal packed up the dishes in the hamper and took them back to the truck, then reappeared with a blanket over his arm.

"I have something to show you," he said. He held out his hand to her.

She stood. "What about Rosie?" The dog was snoring under the chair.

"She'll find us if she wakes up before we get back."

Hal led Gwen to an opening in the woods that flanked the grassy slope and then down a narrow path through the trees and undergrowth. At first, she assumed it had been made by animals —maybe deer—until she noticed some clean cuts in branches that otherwise would have extended into the path.

"Did you make this path?" she asked.

"Rosie found it, I just improved it."

In a minute, they came out into a clearing that was bounded on its far side by a chain link fence, beyond which stretched the airport property. Part of the runway and the windsock were visible, a rise in the ground hiding the airport buildings from view. The pebble-strewn ground was largely free of growth. In the center of the clearing, she could see that some lighter-colored rocks were arranged in a pattern too regular to be natural. She stepped forward and, as she approached, the shape of the arrangement came into view.

She laughed. "A heart!" She looked toward Hal. "Did Rosie help with this, too?"

"She kept me company." He put the folded blanket on the ground. "Speaking of keeping me company ..."

"You scoundrel," she said with amusement.

He glanced at the blanket, then laughed. "That's not what I meant. At least not at the moment." He came to her and took her hands. "I have a question for you."

"Yes."

He raised his eyebrows. "Yes?"

She smiled. "I hope I'm not embarrassing myself, but if you are going to ask me to marry you, the answer is yes."

He laughed and shook his head. "And I thought I was going to be able to surprise you."

"I don't like to be surprised. I like to have a plan and carry it out."

He assumed an offended look. "I'm your plan?"

"No. I have to admit, you were a lovely surprise."

His expression became more serious. "Gwen, I want you to think carefully. Now, when you're twenty-five and I'm forty-five, our age difference doesn't seem like much, but when you're fifty, I'll be seventy. When you're seventy, I'll be—"

"I can do the math, Hal. We've known each other for seven years. We've been dating for four. If I had a problem with our ages, I would have broken it off before now."

He still looked uncertain.

She squeezed his hand. "You didn't buy my love, Hal."

Tears gathered in his eyes. "How did I get so lucky?" he said. He knelt and pulled a small box out of his pocket. He opened it and removed a ring. He took her left hand and slid the ring onto her finger. "Gwen Davis, I'm so glad you already said you'd marry me."

She pulled him to his feet and kissed him, then looked at the ring. The stone was a large yellow diamond, held in place by two tiny platinum projections that tapered smoothly from where they held the stone to the ring itself. She brought the ring close to her eyes.

"Are those ..."

"They're tiny propeller blades," he said. "I designed the ring myself, especially for the Peregrine Falcon."

She shook her head. "How did *I* get so lucky?" She lowered her hand and kissed him again. "I notice you brought a blanket with you."

"I did."

She glanced toward the airport.

"You can't see the clearing from the airport," he said. "And you can't even see it if you're in the pattern. I checked."

She smiled back at him. "You think of everything."

He took her hand and drew her down onto the blanket.

SHE HEARD the sound of an approaching vehicle and turned to see a police cruiser rolling slowly toward her. She opened her fingers and let the scrap of material from Rosie's blanket flutter to the ground. The car stopped and Officer Morelli got out.

"Anything I can help you with, Mrs. Burridge?"

"No, I'm fine. Thank you. What are you doing here?"

"I saw you leave the hangar and walk in this direction. I thought you might need some assistance."

"I appreciate the thought, but I'm fine. Really."

Morelli hooked his thumbs into his belt and looked around. "Is this part of the airport property?"

"No, it belongs to the quarry."

She stopped speaking, hoping he would go away, but he remained there, looking at her sympathetically.

"I came to get the truck," she said.

"Is this your truck?"

"It's my husband's truck. He came here sometimes, especially when he still had his dog. I decided I better not fly after all. I'm going to drive up to Clinton County and my car isn't very reliable."

"Was that your car parked outside the hangar?" He smiled tentatively. "Maybe not reliable, but it sure is good looking. I love those 'vettes. Stingray Grand Sport, am I right?"

"Yes."

He glanced around again. "So why is his truck here?"

She gave a deep sigh. "He came here sometimes when he wanted to be alone. I saw his truck from the air as I was coming into Avondale," she added.

"If he came to the quarry to be alone, how did he end up in the plane with Mr. Calvert?"

He didn't sound like he was interrogating her—he sounded like he was sincerely curious.

"Bryan knew that Hal came here. He might have decided to ask him to come along to the cabin and tracked him down here."

Before Morelli could ask any more questions, she turned toward the pickup. "I have to get going. I need to call Hal's parents before I leave."

"Of course." He stepped forward and opened the driver's door for her. "As Sergeant Cromar said, if there's anything we can do, please let us know."

12

The day after Hal's closed casket funeral, Gwen sat at her desk in the hangar, looking through some papers she had found in Hal's desk related to the airport's operations. When the airport was sold to Turriff Brothers, Russo and Dottie weren't the only ones who would be out of jobs: Avondale hired contractors for landscaping, hangar maintenance, and other airport operations. She shifted her gaze from the papers to the window and the hangars across the ramp. There were also the pilots who would have to find new homes for their planes, undoubtedly at higher rates. She wondered how Arno would handle breaking the news to them. Like a bull in a china shop, she had no doubt.

In fact, Arno was at that moment lumbering across the ramp toward her hangar, looking very bullish. She heaved a sigh. He had been enough of a gentleman not to mention the Turriff Brothers deal to Gwen before Hal's service, and Bryan's the day before, but he was no doubt now ready to move on. She had to be ready to move on as well. On and out.

She heard his heavy knock on the hangar door and called, "Come in."

He stepped in and stood silhouetted against the bright light of the July afternoon.

She held up a hand to shield her eyes from the light. "Arno, would you mind closing the door?"

He pulled the door closed behind him, then crossed to the desk. "Hello, Gwen. Mind if I sit?"

"Of course," she said, and raised an eyebrow when he lowered himself into the chair. At least he had the decency to look uncomfortable.

"So, how are you doing?" he asked.

"Oh, come on, Arno, don't beat around the bush. I know why you're here."

"You do?"

She narrowed her eyes. "Well, I think I do, but far be it from me to make assumptions. Why *are* you here?"

He shifted in his chair. "Before Hal died, he and I had signed a contract. That day, in fact."

"Yes."

He examined her for a moment, then asked, "Did he tell you about it?"

"Yes."

"What did he tell you?"

She sat back. "Please go ahead. I don't want to steal your thunder."

He scowled and shifted again. "We decided to sell the airport."

She looked at him, stone-faced.

"It was a very attractive deal for us," he said.

"I'm sure."

He waited a beat, evidently hoping she'd say more, then plowed ahead. "Gwen, an airport is not a sound financial investment. We bought Avondale twelve years ago because we were two young guys who had made a lot of money from Scanridge Transport and loved planes and didn't have anything better to spend it on. But make no mistake—despite fuel sales and hangar rentals and flying lessons, it's not a money-maker. It's not even self-sustaining. And it's not a matter of just keeping the airport going as-is—we would have some significant expenses coming up. The powers-that-be will pull our license if we don't repave the runway soon. There are already pilots who won't land here because of its condition."

"I'm fully aware of the condition of the runway. I use it a lot more than you do—"

He waved her off. "The point I'm trying to make is that Scanridge Transport is the money-making side of the business. If we sell the airport property to Turriff Brothers, we'll have the money we need to take Scanridge national. It's the perfect opportunity—more and more people are looking to have the things they need delivered to their doorstep, and transportation companies need to be ready to step up. Offer a better delivery experience, even inside-the-home delivery of valuables or perishables ..." His voice trailed off as he noticed her expression. "Gwen, this Turriff Brothers deal is going to be good for you, too. You own Hal's half of Scanridge now—it's going to make us a bundle, I swear."

"I don't need a bundle."

He gave an exasperated sigh. "I'd be happy to sell the airport to someone who would keep it open if they offered a reasonable price, but no one is interested."

"I might be interested."

"Do you know how much Turriff Brothers is offering?"

"Yes."

"Can you match it?"

She hesitated. "Not at the moment."

"We can't wait, Gwen. We can't be forced to spend upwards

of a million bucks on the runway. We'd have to pull that money from Scanridge and that would be disastrous."

"I'm sure Scanridge could weather the storm."

His scowl deepened. "You're not interested in getting more involved in Scanridge, are you?"

"No. I'm sure you're doing fine with Scanridge on your own. I realize that you were largely running it on your own for the last year of Hal's life."

He leaned forward. "Gwen, I don't mind continuing to run Scanridge on my own. You don't have to hang around here. With the money you make from sponsorships, plus what you'll get from Hal's estate, you could go anywhere you want, get a fresh start somewhere else—Arizona, California, Washington."

"I like it here."

"But—"

"Arno, you don't really expect to convince me, do you?"

He sat back in his chair. "No, I suppose not."

"So why are you here?"

He stood and walked to the Extra, his hands in his pockets, then turned back to her. "After I signed the contract that day, Hal took it away with him. He said he wanted to sign it in private. He said he'd give it back to me the next day, with his signature on it."

A ray of hope began to twinkle at the edges of Gwen's consciousness. "And?"

Arno clamped his lips together, then said, "I don't know where the contract is now."

Gwen tried to keep the smile off her face. "You didn't keep a copy?"

"No. And even if I had kept a copy, it wouldn't have his signature on it."

The smile blossomed on her lips. "Isn't that a shame."

"Gwen," he said, clearly trying to control his temper, "it

sounds like Hal told you that he had signed the contract. If he did, then you know that it's what he wanted to have happen. I think you owe it to Hal's memory to act on his last wishes."

She raised her eyebrows. "But how do I know those were his last wishes? He may have told you he would sign, but he might have changed his mind before he did."

"Did he?"

She smiled sweetly. "I guess we'll never know, will we."

13

Ann and Mike sat at the conference table in Mike's West Chester office with Arno Scanlan. The office had formerly housed Mike's financial planning business, but once it became the headquarters of *Ann Kinnear Sensing*, Mike had switched up the decor's previous bright colors for a more subdued palette, as was appropriate for a business where many of the potential clients were recently bereaved.

"Mr. Scanlan," said Mike, "I know you and I discussed your situation on the phone, but it would be helpful for Miss Kinnear to hear it from you first-hand."

"Sure." Arno turned in his chair to face Ann. "It's about my partner, Hal Burridge, who died about a week-and-a-half ago. Hal and I co-owned Scanridge Transport, a regional trucking company, and Avondale Airport." He grimaced. "Made our money on one and spent it on the other. I'll leave you to guess which was which."

"I take lessons at Avondale," said Ann.

"Yes, I've seen you out with Russo. In fact, he was the one who told me about your ..." He glanced around the office.

"Consulting business," Mike prompted.

"Russo recommended me?" asked Ann, surprised.

"We were talking, and I said in passing that there was something I wished I had been able to learn from Hal before he died. Russo said you might be able to ..."

"Contact him," said Mike.

"Yeah."

"Mr. Scanlan," said Mike, "it's natural to be a little uncomfortable. Many of our clients are initially a little uncomfortable about coming to us for help. They are often people who have exhausted other means of resolving their dilemmas and come to Miss Kinnear as a last resort. But I think you will be reassured by the fact that we treat these engagements in a completely straightforward and business-like way. We won't be burning incense or breaking out a Ouija board. I believe our approach will prove completely comfortable to a businessperson like yourself."

Arno glanced around the office. "It does seem like a business-like type of operation."

"Of course, Miss Kinnear heard about Mr. Burridge's death through her association with the airport," continued Mike. "We're sorry for your loss."

"Yes," said Ann. "Very sorry."

Arno heaved a sigh. "Thanks. As you probably know, he died in a plane crash. Bryan Calvert, who was the A&P at Avondale Airport, also died in the crash."

"What an A&P?" asked Mike.

"It stands for airframe and powerplant," said Arno. "Basically an airplane mechanic."

"Is your reason for wanting to contact Mr. Burridge related to your businesses?" asked Mike.

"Yes. The day he died, we had finalized a contract. I signed it, and he took it with him, saying he was going to sign it later that day. He died before he got it back to me, and now I can't find it. I've looked everywhere I can think of—at least the places I can get to. The last time I saw it, it was in a gray folder with silver stripes on it. Hal got those folders for promotional material for his wife, Gwen, but he used them for everything. I've looked through all the files, and any other place I think he might have put it. I'm hoping you can find out from him where it is."

"Are you able to share with us what the contract concerned?"

Arno glanced at Ann, then back at Mike. "It concerned the trucking company," he said.

"Is there anyone else who might know where the contract is?" asked Mike.

"Gwen Burridge might know."

"Have you asked her where it is?"

"Yes."

"What did she say?"

Arno crossed his arms. "What's the problem—you don't like me as a client?"

"We're happy to take you on as a client, Mr. Scanlan," said Mike smoothly, "but I want to make sure that Miss Kinnear's special skills are really needed. I'd hate to have you pay for our services and then find out the contract is sitting in Mr. Burridge's outbox and his wife didn't realize you were looking for it."

After a moment, Arno uncrossed his arms. "Fair enough. Yes, I've asked her, and she says she doesn't know."

"Is it possible she does know but doesn't want to tell you?"

"It's possible."

"Does she disagree with the plan for Scanridge?"

"Maybe she does, maybe she doesn't. But until Hal died and Gwen inherited his assets, the property was his to dispose of, and if he signed a contract indicating his willingness to sell, then I'm guessing I could make that stick, even if she decided to take me to court."

"There are bad feelings between you and your late partner's wife?"

"We've never exactly seen eye-to-eye."

"Has the cause of the plane crash been determined?" asked Ann.

"Not that I've heard," said Arno. "The NTSB won't make the final ruling for a while, but I'm guessing it's going to be night-time disorientation."

"Is that common?" asked Mike.

"More common than you'd think. That's what happened to JFK Junior, and I'm guessing that Clinton County, Pennsylvania, on a moonless night is about as dark as the ocean off the coast of Martha's Vineyard. You're out there with no visual references, your senses are telling you something different from what the instruments are telling you." He shrugged. "Calvert was a good pilot, but it can happen to anyone."

"Might alcohol have been involved?"

"Not that I know of. Calvert was a careful pilot as well as a good one, so I doubt he would have been drinking before a flight. I have no doubt that they would have found alcohol in Hal's blood if they had been able to test ..." His voice trailed off.

"They weren't able to test?" prompted Mike.

"I heard that the bodies were too badly burned to get an accurate reading," said Arno with some reluctance. "But Hal was the passenger, and I'm sure Calvert wouldn't have turned the controls over to him."

"No suspicion of foul play?"

"Not that I've heard of. Plus, I can't imagine a scenario where someone would have wanted to get rid of both Hal Burridge and Bryan Calvert."

"It was Mr. Calvert's plane?"

"Yes."

"Is there anyone who might have wanted to get rid of him,

and Mr. Burridge's death was," Mike cleared his throat delicately, "collateral damage?"

"I can't think of anyone who would have wanted to get rid of Bryan. He wasn't chummy, but the pilots respected his skills and he ran an honest business. That's what the people at Avondale care about."

"I know you might not be in a position to answer this, but how about people outside the airport?"

"Calvert spent almost all his time at the airport, or up at his cabin in Clinton County. He was a loner as far as I could see."

"Anyone who might have wanted to kill Mr. Burridge and didn't mind if Mr. Calvert was collateral damage?"

Arno scowled. "You ask a lot of questions."

"I want to make sure Miss Kinnear doesn't find herself in an awkward situation."

Arno shook his head. "I don't know of anyone who would have wanted to kill Hal."

"You said Mrs. Burridge inherited her husband's assets," said Mike. "Maybe she was looking for some quick cash. Is she in a position where she could have caused the plane to crash?"

Ann suddenly remembered the woman she had seen emerging from the hangar the day of her cancelled lesson, the day that she now knew Russo and Dottie had learned of the crash. "Hal Burridge's wife is the aerobatic pilot based at Avondale."

"That's right," said Arno.

"If she's a pilot and knows airplanes—" began Mike.

"There's always a way to bring a plane down if you want to," said Arno impatiently. "I just don't see her having done it. I'm not a huge fan of Gwen Burridge, but she has money of her own from sponsorships, and if she had wanted more, all she would have had to do was ask Hal." He shook his head. "No, I can't see her as a cold-blooded killer." He smiled humorlessly. "Cold-blooded, yes, but murder seems extreme, even for the Goddess of the Air."

"She calls herself the Goddess of the Air?" asked Ann with a raised eyebrow.

"She calls herself the Peregrine Falcon." He gave a short bark of laughter. "And Hal Burridge was her quarry."

Mike waited, but Arno evidently didn't plan to elaborate. Mike glanced at Ann. "What do you think?"

Ann gave the response that indicated to Mike that she approved accepting the engagement. "I'd be willing to take it on." *It sounds interesting* would have indicated to Mike that she wasn't, in fact, interested.

Mike turned to Arno. "Consider us on the job."

"One thing," said Arno. "I need to make sure this stays among the three of us. I don't want to be reading about it in the *Philadelphia Chronicle*. I don't even want to be hearing it on the airport grapevine. And I especially don't want to hear about it from Gwen Burridge."

Mike's lips tightened. "Mr. Scanlan, if you reviewed the material I sent you, you'll recall it included a copy of the confidentiality agreement, which guarantees that the work we do with you will be done in complete confidence."

"Yes, I saw that. I just wanted to reiterate—"

"It's not necessary to reiterate."

Arno looked from Mike to Ann and back. "All right."

"Where exactly did the crash occur?" asked Mike. "It's most common for Miss Kinnear to make contact at the site of the person's death."

"It's in Clinton County, in the north-central part of the state. The plane went down about three miles from the nearest road. I can get you a map."

Mike tapped a note into his phone. "I'll line up a guide to take Miss Kinnear there. What time did the crash happen?"

"NTSB says around midnight."

"We would probably need to stay overnight for at least one night," Ann said to Mike.

"I'll arrange that," he said, and tapped some more, then glanced up at Arno. "The rate schedule I sent you is acceptable?"

"Yes, it's fine."

"With the bonus if Miss Kinnear is successful locating the contract?"

"Yes."

"Very good. I'll contact you with a proposed date once I confirm some logistical arrangements. Ideally Miss Kinnear will be able to make contact—assuming Mr. Burridge is there to be contacted—on the first visit. If not, we can assess dates for additional visits."

"I'll need to be there. I want to ..." Arno shifted in his seat.

"Talk to him yourself?" said Mike.

"Yes."

"That's fine, as long as we can find a time that's workable for you and Miss Kinnear."

"I'll make myself available."

"Excellent. I'll draw up the final contract and send it to you this afternoon."

They stood and exchanged farewell pleasantries, and Arno lumbered out of the office. They heard his heavy tread descending the stairs.

"I haven't heard the 'many of our clients are a little uncomfortable' speech before," said Ann.

"He seemed a little squeamish."

"I also loved the 'it's not necessary to reiterate' line."

"Can't let the clients think they're calling all the shots."

"And you negotiated a bonus for finding the contract?"

Mike grinned. "That's my favorite part."

14

Scott jumped up from his chair on the deck to slide the screen door open for Mike, who had his hands full with a tray.

"What's the offering for tonight?" asked Scott.

Mike placed the tray on the deck table. "Margaritas and deviled eggs."

"Yum!"

Mike distributed the salt-rimmed glasses, then placed the plate of eggs in the center of the table.

"You only made a dozen," said Ann. "What are you guys going to eat?"

"How someone as skinny as you are can put away a dozen deviled eggs—and not get sick as a dog—is beyond me," said Mike, who quickly placed four egg-halves on his plate.

Ursula snapped into the begging position next to Scott's chair, and he scooped a dollop of filling from one of the eggs and held it out to her to lick.

"Did you talk to Garrick about the documentary yet?" Mike asked Ann as he settled into a chair.

"I did. He's evidently waiting for me to make up my mind before he gives Corey an answer."

"Waiting for you?" Mike crowed. "Who's looking to whom for guidance now?"

"Don't be so self-satisfied," said Ann. "It just means that he doesn't have to be burning brain cells deciding what to do."

"I'm not *self*-satisfied—I'm satisfied for you. I think Masser's starting to realize who the real star is."

"I don't want to be a *star*—" began Ann.

"Kids, kids," said Scott, "can we please not have a *who's the fairest of them all* argument over cocktails?"

They sipped their margaritas, then Ann said, "Speaking of being an unwilling star, did you know there's an *Unofficial Ann Kinnear* YouTube channel?"

"I did," said Mike.

Ann sat forward. "And you didn't tell me?"

"I knew you'd just get yourself all in a lather."

"Why shouldn't I get in a lather? Who knows who this *AnnFan* is who's running it—"

"I know who it is. I researched it when the channel popped up on my Google alerts. It's Mavis."

"Mavis Van Dyke?"

"How many Mavises do you know?"

Ann thought back to all the houses she had visited, and all the bottles of wine she had drunk, with Mavis Van Dyke. Early in Ann's sensing career, Mavis had been her most profitable client. Although Ann hadn't seen her since she had finally found Mavis a home occupied by a friendly spirit, it appeared that Mavis's fascination with Ann's spirit sensing abilities hadn't waned.

"I wouldn't have thought Mavis Van Dyke was technically savvy enough to figure out how to set up a YouTube channel," said Ann.

"I think she probably hired someone to do it for her."

Ann sat back. "I still don't like it."

"It's all very complimentary. If I were putting up a YouTube channel to drum up business, I'd be embarrassed to post stuff that gushy."

She sat forward again. "I don't—"

Scott, evidently in an attempt to avert another argument, said, "Mike told me about your new engagement. It sounds perfect for you. You're getting so interested in aviation, this will give you a whole new perspective." He took a sip of his drink. "The crashing perspective, true, but nonetheless ..."

"I tried calling Walt Federman to see if he could go with you and Scanlan to the site," said Mike. "I thought his aviation knowledge could come in handy. Turns out he's ferrying a plane out to Washington state, but he had an even better option. He knows the guy who acted as a guide for the NTSB investigators: Ellis Tapscott. He's local to the area, a pilot, and evidently an outdoor enthusiast. He can take you and Scanlan there, and he might have some inside information that won't be made public until the official accident report is released. He just has to get out of some summer work-study thing."

"How old is he?"

Mike shrugged. "College age."

"You're sending me into the wilds of Pennsylvania with a college kid?"

"Hey, Walt vouched for him."

She took a sip of margarita. "True."

"In the meantime," Mike continued, picking up his laptop, "I did a little research of my own."

"I thought research into clients or subjects was verboten," said Scott.

"I know I've said that in the past," replied Mike. "I thought we were somehow protecting ourselves from accusations of fraud by not doing research. But if someone doesn't believe Ann can do what she does, then they're unlikely to believe that we didn't do the research, and if they do believe she can do what she does, then they're likely not to care one way or the other. Plus," he added with some satisfaction, "we have so much business coming in we can afford to ignore the disbelievers." He turned to Ann. "What do you think?"

"Sounds good to me—the more information, the better."

"Good." Mike tapped the keyboard. "One of the aviation magazines did a profile of Gwen Burridge a couple of years ago. Sounds like Hal Burridge initially bankrolled her aerobatic and air racing career, although since then she's gotten a bunch of product sponsorships, including Jura Bernois, and she's paying her own way."

"Those are gorgeous watches," said Scott.

"That's for damn sure. If we sold the townhouse, we might be able to afford one for each of us." He tapped some more. "They met when Burridge and Scanlan bought Avondale Airport twelve years ago. She was eighteen and he was thirty-eight. Fell in love and got married seven years later. There's a video." He positioned his laptop so Ann and Scott could see it, then, standing behind them, reached over and started the video.

Two tuxedoed men and a man wearing a clerical collar stood in front of what Ann recognized as the Avondale Airport FBO, which had been greatly spruced up with flowers and bunting. One of the tuxedoed men was Arno Scanlan. The other was a slender, medium-height man with thick brown hair, the waves of which had been tamed by a precision haircut, his sun-darkened skin lined only by a V of smile lines at each eye: Hal Burridge. The camera zoomed in as Arno leaned over and whispered something to Hal, and Hal, whose gaze was fixed on something behind and over the camera, smiled and nodded.

The rumble of an airplane engine could be heard building

in the video, and the camera panned away from the men, catching as it did two groups of onlookers. One group, seated in folding white wooden chairs in front of the FBO, was dressed in formal clothes—the men in suits and ties, many of the women wearing elaborate hats. Another group stood behind streamer-decorated ropes that had been strung between the FBO and the nearest hangar. Most were more informally dressed, but it was possible to glimpse a dress here, a sport coat there. A couple were carrying microphones and video equipment.

The camera tilted upward just in time to catch a plane streak over the airport, a dark metallic blue that sparkled against the cloudless sky.

"The Peregrine Falcon, I presume," said Scott.

The plane shot upward, and the pilot turned on the smoke, leaving a vertical column of white in what must have been nearly stationary air. The smoke turned off, the plane pivoted into a dive, and the smoke turned on again, etching another line parallel to the first as the plane plunged toward the ground. The video picked up a few gasps and exclamations from the onlookers before the smoke turned off and the plane streaked upward again. It maneuvered back toward the columns of smoke, then released another burst that joined the two.

"It's an H!" exclaimed Scott.

The skywriting continued, with the camera periodically tilting back to the members of the crowd, who were laughing delightedly and pointing, and to Hal Burridge, who looked skyward, his hand shading his eyes.

The plane swooped and swerved through the sky: *H ... + ... G*

The crowd whistled and cheered, and the camera caught Arno laughing and clapping a grinning Hal Burridge on the back.

The plane came in for a landing, its decoration clearer now: bands of silver, blue, and white on the fuselage mimicking the underside of a falcon, the wings decorated with stylized feathers, the spinner a bright yellow. It taxied toward a red strip on the ramp.

"That's not smart," said Ann. "The red carpet's going to get sucked up by the prop wash."

Scott leaned forward in his seat and peered at the screen. "I think it's painted on the ground."

The plane powered down and a figure climbed out onto the wing. It was clear from the body-hugging lines of the silver-white flight suit that it was a woman. She pulled a silver helmet from her head and a cascade of auburn waves fell to her shoulders.

"I thought it was some special effect when they did that in the movies," muttered Ann.

Gwen waved to the crowd gathered behind the ropes, which greeted her acknowledgement with whoops and cheers. She dropped the helmet onto the seat she had just vacated and from the other seat picked up a bouquet of flowers, all whites and silvery lavenders, except for one bright yellow flower at its center.

"Why does she always have a little bit of yellow?" asked Mike. "The one yellow rose—the yellow piece on the front of the plane?"

"Peregrine falcons have that little bit of yellow at the top of their beaks," said Scott.

Gwen jumped lightly to the ground as, off-camera, a string quartet struck up a song. She walked slowly up the red strip which, as Scott had guessed, was clearly painted on the asphalt. She reached the spot where Hal, Arno, and the minister stood, the now-quiet crowd forming the backdrop of the shot. She managed to time her arrival just as the last strains of the song died away. Her eyes were shining. Hal beamed at her, wiping a tear from his cheek. They stood side by side and turned to the minister.

"Dearly beloved, we are gathered here today—" the minister began.

Mike pressed *Stop* on the laptop.

"Hey!" protested Scott. "We were just getting to the good part."

Mike rolled his eyes and hit play so they could watch the remainder of the video: a thankfully brief ceremony, after which black-and-white-clad servers emerged from the FBO carrying trays of champagne glasses that they distributed to the invited guests as Hal and Gwen Burridge distributed hugs and kisses. Then Gwen moved to the roped-off area to shake hands and accept several bouquets passed to her from well-wishers before the video ended.

"That was very romantic," said Scott.

"Unfortunately, the honeymoon didn't last," said Mike.

Scott waved his hand. "I don't want to see the post-honeymoon part now, let me enjoy the happy part for a little while first."

Ann was tapping her phone. "Gwen Burridge is going to be performing at an airshow at Avondale Airport this weekend. Maybe we should go check out the Peregrine Falcon in person."

15

The morning of the airshow, Ann took Ursula for a walk early, wanting to take advantage of the relative cool in advance of the spike of heat expected by noon. The highs were forecast to climb steadily over the coming days, from the low eighties into the nineties.

They had just completed the outbound portion of the walk and turned for home when a vintage Buick Grand National slowed and stopped and the driver climbed out. Her hair was styled in the closest thing to a beehive that Ann had seen anywhere other than old movies, nicely set off with a pair of cat-eye glasses. She was wearing a sleeveless yellow blouse, a pair of black and yellow plaid pedal pushers, and yellow flip-flops decorated with rhinestones.

"Ann?" the woman said. "Ann Kinnear?"

Ann racked her brain for who this person could be. She was old enough to have been a teacher in the West Chester elementary school that Ann and Mike had attended, but if she had dressed like that then, Ann would surely remember the look—and the jokes that the kids would have made about it. A friend of her late parents? A client of Mike's former financial planning business whom she had met at his annual client picnic? Again, she thought she would remember the get-up. Maybe the woman was on her way to a costume party.

"Yes," she said guardedly.

"I knew it was you!" said the woman as she stepped onto the sidewalk. "I never drive through this neighborhood, but I had to drop some old cans of paint off at the Art Association and the GPS sent me this way. What am I saying? It was the good Lord who sent me this way so I would see you."

"I'm guessing we've never met," said Ann tiredly.

"Not in person, but I feel like I know you!"

"I'm sorry, I need to get going," said Ann, trying to dodge around the woman, but a hedge on one side and an overturned recycling container on the other blocked her way.

"I saw your video on YouTube," said the woman. "I saw what you did up in Maine."

"I've got to get my dog home," said Ann. She turned to backtrack around the container. The woman followed.

"I read about your dog," she said, "the one in the Adirondacks. He was bigger than this one, right?"

Ann thought with a pang of her dog, Beau—a shaggy shepherd mix—whose spirit was leading a contented canine existence in the woods surrounding her Adirondack cabin. Ursula had appeared at the cabin in Beau's company, and Ann had originally thought that Beau was collecting a pack of fellow spirit dogs—until she reached out and rested her hand on the dachshund's sleek little head. "I'm sure if you do enough Googling, you'll be able to find out," she snapped. She stepped off the sidewalk into the street, figuring that would pose fewer obstacles.

The woman continued to follow, leaving her car, still running, in the middle of the street.

"My husband died last month," said the woman, puffing slightly to keep up with Ann.

Ann tried to rein in her irritation. "I'm very sorry to hear that. You have my condolences."

The woman shrugged. "It wasn't a surprise. He smoked like a chimney. I was cleaning out his workbench and I found a lockbox but no key, and I don't want to pay a locksmith to break it open. You could ask him where the key is."

"My brother handles my schedule. Just go to *annkinnear.com* —his contact information is there."

"We don't need to schedule anything, we can go right now. And I even know where you'd be likely to find him."

Ursula found something intriguing in the gutter and flattened herself onto the ground next to it to get a better sniff. The dog was immovable in that position, unless Ann wanted to drag her down the street by her harness. She bent down and scooped up the dog.

"It's not far," the woman continued. "I could drive you there."

"Ma'am, you really need to—"

The woman held up her hand. "I get it. I wouldn't want to get in a car with someone I didn't know, either. But there wouldn't be any danger in following me. It's not fifteen minutes away." She glanced around. "Where do you live? If you don't want to get in my car with me, I'll follow you to your house so you can get your car."

"Ma'am, I'm not following you." Ann managed to dodge the woman and began walking briskly down the middle of the street in the direction of the townhouse, the woman trailing after her.

"You could meet me there," puffed the woman. She managed to pull ahead of Ann and turned to block her way once again. She could move pretty fast, despite the flip-flops. "Mickey's Bar, right on West Chester Pike."

"You'll need to talk to my brother if you want to arrange an engagement." She'd have to warn Mike not to take on work for any female caller with a pronounced Philly accent.

"I don't need an *engagement*. I just need you to have a quick chat with Mac."

Ann heard an approaching vehicle. She turned with some trepidation, suddenly wondering if the woman had set her up for an ambush, or whether the new arrival might provide an opportunity to end the conversation.

An SUV was negotiating its way around the woman's car. Ann turned back in the direction of the townhouse and tried to sidestep to return to the sidewalk, but the woman managed to block her again.

Ann stopped. "I generally don't do pro bono work."

"What?"

"I don't work for free."

The SUV came to a stop a dozen yards behind Ann.

"Oh, you don't work for *free*, do you? Not even to help a woman who just lost her husband."

Ann heard the door of the SUV thunk closed. Just what she needed—a witness to her argument with this crazy person.

"Ma'am, pretty much everyone I do work for has just had a loved one die. And it is work. It's not a hobby, it's my job."

The woman put her fists on her hips. "Like you couldn't afford to take an hour out of your day."

Ann could feel the beginning vibration of a growl in Ursula's chest.

She turned back toward the SUV. "Sorry for blocking the road, we'll be out of your way in a ... Corey!"

When Ann had last seen Corey Duff at the party he threw for the cast and crew of *The Sense of Death* documentary, his tousle of red hair had been matched with a somewhat unkempt beard and mustache, but now he was clean-shaven. He had lost not only his facial hair but also about twenty pounds.

"Who's he?" asked the woman.

Corey reached the two women. "How are you doing? I'm Corey Duff."

"Betty Mahoney. Are you that guy from the spy movies? The one from Overbrook Park?"

Corey laughed. "Nope, I'm flattered to be mistaken for him, but I believe you're thinking of Sean Fields."

Betty jerked her head at Ann. "Are you her boyfriend?"

"You flatter me again, but I can't claim that privilege."

Ann rolled her eyes.

Betty crossed her arms. "I asked her to come just down the road with me to get one tiny piece of information from my late husband and she refused."

"Well, she's a very busy woman." He turned to Ann. "I'm guessing we're heading in the same direction. Want a lift?"

"You bet."

She and Corey started back toward his SUV, the woman trailing behind them.

"Someone gets a little famous," said Betty, "and suddenly she's too good for the rest of us."

Corey opened the passenger door of the SUV and Ann climbed in.

"Just like you, Mr. Overbrook Park. You leave for Hollywood and when you come back to Philly you decide to use a fake name."

Corey went to the driver's side and climbed in.

Betty fished a phone out of her back pocket and aimed it at the car. "I'm taking a picture so I can tell people what Ann Kinnear and the spy movie guy are really like."

Corey eased the SUV past Betty, who was still pointing her phone at the car. He gave her a cheerful wave. Ann also raised her hand, although more half-heartedly.

"Corey, what are you doing here?" she asked as he accelerated down the street.

"Nice to see you," he said. "Cute dog."

"Thanks. Nice to see you, too. But what are you doing here?"

"I thought I might be more convincing in person than over the phone."

Ann glanced in the rearview mirror. Betty was hurrying back to her car. "Can we drive around a little bit? I don't want to lead her right back to the townhouse."

"Sure thing."

When he reached the end of the street, the GPS in the dash instructed him to turn left. He turned right.

"If we can lose her, want to grab some coffee?" he asked. "A hoagie? Cheesesteak? It is not possible to get a good cheesesteak in L.A. I'll bet there are good diners around here."

"I can't. Mike and Scott and I are going to an airshow."

"Sounds fun."

"It's for an engagement."

"Still sounds fun."

She raised an eyebrow. "Want to come along?"

He grinned. "Sure."

She looked in the rearview mirror. "I think we lost her."

"You know, the video she took is probably already up on social media," he said.

Ann groaned.

"Now she has a platform to describe what a jerk Ann Kinnear is. She'll own the story. *Your* story. When we do the documentary—"

"Don't jump the gun—I'm still thinking about it."

"You've been thinking about it for almost two weeks."

"It's complicated."

"How complicated could it be? I remember you telling me after we wrapped *The Sense of Death* that you appreciated having the chance to tell your side of the story. This will be the same, except better because it will just be you and Masser—the two best-known spirit sensers in the country. It would be therapeutic for you."

"Plus, you don't get funding unless I sign up, right?"

He grinned again, more sheepishly this time. "That, too."

16

C orey drove them to Avondale Airport in his rental SUV, Ann in front, Mike, Scott, and Ursula in back. Volunteers wearing yellow vests directed them to a mowed field that was functioning as a temporary parking lot. Families unloaded foldable chairs and coolers from the backs of minivans. White-haired men, many wearing baseball hats with military insignia, arrived singly or with a buddy or wife. A banner strung across the drive read *Welcome to the 20th Annual Avondale Airport Community Day*.

Ann had attended airshows at Atlantic City and Reading and, in comparison to those, this one was small—an event no doubt aimed at maintaining good relations with the neighbors who put up with the drone of arriving and departing planes. A row of classic cars was lined up behind the hangars, hoods open, chrome polished to a high sheen. A line of kids waited at the face-painting booth, and many of those who had already visited it sported a bird-of-prey design. A bit further on, food trucks offered lemonade, hamburgers, cheese fries, gyros, and, Mike's favorite, funnel cake.

"How about setting up over there?" asked Scott, pointing to a small hill near the hangars. "That will give us a good view of the performances, plus good people-watching." He glanced skyward. "And we should get a little shade from the hangar as the sun moves."

Scott spread two blankets on the rise. Mike and Scott sat on one, Corey and Ann on the other. Scott broke off a tiny piece of Mike's funnel cake and dusted off the powdered sugar.

"I didn't know you didn't like powdered sugar," said Mike, popping a piece in his mouth and leaving a scattering of sugar on his shirt. "I would have asked them to only put it on half."

"I don't mind it, but I don't think it would be good for Ursula." Scott handed the piece over to the dog, who snapped it up.

"Hey!" protested Mike.

"It's such a tiny piece," said Scott, "you wouldn't even have missed it if you hadn't seen me take it."

A glider performance was in progress, accompanied by orchestral music played over the airport's PA system, the smoke emitted from the glider's wingtips tracing graceful arcs through the cloudless sky. Next, a Cessna 175 swooped through a tow banner demonstration accompanied by the local high school marching band oompahing out a Sousa tune. That was followed by a dogfight between a pair of startlingly large, loud, and realistic-looking radio-controlled planes. Then there was a break in the aerial festivities while prizes were awarded in the classic cars display.

"You want to go check out the cars?" Corey asked Ann.

"Old cars aren't really my thing," she said, "I'm mainly here for the planes."

"That's right, you said you were taking flying lessons."

"Actually, I'm taking lessons here."

"No kidding—that's cool." Corey looked around the airport with renewed interest. "We could bake that into the documentary."

"Corey," said Ann, "don't be a pest."

"Oh, go ahead, be a pest," said Mike, who was lying on the blanket, his hat over his face. "Maybe you can wear her down."

"Mind your own business," said Ann to Mike.

"It is my business—literally. Minding it is what you're paying me for."

"Well, if you don't want to see the cars," said Corey to Ann, "maybe you could show me around the airport. Seems like a charming place."

"Sure," she said, happy for the opportunity to deflect Corey's attention to something other than the documentary. She turned to Mike and Scott. "We'll be back in a little bit."

She showed him the Warrior she flew for her lessons and tested her retention of the facts she had been packing into her brain, giving him a run-down of the functions of the plane's components and the purposes of the various instruments. They wandered up and down the rows of hangars, some of which had their doors open, the planes' owners lounging in webbed lawn chairs, anxious to expound on their crafts' virtues.

As Ann and Corey approached the FBO, where Dottie was manning a table of brochures beneath a jaunty *Learn to Fly Here!* flag, Arno emerged. Ann was faced with the same dilemma that she imagined psychiatrists and gynecologists faced when they encountered clients in public: whether or not to acknowledge them. Arno made the decision for her by changing direction when he noticed her. She consoled herself with the thought that perhaps his disappearance was driven more by his desire for secrecy than by embarrassment at her profession.

A crowd was starting to form by the ropes near a free-standing hangar.

"Let's go see what all the excitement is about," said Corey.

Ann saw Russo standing on the other side of the ropes holding a small video camera at his side. His polo shirt was inexplicably sweat stain-free. He spotted Ann, waved, and approached the barrier.

"Playing videographer today," he said as he reached them.

"Corey, this is my flying instructor, Russo," she said. "Russo, this is Corey Duff."

"Boyfriend?" asked Russo.

"Do you have no filters between your brain and your mouth?" said Ann. "Corey directed a documentary I was in a couple of years ago."

"No reason he couldn't also be a boyfriend," said Russo cheerfully. "Doing a documentary on the Peregrine Falcon?" he asked Corey.

"I'm trying to talk Ann into doing another documentary, but she's playing hard to get." He gave Ann a grin. "Maybe I should switch my attention to this Peregrine Falcon. What is it?"

"Not what—who," said Russo. "You'll see for yourself pretty soon."

The crowd at the ropes grew and then a voice boomed over the loudspeakers. "Ladies and gentlemen, may I have your attention please."

The crowd quieted, a few remaining voices silenced by shushing noises.

"As some of you may know, Hal Burridge, one of the owners of Avondale Airport, and Bryan Calvert, who ran Avondale's maintenance shop, were killed two weeks ago in a tragic accident. They were both instrumental in making Avondale the place it is today—a thriving general aviation airport with close ties to the communities it serves. In their memory, we would like to observe a minute of silence."

The white-haired veterans removed their caps, the younger men following their example a few moments later. The people in the crowd dropped their gazes to the ground.

After half a minute, Ann became aware of a faint buzz,

becoming less faint with each passing second. She looked up, joined by others in the crowd who had also heard the sound, and saw the dots of two rapidly approaching planes. The buzz became a roar as two World War 2-era fighter planes swept over the airport, then split apart in graceful arcs, one disappearing to the east and one to the west.

"Fantastic," Corey murmured.

"Thank you," came the announcer's solemn voice. Then he continued in far more enthusiastic tones. "And now it's time for today's headline event, the performance you've all been waiting for—a performance that is dedicated to the memory of Hal Burridge and Bryan Calvert. Let's give a warm Avondale welcome to our hometown girl, the Peregrine Falcon herself ... Gwen Burridge!"

Gwen emerged from the freestanding hangar, hand raised to the enthusiastically applauding crowd. The colors of her flight suit were muted: dark gray with lighter gray trim, the only color a band of yellow-gold at the neck. The large, round sunglasses she wore mimicked the bright black eye of a predator bird. She was followed by a young police officer.

"I realize that Gwen's a big wheel on the airshow circuit," said Ann to Russo, "but police protection seems excessive."

"Arno usually asks for a couple of cops for the shows," said Russo, "mainly to keep people away from the runway. That's Rob Morelli, he was one of the guys who came to the airport to let Gwen know about Hal and Bryan. He probably asked for the airshow assignment—I think he's got a little bit of a crush."

Gwen stopped to shake hands with an older couple. The man pulled out a phone and Gwen took it, then waved Morelli over and handed him the camera. She leaned over the rope to pose with the couple as the officer snapped a few photos.

Russo laughed. "Arno's not going to be happy about that.

Morelli's supposed to be doing crowd control, not playing paparazzi."

After shaking hands with a few more fans, Gwen continued toward her plane, which had been staged in a roped-off section of the ramp. She was followed by a little girl carrying a metallic gray helmet and a woman who was probably the girl's mother. When Gwen reached the plane, she removed her sunglasses and handed them to the mother, then took the helmet from the girl and slipped it on over her auburn waves. She bent to give the girl a kiss on the cheek, then flipped the helmet's darkened visor down over her face.

"That get-up's got to be hot," said Ann.

"It's a great look, though," said Corey. "She's playing to the crowd."

Gwen stepped onto the wing of the plane, gave another wave to the crowd, then lowered herself into the cockpit and closed the canopy. The sound of the plane's engine firing up rumbled across the airport. Morelli retreated to the hangar, near where Russo, Ann, and Corey stood.

"What kind of plane is that?" asked Corey.

"An Extra 330LX," said Russo.

"What's 'extra' about it?"

"That's the designer's name—Walter Extra—but the name fits. Three-hundred-and-forty horses driving a carbon fiber airframe that weighs less than two thousand pounds—a lot less than your average car."

The plane began taxiing toward the runway.

Russo raised the camera. "Corey, next time you come to Avondale, bring your documentary crew along so I don't have to play cameraman."

"Will do," said Corey as Russo stepped away from the rope and raised the video camera to his eye to track the plane down the taxiway.

"Do you know Gwen Burridge?" Corey asked Ann, his eyes still on the plane.

"Not personally," said Ann.

"Really? I thought she must be your client, considering that her husband just died."

"Corey, don't try to trick me into telling you stuff that isn't any of your business."

He shrugged. "Not trying to trick you, but it was a logical assumption." He looked toward where the police officer now stood next to the hangar. "Mind if I talk to this Morelli guy?"

"Why? Hoping you can pump him for information about my confidential engagement?"

"No. The idea of doing a piece about a female aerobatic pilot isn't a bad one—*after* the one about you and Masser, of course—and it would be interesting to know what her fans think about her."

"I think it's pretty clear what her fans think about her," replied Ann, "but if you want to talk to him, be my guest."

Ann followed Corey to where Morelli stood.

"Good afternoon, Officer. Keeping an eye on Ms. Burridge?" asked Corey.

Morelli turned toward him. "Yes, sir. Just helping out where I can."

"Looking forward to the performance?"

"You bet—I've been a fan of Gwen Burridge for years," he replied with a grin.

"I understand you were one of the people who notified her of her husband's death."

Ann jabbed an elbow into his side and Corey suppressed a grunt.

Morelli's grin faded. "Yes. That was my first experience with being on a notification team."

"That must have been difficult."

"Yes, but not as hard as if she had fallen apart. She was very brave about it. That woman has nerves of steel."

As if on cue, Gwen's Extra roared down the runway and then popped into the air in a nearly vertical climb. The crowd whooped and cheered.

"She seemed more surprised by Mr. Calvert's death," Morelli continued, his eyes following the plane, "although that might be because her husband was ..." He blushed and glanced back at Corey and Ann. "Well, I understand her husband had been having problems over the last year or so. Maybe she wasn't so surprised that something had happened to him."

He turned back to the performance as Gwen's plane streaked past the crowd fifteen feet above the runway and upside down. Morelli joined in the crowd's enthusiastic applause.

"Sometimes people have a delayed reaction to that sort of news," he continued, his eyes following the plane as it disappeared behind some trees, "so when Sergeant Cromar left, I stayed around in case Ms. Burridge needed anything."

"And did she?" Corey asked.

"I thought she did, but it turned out I was wrong." Gwen's plane reappeared, corkscrewing skyward, trailing a path of white smoke. "She went over to the quarry after Sergeant Cromar left—walked over from the airport. I was worried about her—you never know what people might do when they've just gotten terrible news—so I drove over there to see if she needed anything. The back gate was unlocked so I went in. She said she was getting her husband's pickup truck so she could drive up to Clinton County, where the crash took place. She had everything under control."

"Why was her husband's pickup at the quarry?" asked Ann.

Morelli shrugged. "I guess he liked hanging out there. You wouldn't expect it, being that it's a quarry, but the area around the old pit is nice. I swing by there on my patrols sometimes. In any case, she said she saw his truck there when she was coming into Avondale to land."

"That's quite a story," said Corey. "Makes me even more interested in her as a documentary subject."

"Documentary?" asked Morelli, blushing. "Maybe I shouldn't have—"

Corey held up his hand. "It won't go any further, but it's a great illustration of her character. Are you a pilot yourself?"

"Hope to be someday," said Morelli. "I'm saving up for lessons."

Corey nodded toward where Gwen's plane was slowing in a climb. "You've got an impressive role model right there."

"She is an impressive lady," said Morelli. "I sure am glad she felt up for performing today."

For a moment, the plane hung suspended at the apex of the climb, then began to drop tail-first. After a few heart-stopping seconds, it banked out of its seemingly uncontrolled descent and shot forward, snapping through a four-point roll.

Morelli shook his head. "Nerves of steel."

GWEN CONCLUDED her performance with what was evidently her signature move: the hunting dive, where she mimicked the falcon's stoop by diving toward the runway and pulling up at the last moment, to the gratified shrieks and gasps of the audience. As she brought the Extra in for a landing, Ann turned away from the performance and started back to where they had left Mike and Scott.

Corey followed. "Impressive."

"And obviously she enjoys the attention," said Ann. "Why don't you just do the documentary about Gwen Burridge and forget about the one with me and Garrick?"

"Do I sense a bit of jealousy?" he teased.

"No, Corey, you sense a bit of irritation. I don't know why you keep banging away at the spirit sensing topic when you have a ready and, I'm sure, willing subject right there."

"Because my backers want you and Garrick," he replied. "I'm sure I could find backers for a documentary on the Peregrine Falcon eventually, but it would take time. You and Garrick are the hot ticket. I want to strike while that iron is hot."

"Flattering."

"Ann," he said, exasperated, "you and Garrick are the perfect subjects. The time is right, the topic is fascinating, it would be great for my business, it would be great for your business. And, I think, it would be great for you personally."

She stopped walking "Oh? Why's that?"

"Because the more people who see you demonstrate your talent under an objective lens, the more ammunition you'll have to combat the people who think it's crazy."

"Or that I'm crazy."

"That too."

"Or a liar."

"Ann ..."

"Corey, maybe I'm past caring if someone thinks I'm crazy or a liar."

She did an about face and stalked away.

17

W hen Corey pulled the SUV up in front of Mike and Scott's townhouse, Mike, who was in the passenger seat that Ann had insisted he take, said, "Care to come in for a drink, Corey? I've been experimenting with cocktail-and-hors d'oeuvres pairings. I could whip up a batch of Grasshoppers—I think they'd be good with gingersnaps."

Ann glared at him from the back seat.

Corey checked the clock in the dashboard. "I'd love to, Mike, but I'm supposed to be in New York City for a late dinner."

"Work?" asked Scott.

"It's to discuss project funding," he said. He glanced toward Ann. "In the hopes that the project will go forward."

"Don't hold your breath," muttered Ann.

"But don't count us out either," said Mike hastily. "It was great seeing you, Corey. I hope we'll have an excuse to be seeing more of you in the future."

"Yes," said Scott, "come by for the weekend some time, we have a spare room. Ow!"

"Yeah, I got the elbow myself," said Corey with a rueful smile.

"You are all hopeless," said Ann, climbing out of the vehicle.

Mike and Scott got out of the SUV and Scott placed Ursula on the ground. They watched Corey pull away.

"Seems like he's doing well for himself," said Mike. "Business dinner in the Big Apple, fancy wheels."

"I'm sure it's a rental."

"Those things don't come cheap, even to rent."

"Yeah, he's the golden boy, all right." Ann turned and headed for the townhouse, Mike and Scott following.

"If he took the time—and the expense—of stopping off to see you on his way to New York for a business meeting, he must really want you for his show," said Mike.

"He seems very nice," said Scott. "Handsome, too."

"Will the two of you just knock it off?"

She was sweaty and grimy from her day at the airport and went upstairs to shower. When she took off her T-shirt, she saw that her arms and neck had burned. No sleeveless or scoop-neck shirts for her until the farmer's tan faded.

When she came downstairs, Mike had prepared a round of Grasshoppers.

"Is it supposed to be that color?" asked Ann.

"Of course. Otherwise they wouldn't call it a Grasshopper," said Mike.

Ann took a sip and made a face. "It tastes like chocolate mint ice cream."

"Is that bad?" asked Scott, picking up his glass. "I like chocolate mint ice cream."

"I don't want to get my alcohol from something that tastes like a kid's dessert," she said, setting the drink aside. "I'm having a beer."

"Well, aren't you too cool for school," said Mike. He took a sip of the Grasshopper. "Hmm. Maybe you're right. I'll switch to beer, too."

Scott contemplated his first sip. "It might be better as an after-dinner drink," he admitted. "I'm putting mine in the fridge for later. Get a beer for me as well, would you, sweetie?"

Mike got three bottles of Headwaters Pale Ale from the refrigerator and handed them around. "Porch?"

"Let's sit in the living room," said Ann. "I just took a shower and don't feel like getting all sweaty again."

As they went living room, Mike's phone pinged. He pulled it out of his pocket and tapped, then said, "Do you have a secret dating life you're not telling us about?"

"What are you talking about? I have no dating life."

He handed her his phone, obviously trying to suppress a smile. It was open to a website called *Secret Romances*. She read the headline.

Are Actor Sean Green and Spirit Senser Ann Kinnear an Item?

Under it was a photo of Corey and Ann, clearly taken as Corey maneuvered the SUV around Betty Mahoney. Corey was waving cheerfully. Ann's raised hand almost but not quite blocked her scowl. Ursula's head was visible, her stubby front legs braced against the top of the door.

"What the hell?" said Ann.

"What?" asked Scott.

She passed him the phone.

"Wow," he said. "Well, Corey does look a lot like Sean Green in that picture."

"What does the article say?" asked Mike.

Scott scanned the article. "Evidently this woman encountered Ann out for a walk with Ursula and was talking to her when 'Sean' arrived and whisked Ann away."

"You didn't tell me about that," said Mike to Ann.

"I'm not in the habit of reporting back to you about every

weird encounter I have." She turned to Scott. "What else does it say?"

"The woman who took the picture seems a little ... peeved with you."

"Great." Ann took a gulp of beer.

The phone buzzed again, and Scott handed it back to Mike.

Mike tapped and put the phone to his ear. "Ann Kinnear Sensing, this is Mike Kinnear." After a moment, he said, "Hello, Mr. Abbott." He made a sour face at Ann. "Yes, I just saw that myself, but I think if you look closely, you'll see that it's not actually Sean Green ..." He stood and his voice trailed away as he headed toward his office.

"Lincoln Abbott of the *Chronicle*?" asked Scott.

"That would be my guess, based on his expression," said Ann.

After a few minutes, Mike emerged from his office.

"What was that all about?" asked Ann.

"He wanted to know if you're dating Sean Green."

"Good lord," muttered Ann.

Mike gestured toward their beer bottles. "Ready for refills?"

Getting *yeses* from both of them, he disappeared into the kitchen and returned a moment later with three bottles.

"The man's like a terrier with a bone," he said.

Ursula's ears pricked up at the word "bone."

"Ready to see the unhappy Burridges?" Mike continued.

"Sure," said Ann, "why not. It will match my mood."

Scott stood. "I had such a nice time today, I don't feel like ruining my mood with a depressing video. I'm going to get Ursula a B-O-N-E since you said the b-word in front of her."

Scott and Ursula retired to the kitchen while Mike hooked his laptop up to the TV. He pulled up a video from the *Philadelphia Chronicle* website. A soberly dressed reporter stood across the street from a church, holding an umbrella against a light drizzle.

"Today the medical and aviation communities mourned the loss of one of their own: Dr. Preston Gilman, pilot and enthusiastic supporter of general aviation in Chester County." He stepped to one side and the camera zoomed in on the mourners leaving the church. "St. Bartholomew Church in Kennett Square was filled to capacity with Dr. Gilman's many friends and admirers."

Mike muted the commentary as the segment showed mourners leaving the church and opening their umbrellas against the rain. After a few seconds, he said, "Here come the Burridges."

If Ann hadn't known the two people emerging from the church were Hal and Gwen Burridge, she wouldn't have realized that they were a couple. Gwen stepped out of the shadowed interior of the church's vestibule first, slipping on a pair of large, round sunglasses before starting down the steps.

"A little dark for sunglasses, don't you think?" she said.

"If Preston Gilman was so beloved, maybe she had been crying and her makeup was smeared," said Mike.

A moment later, Hal appeared. He unfurled an umbrella and moved toward his wife to hold it over her head, but Gwen was already striding away from the church steps, head held high, the collar of her silver-gray raincoat turned up against the drizzle, her hair pulled back in a severe, and rain-proof, bun. Her husband followed her for a few steps, evidently trying to catch up, then stopped, dropped his head, folded his umbrella, then followed her off-camera.

The view switched to the reporter interviewing some of the mourners. The third person to appear on camera was Gwen Burridge. The reporter had evidently caught up with the

Burridges just as they were getting ready to get into a Honda Ridgeline. Mike unmuted the sound.

"—understand you had a long association with Dr. Gilman," the reporter was saying.

"Yes," said Gwen, "Preston was a close friend, and a great support to me throughout my aviation career. He will be sorely missed in the aviation community." She turned to her husband. "Isn't that right, darling?"

Ann had rarely seen a person look as miserable as Hal Burridge looked, his face drawn, his eyes bloodshot, his hair plastered to his scalp by the rain.

"Yes. Sorely missed," he said, then reached to open the Ridgeline's door for his wife.

Mike paused the video. "What do you think of that? Not exactly the happy couple anymore."

"Well, they were at a funeral."

"But did you see their body language?" asked Scott from the doorway. "Did you see how far apart they were walking, the fact that she didn't wait for him when they left the church?"

"I thought you didn't want to ruin your airshow mood," said Mike as Scott sat down on the couch next to Ann.

Scott shrugged. "I got curious."

"When was that video from?" Ann asked Mike.

"About a year ago," said Mike. "Here's something more recent."

Mike pulled up a photo captioned *Gwen Burridge, the Peregrine Falcon, enjoys the show after her performance at the Fond du Lac Airshow.* She was standing on a raised viewing platform, her eyes shielded by the ever-present sunglasses, her mouth a thin line. Hal Burridge stood at her side, noticeably thinner than he had been in the previous video. He gripped a rolled brochure or program tightly in his hands and leaned toward his wife, his open mouth near her ear.

Gwen's face was turned not toward her husband or even toward the officials and other performers with whom she shared the stage, but skyward.

"Checking out the competition," said Ann.

"Or just enjoying the show," said Mike. "Why do you have such a bug up your ass about Gwen Burridge?"

"I don't have a bug up my ass. Look at her—she's not enjoying anything."

"When was that?" asked Scott.

"Just about a month ago."

"Poor man," said Scott. "He looks terrible. What could have happened?"

"Maybe marital difficulties." Mike took a sip of beer. "Maybe he should have hooked up with someone closer to his own age."

"Don't be silly," said Scott. "Age has nothing to do with it." He turned to Ann. "When you contact him, you can ask him."

18

Gwen entered Hal's office, glass of Pellegrino in hand, and flicked on the lights, flooding the room with light. No atmospheric mood lighting for her.

She had never felt the need for an office other than her desks at the airport—one in the hangar, one in the FBO for when the Pennsylvania winter made the hangar too cold even for her. Of the computers available in the house, the one in Hal's office, equipped with a large monitor, was more pleasant to use than her laptop.

When she had found out that Arno didn't have the signed contract, she had looked through every file on the desk and in its drawers for the document. No joy. She had finally remembered the combination to Hal's safe—the digits in the Extra's tail number—but with the same result.

She had gone through Hal's offices at the airport and Scanridge, and Dottie's filing cabinets in the FBO. She suspected Arno was doing the same. Whoever laid their hands on the contract first could ensure that their hopes for Avondale—as a thriving general aviation airport or a soulless development—was the one that came to fruition.

She'd have no compunction about destroying the contract if she was the one to locate it.

She crossed to Hal's desk and sank with a sigh into his chair.

She was relieved that the airshow had occurred as planned, especially since it was the twentieth of the annual Community Day events. She remembered attending the first one as a ten-year-old, gawking at the planes, sidling up to the hangars to listen to the pilot's talk. She had wandered away from her parents in search of the source of the throaty roar emanating from the vicinity of the hangars and had found a cherry red Stearman warming up for its performance. When her parents finally found her, she was grilling an amused pilot about why the plane had two sets of wings and why the little wheel was in the back. When they told her that it was time to go, she had been so distraught at the prospect of missing the Stearman's performance that they had eventually agreed, with mutual sighs, to postpone their departure.

When Hal and Arno had bought the airport, she had convinced Hal to continue the tradition. The residents of the neighboring towns and developments looked forward to it every year, but she wouldn't have put it past Arno to cancel it if the Turriff Brothers deal had gone through. The event had, in fact, been a great success, almost despite his best efforts to the contrary. Russo had told her that Arno had taken Officer Morelli to task for helping with the fan photos. It wasn't like he was needed to control an unruly crowd. They were there to see the Peregrine Falcon fly, not to make trouble. And it was clear that the attendees had been moved by the tribute to Hal and Bryan. The pilots who owned the vintage fighters were not only colleagues of Gwen's but also had been friends of both men and were happy to participate in the fly-over.

After her performance, and after the Extra had been rolled into the hangar, she had taken the few kids and teenagers who had signed up for the opportunity on a tour of the hangar. Their favorite part had been learning that Gwen had an extra engine for the Lancair, and that after the White Lake Air Races, she had the spare installed before flying home. She didn't want to rely on an engine that had taken a beating in the race to get her back to Avondale, on the other side of the country. After they dispersed, Dottie escorted an ancient man with a walker across the ramp to have his photo taken with Gwen in front of the Extra. She showed him the plane's controls and he told her of his war-time experience as a flier. As always at the Avondale events, there was a large contingent of veterans among the attendees.

She had signed a program for him. Then, in what she felt was an inspired move, she asked him to sign her helmet. Dottie had captured his embarrassed pride on video, which was already up on the airport's Facebook page. Gwen might have wished that his scrawled signature was not quite so large, but soon she'd be able to switch back to her usual, more brightly colored flight gear and would probably retire that darker helmet.

She powered up Hal's large monitor and inserted the memory card containing the video that Russo had taken into the computer. When she was on the road, Bryan had always videoed her performances; when she was at Avondale, Hal had always been the videographer. Today she had pressed Russo into service.

She had debuted Rob Holland's Frisbee maneuver at the airshow. She knew it would be a crowd-pleaser: audiences loved any maneuver that looked like the pilot had lost control. And Avondale was a great place to try out new additions to the performance. While no one in that crowd would know enough to be suitably impressed, no one was likely to realize if she got it wrong, assuming she didn't get it wrong with catastrophic consequences. She skipped through the video until she got to the maneuver.

As the Extra approached the center box, it traded altitude for speed in a Cuban eight, then slewed around, wings parallel to the ground, like an out-of-control car spinning on ice. The video picked up some gasps from the crowd, then relieved laughter and some scattered applause as she pushed the nose down into a hammerhead.

She crossed her arms, displeased. She hadn't entered the Frisbee fast enough. She needed to see Holland do it. She tapped some searches into the browser but couldn't find a view from the angle she needed.

She had a bootleg video of one of Holland's performances that provided the perspective she was looking for. She went to the bookshelves that held DVDs of her aerobatic video collection and pulled out the half-dozen cases devoted to Holland's performances. She had turned to go back to the desk when something caught her peripheral vision and she turned back to the shelf.

She pulled out another jewel case, then another, then grabbed a handful and set them on the floor. Her heart hammering, she pulled out what she had seen behind them: one of the gray-and-silver folders Hal had ordered for her marketing materials, with *Gwen Burridge: The Peregrine Falcon* embossed on the front.

The contents of the folder seemed like the right shape and weight for a contract.

She flipped open the folder, and almost groaned with disappointment. It was a magazine, a startling close-up of an eyeball staring out from its cover. A few Post-it Notes fringed the edge.

In addition to the magazine, a memory card, identical to the one Russo had given her of that day's performance, was taped to the inside of the folder. She pulled it off the folder and put it in her pocket.

She sank into the desk chair and slid her finger into one of the magazine's tabbed pages and flipped it open. She knew what she would find. She scanned the page listlessly. Nothing she didn't already know.

She flipped the folder closed and sat staring across the room. She knew why he had hidden it, why he had gone to the trouble of obtaining a paper copy of the magazine rather than accessing the content online. There were some searches that one didn't want a record of.

She pulled the paper shredder out from under the desk and, tearing out a few pages at a time, fed the magazine into the machine.

19

Two days after the airshow, Ann was on her way to Clinton County with Arno in his Beechcraft Bonanza. They were traveling light. Ellis Tapscott, the young man Mike had hired to guide them to the crash site, had advised Ann and Arno to bring just a couple of changes of underwear and socks and whatever toiletries they deemed vital for a hike into the woods. He would provide the rest of the equipment and supplies.

They were also traveling dog-free, despite the fact that Scott had offered to have Ursula accompany Ann on the trip. In the wake of a previous engagement, Ursula's demonstrated spirit-sensing skill had alerted Ann to the presence of the ghostly force that was responsible for a series of mishaps, ranging from a burned hand to a car wreck-induced concussion.

"She could keep an eye out for Hal Burridge," said Scott.

Ann looked at where Ursula sat at the top of the little stairway Scott had constructed so that she could look out the front windows of the townhouse. "I'd hate to tear her away from her neighborhood watch responsibilities."

"Maybe she'd enjoy a change of scenery," said Scott uncertainly.

"I don't think she'd enjoy a hike through the woods. Especially those woods."

"Those stubby legs can go for miles. I know—she wears me out on walks sometimes."

"And we'd be roughing it at the campsite. No fancy dog food for dinner."

Ursula sprang up from her perch, hurried down the stairway, and disappeared into the kitchen.

"You said the d-word," said Scott. "Now I have to give her a snack."

He followed the dog into the kitchen.

Now, as Ann and Arno flew northwest and the cities, towns, and farmland of southeastern Pennsylvania gave way to the forested expanses of the central part of the state, she was doubly glad that the dog was ensconced in the air-conditioned comfort of the townhouse. Stripes of forested ridges ran southwest to northeast, marching into a heat-hazed distance, ridges that eventually became the Pocono Mountains, then the Catskills, and finally the Adirondacks. Puffy white clouds floating a few thousand feet above them only occasionally blocked the sun that beat down through the plane's windscreen, although the cooler air at their altitude helped keep the temperature bearable. The drone of radio chatter and the thrum of the engine had a soporific effect, and Ann felt no need to fight the urge to nod off, knowing that she'd likely be having a late night at the crash site.

She was woken by a deadpan female voice saying, "Pull up. Pull up."

She jerked upright.

"No worries," said Arno. "It's just the terrain awareness system being alarmist."

She glanced around. The system had obviously been triggered by the proximity of the hills into which the Bonanza was descending as Arno lined up for the runway.

The Bonanza touched down and they taxied toward the FBO. As Arno powered down the plane in the tie-down area, a young man stepped through a gate in the chain link fence that separated the ramp from a small parking area and made his way toward the plane. Ann popped open the Bonanza's door and climbed out as Arno completed his shutdown checklist.

"Hi, I'm Ellis. You must be Ann. Welcome to Clinton County."

If Ann hadn't known that Ellis was a college student, she would have guessed him to be in high school based on his slight build and eager expression. She wondered if he was old enough to drink.

"First time to this part of the state?" Ellis asked.

"I think State College is as far northwest as I've gotten before," she replied.

"Probably a couple of degrees cooler here than it is back in Chester County," he said.

Ann glanced around the plane, at the waves of heat shimmering off the pavement under the late-morning sun. "Maybe once we get off the ramp."

Arno climbed out and further introductions were made.

Arno removed their small bags from the back of the Bonanza and, before he could object, Ellis had grabbed them and was walking briskly back toward the gate. "Nice day for a hike!" he called over his shoulder.

Arno and Ann were just finishing putting the canvas cover on the Bonanza when Ann heard the buzz of an airplane on approach to the runway. She turned and shaded her eyes with her hand.

"I've seen that plane around Avondale."

Arno followed her gaze. "Shit," he hissed. "That's Gwen's Lancair. How did she know we were coming here? I didn't see her car at the airport." He watched as the plane touched down with a squeak of wheels on asphalt, then he turned back toward Ellis's SUV. "Let's get out of here." He strode off toward the vehicle.

"Really?" Ann called after him. "If the crash site is nearby, don't you think she'll assume we're going there? Don't you think she'll follow us?"

Arno stopped, then reluctantly returned to where Ann stood. "Yeah, seems like the kind of thing she'd do," he growled. After a moment, he said, "She can't know why we're here. She shouldn't even know what you do."

"Fine. What do you suggest?"

Arno jammed his hands into his pockets and looked toward where Ellis was waiting for them by the SUV. "Does Ellis know why we're here?"

"Mike just told him we wanted to visit the crash site but nothing about why."

"We'll tell her I'm here to pay my respects to Hal, Ellis is my guide, and you're ... Ellis's girlfriend."

"I'm ten years older than he is."

He shrugged. "May-September romance. She'll understand that."

"Great," muttered Ann.

"Hey, Ellis," Arno called.

Ellis swung shut the back door of a Chevy Tahoe then jogged toward them, simultaneously watching with appreciation as the Lancair taxied toward the FBO. The plane was decorated in a similar color scheme to the Extra, but bolder—the fuselage silver with bands of metallic blue running its length, the cowling marked with a yellow-gold triangle running from spinner to windscreen.

"Man, check that out," Ellis said as he reached them.

"Yeah. That's Gwen Burridge—"

"*The* Gwen Burridge?" said Ellis, shading his eyes for a better look at the plane.

"Yes, *the* Gwen Burridge," snapped Arno. "Listen, as far as Ms. Burridge is concerned, Ann is your girlfriend, okay?"

"Why—?"

"Just humor me," said Arno.

Ellis glanced over at Ann, who smiled wanly. "Uh ... sure."

They watched as Gwen shut down, climbed out of the plane, and strode toward them.

"What are you doing here?" called Arno as she approached them. "You followed me?"

"I saw you were headed in this direction and I was curious as to why you were on your way to the crash site."

"What are you doing, watching every plane that leaves Avondale?"

"Even better." Gwen held up her phone as she reached them. "I have your Bonanza programmed into FlightAware."

"Jesus Christ," Arno muttered.

"So," she said, adjusting her large, round sunglasses, "care to tell me what you're doing up here? And who your friends are?"

"I wanted to visit the crash site to pay my respects. This young man and his ..." He hesitated. "... friend are going to take me there."

Gwen glanced from Ellis to Ann and gave them a curt nod. "I'm coming, too."

"We're camping at the site. Unless you've got a sleeping bag stashed in the Lancair, I don't think you're exactly equipped for an overnight stay in the woods."

"I have some equipment you can use, Ms. Burridge," said Ellis.

Arno glared at him.

Gwen's lips curled up in a smile. "Why, thank you—"

"Ellis. Ellis Tapscott."

"Thank you, Ellis, that's very thoughtful of you." She turned the smile on Arno. "You see, Arno—no problem in terms of equipment. Just let me arrange a hangar for the plane. I don't want it left out overnight."

Gwen turned and jogged back to the FBO.

"We could leave while she's sweet-talking some airport manager into clearing a hangar for her plane," said Arno.

Ellis looked shocked.

"If she can sweet-talk her way into hangar space, I'm sure she could sweet-talk someone into driving her to the site," said Ann.

"Fine, we'll wait for her." Arno stalked over to the Tahoe, climbed into the front passenger seat, and slammed the door behind him.

"Why are we supposed to tell Ms. Burridge that you're my girlfriend?" asked Ellis.

Ann shrugged. "Maybe Arno doesn't want her to think I'm his girlfriend."

"A little young for him, aren't you?"

Ann smiled at him. "Thank you, Ellis."

"She's not his girlfriend, is she?"

"Definitely not."

"Yeah, that would be even weirder than you being his girlfriend."

"I'm about the same age she is, you know."

"Oh. Sorry," he said, blushing.

Ann followed Arno to the Tahoe and got in the back seat, leaving Ellis on the ramp to wait for Gwen.

They sat in silence for about a quarter of an hour, Ann

watching planes arriving and departing, Arno tapping on his phone. Then the back door opened, Ellis standing aside to let Gwen in.

"They found some space for the Lancair," he said cheerfully.

"They always find space for the Lancair," said Gwen.

20

Half an hour after leaving the airport, Ellis steered the Tahoe off the two-lane highway onto a pull-off. "This is the closest we can drive to the site—we'll hike in from here."

Arno looked into the woods. "How far is it?"

"About three miles."

"I don't suppose there's a path."

"Nope," said Ellis cheerfully.

"Good times," muttered Arno.

Ellis pulled three packs out of the back of the Tahoe, gave them each a hiking stick, then assembled a fourth pack for Gwen from his spare supplies.

They shouldered the packs and started through the woods— Ellis in front, followed by Gwen, and then Ann, with Arno bringing up the rear. The temperature dropped to a more bearable level under the trees' canopy, and the shade cast by the branches meant that understory growth was fairly sparse. Every twenty-five yards or so, Ellis pulled from his pocket a strip of bright yellow plastic, like narrow crime scene tape, and tied it to a tree.

"Just in case anyone needs to get back to the car without me," he explained.

The ground angled gradually upward, and soon Ann was mopping beads of sweat off her upper lip and neck despite the relatively cooler temperature in the woods.

Ahead of her, sweat stuck Gwen's shirt to her back. Ann noted that Gwen's clothing colors were brand-right even when she couldn't expect to be beset by adoring fans: a white T-shirt with gray linen pants and dark purple espadrilles. By the time they got to the crash site, she was going to regret that she hadn't chosen hiking boots that morning. However, despite the fact that the shoes were ill-suited for the terrain, Gwen scrambled along without complaint.

Arno, on the other hand, while not complaining, was having a harder time with the hike. As the slope steepened, his breathing became more labored and he fell further behind the group. Evidently running a trucking company and an airport didn't involve a lot of physical activity.

In the stretches where the trees thinned sufficiently for them to walk two abreast, Ellis would drop back to walk beside Gwen. Ann could hear snatches of his conversation drifting back to her: *aerobatics ... Lancair ... Extra*. Ellis wasn't being very attentive to his presumed girlfriend, she thought irritably.

Not wanting to leave Arno behind, Ann slowed her pace to meet his.

"You don't need to wait up for me," he wheezed.

"I figured I'd give my boyfriend a chance to chat privately with his new crush."

Arno was evidently unwilling to expend any of his limited breathing capacity on idle chat, so they walked in silence. After a minute, Ellis glanced back and stopped.

"Everything okay?" he called back.

Arno waved him on. "You go ahead. We'll catch up with you."

Ellis hesitated for a moment, then gave a thumbs up and picked up his pace to catch up with Gwen, who had kept walking.

Arno sat down heavily on a rock. "Jesus. I have to get back to the gym."

Ann, not objecting to an opportunity to take a break, slipped off her pack and sat on a nearby log.

"What are we going to do when we get to the site?" she asked.

"Go through with the whole 'paying my respects' rigamarole, I suppose."

Ann raised an eyebrow.

He sighed. "I didn't mean that to come out sounding so disrespectful. Hal was a friend as well as a business partner—we were at Penn together, roommates freshman and sophomore years—but what difference could it make to him? I figure that kind of stuff is more for the people who are still alive than the people who are dead." He gave an ironic laugh. "Although obviously I may have to rethink that position if this trip is actually successful. We can ask Hal what he thinks."

"I did contact a guy once who was pretty pissed that his wife failed to include one of the hymns he had specified for his funeral service."

"No kidding? Well, I suppose if he told her that's what he wanted ..." Arno pushed himself to his feet. "Let's not let Gwen and the Tapscott kid get too far ahead."

Ann hoisted her pack and they set off after Gwen and Ellis.

The ground became somewhat rockier and Ann had to choose her foot placement more carefully. She had only taken a few steps into the rocky stretch when she heard an exclamation of surprise and a whump behind her. She turned to see Arno on the ground, gripping his knee.

"Goddammit!"

"Are you okay?"

"Twisted my knee."

Ann made her way back to him as he shrugged out of his backpack and climbed awkwardly to his feet with the aid of his walking stick. He gingerly tested his weight on his leg and winced. "Dammit." He hobbled over to a rock and lowered himself onto it. "I'm never going to be able to make it to the crash site."

Ann glanced up the slope to where she could just see Ellis and Gwen moving between the trees. "Want me to go get Ellis?"

"Not yet. They'll turn around eventually when they figure out we're not following." He glared after the disappearing forms, then moved his leg experimentally. "It's just twisted. I'll rest it for a couple of hours and then get back to the car. Good thing Tapscott put those markers up." He was silent for a moment, then continued. "We need an explanation for why you're continuing on without me."

They were silent for a few moments, then Ann said, "We could tell them that you wanted to leave a memento at the site, and you want me to do that for you. Or, maybe more believably, you want Ellis to do that for you since I'm just the elderly girlfriend tagging along."

That elicited a faint smile from Arno. "Desperation is the mother of invention, right?"

She laughed. "Something like that. Do you have anything that we could use as the memento?"

He thought for a moment, then pulled a keyring out of his pocket. He removed a key fob from the ring and turned it in his hand, running his thumb over it. "I hate to give it up, but it's the only thing I have with me that would make a believable memento." He handed it to Ann.

It was a brass oval with a vintage prop plane engraved on one side and *Avondale Airport - Burridge & Scanlan* on the other.

"Hal had one just like it," he said. "I understand it's what the police showed Gwen to get a tentative ID." He brightened. "Maybe you wouldn't actually need to leave it there, maybe you can sneak it back to me."

"Sure, I'll try."

"You'll need to find a way to talk to Hal without Gwen being around."

"Okay."

"Ask him where the contract is."

"Right."

"I don't need him to tell you any details about the contract—just where it is. Let him know that."

She raised an eyebrow. "Afraid I'm going to horn in on your trucking business?"

Arno waved a hand. "No, of course not. Just habit. I'm used to operating my businesses on a need to know basis."

"We need to plan for the possibility that I can't communicate with Hal but can communicate with Bryan Calvert," said Ann.

"Isn't it an all-or-nothing-type deal?"

"Not necessarily."

"I can't imagine that Calvert would know where the contract is, but if you can't get in touch with Hal, you might as well ask him."

"Arno, why doesn't Gwen want you to find the Scanridge contract?"

He massaged his knee, examining his leg as he slowly straightened and bent it. "Like I said, we've never seen eye-to-eye on things. The fact that I want it might be enough motivation for her to want to keep it from me."

"What is it between the two of you?"

He sighed. "When Hal and I were thinking about buying Avondale, it was a lark, you know? We were in our late thirties, had just made a bundle from Scanridge, had energy to burn, and figured it was no problem to run a small GA airport basically in our spare time. Then he met eighteen-year-old Gwen Davis manning the desk at the FBO and ..." He shook his head. "I had never believed in love at first sight, especially for Hal, who had always been such a level-headed guy—plus, at the time he was pretty serious with a woman closer to his own age —but he fell hard. I figured it was just a temporary infatuation, but once he fell, he ..." He gave a short laugh. "He stayed felled. The Falcon got her talons into him and didn't let go. Although she wasn't the Peregrine Falcon at the time, she was just pretty Gwen Davis, sweeping hangars in exchange for rides." He shifted his leg and winced. "She's been dining out on that story for years."

"So she was a gold-digger?"

There was a long pause, then Arno said, "I'm not going to badmouth Gwen—at least not more than I already have—but I don't think anyone would deny that Hal never had the same focus on Scanridge once he met her. Especially in the last year, he really lost his interest in the business. Hell, it seemed like he had lost his interest in just about everything. He was drinking. A lot. I was having to pick up the slack, and I think he felt bad about it. Plus, you screw up running an airport or a trucking operation, it can literally be a matter of life and death."

"What happened a year ago?"

He shrugged. "On the outs with Gwen? I'm really not sure."

Ann heard a call from up the hill. "You guys all right?"

She turned to see Ellis making his way toward them, followed by Gwen.

"I twisted my knee," said Arno as the pair reached them.

"You guys are going to have to go on without me. I gave Ann something I'd like to have left at the crash site."

Ann held up the key fob.

"How touching," said Gwen. "So it's just going to be me, Mrs. Robinson, and Benjamin Braddock here officiating at the ceremony?"

"What does that mean?" whispered Ellis to Ann.

She shushed him with a gesture.

"I'm not the one who invited you along," said Arno to Gwen. "In fact, since you don't need to be keeping an eye on me at the crash site anymore, maybe we can let Ellis and Ann go on to leave the key fob and you can come back to the car with me. I'll drive you back to Lock Haven. It's not too late for you to get back to Avondale before dark."

"Come on, Arno, you think I don't know Ann Kinnear, the most gossiped-about flight school student at Avondale Airport? I'm guessing you're hoping she'll be able to have a little post-mortem chat with Hal."

Arno's face turned an alarming shade of red. "He was my friend, I guess I have a right to experiment with—" He waved his hand at Ann.

Gwen raised an eyebrow. "I never figured you to have enough imagination—or to be gullible enough—to believe in that kind of thing."

"If you're so skeptical that she can do what she says, why don't you save your fancy shoes and turn around yourself."

"I'm curious to see how this circus plays out."

Arno tried to stand and fell back with a grimace. "I can't keep you from following them, although God knows I'd love to try, but Kinnear's here on my dime and I expect her to be able to discharge the job without interference from you."

"I'm standing right here, you know," said Ann.

They ignored her. "That's fine with me," said Gwen to Arno.

"If I actually thought for a minute that she was going to be able to communicate with my husband, I'd have been up here with her a week ago."

"Communicate with Gwen's husband?" asked Ellis.

"Didn't you know?" said Gwen. "Ann talks to dead people."

Ellis's eyebrows rose. "Really?"

"That's the claim. So," Gwen continued, turning to Arno with a smile, "I guess Ann's not such a close friend of Ellis's after all."

21

They agreed that Arno would drive Ellis's Tahoe to a motel in Lock Haven, then return to pick them up the next day.

"We can call you when we're getting ready to leave the site so you know when to pick us up tomorrow," said Ann.

"Probably not," said Ellis. "Cell service will be pretty spotty at the crash site, but it should be better by the road. Arno, we'll call you as soon as we're close to the pick-up point." He handed Arno one of the yellow plastic ribbons. "Tie this to a tree next to the pull-off so you can find it when you come back tomorrow. You can leave your backpack here—just take what you need to get back to the car, and I can pick it up on the way back." He rummaged in his backpack and produced a cold pack. "Just squeeze this to activate it—that should help keep down any swelling." Finally, he handed over his hiking stick. "Having two sticks will be better for balance."

"Appreciate it," grumbled Arno, trying valiantly to be gracious.

Ellis and Gwen turned and began climbing the hill again. When they were out of earshot, Arno turned to Ann. "If you talk with Hal and find out where the contract is, even if you think you're alone, Gwen might be eavesdropping. There's a bonus in it for you if you hike back toward the road far enough that you can call me and tell me where it is. I could fly back to Chester County, get it, and come back for you in the morning."

"You want me to hike through the woods in the middle of the night?"

"I'd make it worth your while."

"If you're so suspicious of Gwen, what makes you think she wouldn't just follow me and call someone back in Chester County—Russo or Dottie—to get to the contract before you could?"

He shook his head. "She's not likely to venture through the woods at night. For someone as fearless in the air as she is, she's a bit of a scaredy-cat on the ground."

Ann would have been perfectly comfortable taking a midnight stroll through the woods near her home in the Adirondacks, but less so in an area with which she was unfamiliar. "I think anyone wandering around here in the dark is asking for trouble. I'll be careful that Gwen can't overhear any conversation I have with Hal."

Arno appeared ready to argue, then nodded, resigned. "Just keep an eye on her."

Ann left Arno settling himself on a log to rest his leg before heading back to the road and hurried to catch up with Ellis and Gwen. Ellis's yellow markers were already proving helpful, since the pair was out of sight.

She caught up with them a few minutes later, in time to hear Ellis ask Gwen, "So what would you be doing today if you weren't up here in Clinton County?"

"Probably getting the Lancair ready for the White Lake Air Races next month."

"That's super impressive that you do air racing and aerobatics."

"Thank you," said Gwen as she picked her way through a muddy stretch.

"What's the difference between racing and aerobatics?"

"You pay money to race, you earn money when you perform. When you race, all your fellow pilots tell you where you screwed up, when you perform, all your fans tell you how great you are." She unhooked her shirt from a briar. "It's harder to find a women's restroom on the racecourse than at an airshow."

"So why do you keep racing?"

She smiled. "Because I'm great at it."

AN HOUR LATER, they crossed a small stream, Ellis and Gwen in the lead, Ann trailing a dozen yards behind. Fifty yards further on, they came to a clearing.

Ellis swung his pack off his back.

"The crash site is right over that rise," he said, pointing up the hill. "We'll set up camp here."

Although the impact site itself was hidden by the contours of the ground, Ann could see that the tops of some of the trees beyond the rise were splintered and their trunks charred.

Gwen swung her pack off her back with a groan of relief. The sleeve of her T-shirt was torn, the hems of her pants were muddy, and she was limping badly. Even Ann, despite being more suitably outfitted, was grateful to be able to drop her backpack.

"I'm heading back to the stream," said Gwen.

"You'll need to treat the water before you drink it," said Ellis. "There's a squeeze bottle in your pack. I can show you how to use it."

"At the moment I'm less interested in drinking it than I am in soaking my feet in it," she said, and began picking her way gingerly back toward the stream.

Ann wished she had thought of this herself but didn't feel like tagging along after Gwen. She sat down on the ground and pulled off her hiking boots as Ellis busied himself getting the camp set up.

"Why didn't Arno want Gwen to come up here with us?" he asked as he lugged a couple of logs over to provide seating. "If he wanted to have a sort of memorial service up here, it seems like he should have involved her."

"I don't think they're too fond of each other." Not being in the mood to justify Arno's actions to Ellis, she said, "So, you were up here with the NTSB team?"

"Yes. I showed them the easiest route and escorted investigators to and from the site."

"Do you have any inside scoop about the crash?"

"Not really. I haven't talked much with the folks I met from the NTSB since they left. I did download the preliminary report, though." He pulled out his phone, tapped, and handed it to Ann.

She relocated from the ground to one of the logs Ellis had dragged over. Ellis sat down beside her as she read.

The airplane impacted terrain at about 2350 Eastern time. The private pilot / owner and pilot-rated passenger were fatally injured. The aircraft was destroyed by impact forces and a post impact fire. Dark night visual conditions prevailed; no flight plan had been filed.

The wreckage was located within steep hilly terrain, just below a ridge line extending southwest to northeast, and included the fuselage, empennage, both wings, and the engine and propeller assembly. Curling of the propeller indicated that it was rotating at the time of impact. The condition of the accident site was consistent with the airplane striking the ground at a high velocity and steep angle in a left wing low attitude.

Fuel smell was present at the accident site. Residual fuel was tested; no water was detected.

"They don't say what caused the crash," said Ann.

"It can take a year or more for the NTSB to issue a final report, but you can tell some things from the preliminary report. He didn't lose the engine because the prop was turning when the plane hit the ground. He didn't run out of fuel because you could smell fuel at the crash site. I remember the smell, it was strong—the plane had auxiliary tanks and they must have been full when he took off. The fire was fierce—the scorch marks go high up the tree trunks. They must have come almost straight down based on the relatively small area where the trees show damage."

They turned toward the crash site and both jumped when they saw Gwen only a few feet away, walking gingerly over the ground in her bare feet, her espadrilles hanging from her fingers. She walked past them and sat down on a rock.

Ellis's face reddened. "Sorry, I didn't know you were there."

"It's fine," she snapped. "I can interpret an accident brief as well as you can."

"We can talk about something else."

"Don't change the topic on my account."

"How did they get the wreckage out of here?" asked Ann, hoping this constituted not changing the topic, but at least moving its focus to a slightly less grisly subject than Gwen's husband's demise: *blunt force and thermal trauma*, as she had heard such a death referred to in news articles.

"By helicopter," said Ellis. "They chop up the plane and take it out in bags."

"Too bad we couldn't have come in by helicopter," said Ann.

"As soon as you learn to rappel out of one, you can try it out," muttered Gwen.

"So, what's the plan now that we're here?" asked Ellis.

"Arno wanted me to try to contact Hal," said Ann, "as well as to leave behind the memento," she added hastily. "I'll check out the site and see if Hal's there," she tried to ignore Gwen's eye roll, "and if he's not there now, I'll go back at the time of the crash. People usually appear at the time as well as the location of their deaths."

"Knock yourself out," said Gwen.

Leaving Gwen massaging her feet and Ellis getting their camp set up, Ann trudged up the hill toward the crash site. She wasn't sure which was more aggravating—disbelief like Gwen's or excessive enthusiasm like Betty Mahoney's. Ann knew there were many more of both types whom she never encountered, since Mike usually ran interference for her, as he had done since they were children. She needed to keep that in mind when she got irritated with him for his own excesses, like his enthusiasm for Corey's documentary.

Although he was going to have to dial it back if he didn't want to make her turn Corey down just to be ornery. If she had agreed to the project already, would Corey have been lobbying to follow her up to the Clinton County crash site, equipment and supplies in tow? Would she have had a camera pointed at her as she sat here waiting, perhaps in vain, for Hal Burridge to make an appearance? She shuddered at the thought.

When she crested the rise, the scene was startling, even after having read the preliminary accident report and heard Ellis's commentary. All vegetation had been burned away in a circle fifty yards in diameter, at the center of which lay the depression marking the plane's point of impact. Even the soil had been charred into sooty granules. Outside the circle, the lower branches of the towering trees that surrounded the site were blackened and shriveled. She thought back to Arno's comment that the bodies had been too badly burned to determine if Bryan Calvert had been drinking before the flight. She hoped that, if she was able to contact Hal or Bryan, they would look as they had before the crash, not after the high-speed impact and fire. She had experienced both scenarios.

She crossed the charred ground and stepped down into the depression, then made a slow three-hundred-and-sixty-degree turn. She stood still and listened but could only hear the twitter of birds and the whisper of a distant jet.

"Hal?"

She let a minute tick by.

"Hal Burridge?"

Nothing.

She glanced at her watch. She'd give it an hour, then go back to the campsite.

With a sigh, she climbed out of the depression. She brushed at the blackened bark of a downed tree, leaving a greasy smear of soot on her hand. She wiped her hand on her pants, then sat down on the log to wait and watch.

———

22

Ellis proved to be the perfect host. After helping Gwen patch up her blistered feet with moleskin from his seemingly bottomless backpack, he arranged logs around a dormant fire pit to provide comfortable seating, and hung three hammocks, complete with mosquito netting. He prepared a dinner of fairly decent no-cook tacos. For dessert, he had dark chocolate and some blueberries he had picked near the stream. After that, he produced a deck of cards, although he was unable to entice Gwen or Ann to play.

When darkness fell, he built a small fire.

"I don't think we're going to have an issue with keeping warm," said Ann. "I can't believe it's going to go much below seventy tonight."

"I know," he said, "but I like the way it looks."

"I need to pee," said Gwen, casting a glance toward the trees. "Can I borrow the flashlight?"

"Sure," said Ellis. He passed her the flashlight.

She switched it on and took a few hesitant steps toward the trees, then paused when she reached the limit of the fire's illumination.

"We won't look, if that's what you're worried about," said Ann.

"Gee, thanks," said Gwen, not bothering to look at Ann. "That was definitely top of mind for me."

Gwen walked slowly toward the edge of the clearing, following the pool of illumination from the flashlight with what seemed to Ann to be exaggerated caution.

Ann turned back to the fire, although she could still see the flashlight beam moving among the trees in her peripheral vision. A few moments later, there was a muffled crash and the light swung crazily into the tree branches and then disappeared.

"Shit!" they heard from the woods.

Ellis jumped to his feet and ran toward the woods, Ann following more slowly. Although the campfire's glow reached almost to the edges of the clearing, there was no point in risking another person falling.

When she reached Gwen and Ellis, Gwen was getting to her feet and brushing leaves off her pants and shirt.

Ellis found the flashlight under a bush and handed it to Gwen.

She flicked it on. "I just got my foot caught in a branch. Or maybe a tree root."

Ann scanned the ground, which as far as she could see was devoid of branches or tree roots.

"Need any help?" asked Ellis.

"No, Ellis," Gwen replied testily, "contrary to appearances, I can pee on my own."

Ellis's blush was visible even in the dim light. "Sorry, I didn't mean that—"

She waved a hand. "I know. I'm fine. I'll be back to the camp-site in a minute."

"Sure, sure, no problem," said Ellis.

Ann followed him back to the fire. In a few minutes she saw

the flashlight moving back toward the campsite at an even more sedate pace than on the outward trip.

There was another scuffle of leaves, another thump, and then an irritated, "I'm fine!"

"Maybe she's been drinking," said Ann to Ellis.

"I didn't bring anything alcoholic."

"Maybe she brought a flask," said Ann. A flask would have been a good idea.

A minute later, Gwen rejoined them, her clothes somewhat muddier than they had been after her first fall. "I'll hold onto this if that's okay," she said to Ellis, indicating the flashlight.

"Sure, no problem."

Gwen lowered herself onto one of the logs. "So, Ellis, you're a pilot?"

"Yup. Just got my own plane—a 1946 Stinson 108. November niner three five five."

"Good for you," said Gwen.

"I've never heard of that kind of plane," said Ann.

"It's a classic. Good looking, handles great, docile in a stall. Plus," he added, "you can find them cheap. I like to fly low and slow." He smiled at Gwen. "Not you, though."

"No," she said. "I like to fly low and fast."

He waited a beat, evidently hoping for more details, but Gwen stared into the flames of the campfire. He turned to Ann.

"You're quite a celebrity yourself, Ann," he said, evidently taking seriously his responsibility to involve all his guests in the conversation. "I looked you up when we were waiting for the folks at the airport to find a hangar for Gwen's Lancair. I watched the videos on your YouTube channel."

Ann groaned. "Not the YouTube channel."

"You don't like your YouTube channel?" he asked.

"I didn't set it up—a previous client did. Without getting permission."

"It must be good for your business, right?"

"I guess so, although it wouldn't be my preferred way of drumming up customers."

"How would you prefer to drum up customers?" asked Gwen.

"Word of mouth. Referrals."

Gwen laughed. "There's a whole network of you guys?"

Ann shrugged. "There are a few."

"And where do you stand in the rankings?"

Ellis shifted uncomfortably.

Ann gazed at Gwen for a moment, then said, "Third in the US."

Gwen looked surprised. "Third? Who's second and first?"

"A woman in New Mexico and Garrick Masser."

"Why do you suppose Arno didn't hire one of them?"

"Because they're in New Mexico and Maine and I'm in Pennsylvania. Because neither of them would likely agree to hike through the woods to a remote airplane crash site. And because neither of them takes flying lessons at Avondale Airport."

She was gratified that that seemed to shut Gwen up, but her satisfaction was short-lived.

After half a minute, Gwen said, "I don't know why you're unhappy about someone setting up a YouTube channel. It shows that your fans appreciate you. You're a public figure, you owe the public a good show."

"I'm a professional, not a performer. I have clients, not an audience."

"We're all performers for an audience, some of us are just more comfortable with it than others," said Gwen. She turned to Ellis. "What do you think of Ann's profession?"

He glanced between Gwen and Ann, clearly not interested in getting in the middle of this argument, then shrugged. "Like they say, more things in heaven and earth ..." He gazed into the fire and, after a moment, continued. "My dad died my senior year of high school. It was pretty rough. It was just a couple of months before graduation and I was pretty upset about the fact that he wouldn't be there." He poked the fire with a stick. "It was raining on graduation day and they had the ceremony in the gym. It was a pretty small class but there wasn't a lot of room in the bleachers. They handed out tickets for the families, and I remember when my mom opened the envelope, there were three tickets in there. One for my mom, one for my sister, and one—" He cleared his throat, then wiped his nose with the back of his hand. "They had forgotten that my dad didn't need a ticket. Anyhow, after I got my diploma and went back to my seat, I looked over at where my mom and my sister were sitting ..." He stopped speaking, and his eyes sparkled in the firelight. "I saw my dad sitting next to them. He waved at me."

The two women exchanged a look.

"That must have meant a lot to you," said Ann.

"Yeah." He was silent for a moment, then continued. "So, do I believe someone could communicate with dead people? Yeah, I think I do."

23

A nn became aware of a male voice murmuring her name against the backdrop of a soft and vaguely familiar chiming sound. She was just battling out of sleep, the murmur of her name continuing, when she was jarred to full wakefulness by a sharp *Ann!*

She sat up, trying to orient herself to the dark, outdoor, and unfamiliar surroundings.

"Your alarm's going off," said Gwen irritably. "*Been* going off," she added.

"Just for a minute," said Ellis. "Not even."

Ann jabbed the chiming alarm app into silence and rubbed her face. The hike in the heat had worn her out. She climbed to her feet. "I'm going to head up there," she shot a look at Gwen, "for my *confidential* engagement."

Gwen waved her hand. "You go ahead and have your little chat with Hal. I can guess what Arno wants you to talk with him about."

"Oh? And what's that?"

"Something I'd have thought you would want to stay out of the middle of."

Ann waited to see if Gwen would say more, but when she was silent, Ann shrugged and climbed the hill toward the crash site.

The site was even more eerie in the darkness, illuminated only by the narrow beam of the flashlight. As she cast the beam across the clearing that the fire had burned into the forest, it caught the skeletal fingers of a shrub here, the fire-blackened soil of the impact point there. She looked back in the direction of the campsite. The fire itself was hidden by the slight rise, but its light danced cheerfully in the branches of the trees. She was glad Ellis had built a fire despite the warmth of the night.

She turned back to the charred clearing. "Hal? Hal Burridge?" she called softly.

There was no response.

She sat down on the log she had occupied earlier and switched off the flashlight. The jittery shadows it had cast disappeared, replaced by the soothing silver light of the full moon. The singed undergrowth surrounding the clearing morphed into a smooth palette of light blacks and dark grays, the broken trees drawing the eye up to the purple-black sky. Ann had always enjoyed being outdoors in the moonlight, and she had spent many a night lying in a hammock on the dock of her Adirondack cabin staring at a gallery of stars stretching from tree-lined horizon to tree-line horizon, their light doubled in the still water of Loon Pond.

The stars weren't the only thing that brought to mind the Adirondacks—the temperature was also noticeably cooler here than at the campsite. It was a good sign—the presence of a spirit was often accompanied by an otherwise unexplainable drop in temperature. She rubbed her arms. She should have brought a long-sleeved shirt with her to her vigil.

She felt her eyelids drooping and hauled herself to her feet. She couldn't afford to sleep through the appearance of one or both of the crash victims. She scrubbed her face with her hands. What she should really have brought was a flask of espresso.

She circled the impact area, picking her way carefully over the ground by the light of the moon, not wanting to ruin her night vision by turning on the flashlight. She completed the circuit and was contemplating whether she could risk sitting down again when her attention was drawn by a flicker of light on the other side of the impact site. The light drew closer and gradually resolved itself into a man. She recognized him from the photo that Mike had obtained from Arno: Bryan Calvert. And, fortunately, in his pre-crash appearance.

"Hi, I'm Ann Kinnear. You're Bryan Calvert, right?"

"Yes." He was quite vivid—almost life-like, if one were to set aside the fact that he was providing his own illumination. His voice was a little distorted but perfectly understandable. "How come you can see me? Are you ...?"

"I'm not dead. It's a skill I have."

"What are you doing here?" His tone was guarded. He was clearly not altogether enthusiastic about her arrival.

Ann considered her approach and decided she would keep her options open until she had a chance to assess whether Hal as well as Bryan was present.

"I was asked to bring a memento to the site." She got the brass key fob out of her pocket and held it up for his inspection.

Bryan stepped closer to examine it. "Is that Hal's? How did you get that?" His attention shifted from the key fob to Ann. "Hey, you're Russo's student. The psychic."

"That's right."

Bryan gave a sardonic laugh—a strange, rippling sound, like a distant stream. "Man, I didn't think you could really do it." He raised a hand. "Not that I'm complaining. Who asked you to leave the memento? Gwen?"

"No. Arno asked me to bring it here."

"It's Arno's key fob?" His expression hardened. "It's even less the kind of thing I would expect from him."

Ann shrugged. "Sometimes people react to tragedy in ways you don't expect."

He crossed his arms and contemplated her. "Does Gwen know you're here?"

She hesitated. "Yes."

"Yes ...?"

"Yes, she knows I'm here." After a pause, she added, "She's here, too."

He straightened and looked around. "Where? I want to speak with her."

Ann weighed her options. Funding a chat between Gwen and Bryan Calvert was clearly not Arno's goal. Plus, if Hal did show up, Ann would have to find a way to get rid of Gwen so she could talk with him. "She doesn't believe in what I do. She would probably think I'm making up your side of the conversation."

"Not if you tell her something only I would know."

Was there any harm in facilitating a conversation between Bryan and Gwen? Maybe she'd hear something that would point the way to the Scanridge contract. Plus, she had to admit she was curious about what Gwen's reaction would be. Ann pulled her phone out: *No service*. No way to check with Arno. She slipped the phone back into her pocket.

Bryan Calvert seemed like a no-nonsense guy. She'd take a no-nonsense approach. "I'm here on a job. I need to know if Hal Burridge is here. If possible, I need to speak with him. If you can help me with that, I'll help you speak with Gwen."

"How do I know I need your help? Maybe I can communicate with her myself."

Ann raised an eyebrow. "You're welcome to try."

"Where is she?"

Ann nodded toward the lights flickering in the trees surrounding the campfire. "Over there. She's with our guide. Try not to alarm him."

Bryan nodded, and strode off toward the rise that led to the campsite. Evidently, he wasn't worried about tripping on a branch or tree root.

Ann sat down on the log. After about five minutes, Bryan's flickering form reappeared over the hill and descended the hill to the crash site.

"Okay, fine," he said. "What do you want to know about Hal?"

Ann waved a hand toward the other end of the log on which she sat. "Have a seat?"

"Sure." He lowered himself onto the log.

"Have you seen him?"

"No. Would you expect me to have seen him?"

"People's spirits don't always stay around, but if he did stay around, it would likely be at the location of his death."

Bryan was silent for a moment, then said, "Good to know."

"Are you surprised Hal isn't here?"

"Not particularly."

"I just thought that if the two of you had been close, it might make sense that he would be here, too."

"He was my boss."

"But you were taking him to your cabin with you. That suggests that you were friends, too."

She thought she perceived some change of expression, but in the odd Bryan-generated light, she couldn't tell what it was.

"Did he ever talk about his businesses with you?" she asked. "About the trucking company?"

"Scanridge? No."

"Maybe during the flight? Something about changes to the business?"

He didn't answer and she was about to repeat her question when he stood. "Something about the business?"

"Something about Scanridge?" she prompted.

He moved toward her again, and she shivered. "You're not really here to leave a memento at the site, are you. Arno could have hired anyone to do that. Why isn't he here himself?"

"He intended to be here, but he hurt his leg during the hike to the site."

"And he invited Gwen along?"

"She was a late addition to the party. A self-invited addition."

"I want to talk to her now. You said you'd help me if I answered your questions—it's not my fault that Hal wasn't around for me to provide an introduction, or that I don't know what his plans for Scanridge were."

Ann tried to think of other tacks she could take, but if Bryan didn't know anything about the Scanridge contract—or knew but didn't want to tell her—it seemed like a dead end. "Okay, let me see if she'll come over. Wait here."

"I can come with you."

"As I'm sure you saw, the guide is at the campsite. Arno would like to keep any conversation that happens as private as possible."

"So, tell him to go somewhere else while we talk. He's a guide, right? Walking around in the woods is likely going to be a whole lot easier for him than for Gwen. And for you."

Ann thought back to the falls Gwen had taken in the woods. "Okay, fine. Just give me a few minutes to explain to them what's going on, then come on over."

24

W hen Ann reached the campsite, Ellis was reading by the firelight—a hardcover copy of Wolfgang Langewiesche's *Stick and Rudder: An Explanation of the Art of Flying*—while Gwen sat staring into the flames. They turned as she approached.

"Any luck?" asked Ellis.

"No sign of Hal yet, but Bryan Calvert's there."

She was gratified to see Gwen's smirk freeze.

"He says he wants to come over here and talk to Gwen," she continued.

Gwen stood and examined her for a moment. "You know, Bryan Calvert was a friend of mine. If you're screwing with me—"

"I'm not screwing with you. If you want to talk with him, I'll mediate. If not, I'll let him know you're not interested."

Gwen scowled. "Fine. I'll talk with him," she said, her tone freighted with skepticism.

"Ellis, I hate to ask this," said Ann, "but Arno is a stickler for confidentiality. Would you mind taking a walk while we talk?"

Ellis appeared ready to protest, then flipped the book closed.

"Fine. I guess I was the last person to believe that this was all about leaving a brass key ring at the crash site." Still carrying the book, he slipped the flashlight into his pocket, then headed off through the moonlit night in the opposite direction from the crash site.

Gwen crossed her arms. "Now what?"

"We wait here for Bryan to come."

Gwen scanned the surrounding woods. A few minutes passed. She resumed her seat on the log with a theatrical sigh.

Ann was beginning to wonder if Bryan had changed his mind. She was formulating a plan for addressing Gwen's response to that news when she sensed a movement on the slope leading to the crash site, a flicker in the trees not caused by the campfire or a flashlight.

"Bryan?" she called.

Gwen jumped up and followed the direction of her gaze.

In a moment, Bryan moved into the circle of light cast by the fire.

"Hello, Gwen," he said.

Gwen was scanning the area toward which Ann had been looking. "Where is he?"

Ann gestured to where Bryan stood. "He's standing next to that log. He says hello."

Gwen turned toward the log and scanned the area. "I don't see anything."

"Not surprising," replied Ann drily.

Gwen shot her a look, then turned back toward where Ann had indicated Bryan was standing. "How do I know you're not making this up?"

Ann turned to Bryan. "Can you hear what she's saying?"

"No. I can see that she's saying something but not what it is."

"She's not entirely bought into the idea that you're here. Can you give me something else to tell her to prove it's you?"

Bryan considered, then said, "Tell her if the ailerons get too snatchy again, she'll need to adjust the spades to get a better center."

When Ann conveyed the message, she was gratified to see Gwen's eyes widen. After a moment, however, her eyes narrowed. "Maybe Bryan told you that when he was alive. Maybe you visited the shop after one of your lessons."

"Don't you think Bryan would have mentioned if he had been shooting the shit about your airplane with Avondale Airport's most gossiped-about flight school student?" asked Ann, exasperated.

Gwen shrugged. "Maybe he felt guilty about it and didn't want me to know."

"Still not bought in, I take it," said Bryan.

Ann nodded.

Bryan thought for a moment, then grinned. "Tell her it's a good thing the tail of the Extra can support a hundred and forty pounds."

Ann turned to Gwen. "He says it's a good thing the tail of the Extra can support a hundred and forty pounds."

Gwen folded her arms and looked speculatively at Ann. Finally, she said, "Okay, I can't imagine a scenario where he would have mentioned that in casual conversation." She looked back toward where Bryan stood. "Bryan, it's really you?"

"It is," said Ann, not bothering to convey Gwen's comment. "Let's sit down."

When they were settled on the log seats, the conversation resumed, and Ann mediated.

"So, you decided to take Hal with you to the cabin," said Gwen.

Bryan nodded. "Yes."

"I'm glad you did," Gwen continued. "He's been so depressed lately. And I'm glad you knew to look for him at the quarry."

"How did you know to look for him there?" interjected Ann.

Gwen shot her a look. "Aren't you just supposed to be translating?"

"Okay, fine," muttered Ann.

Gwen turned back to Bryan.

"Yeah," he said. "Good thing I knew to look for him at the quarry."

"There was a fire after the crash," said Gwen. "It burned everything. *Everything.* The only things they had to help identify you and Hal were your belt buckle and Hal's Avondale key fob."

He nodded. "Yeah, I can imagine with the auxiliary tanks that would have been quite a blaze."

She glanced into the surrounding woods. "You haven't seen Hal here?"

"No." Bryan paused, then continued. "But you should have seen him on the flight—talking and talking. You know how he was."

Ann turned toward Gwen as she conveyed Bryan's comment, and even in the flickering light of the fire, it seemed to her that Gwen's face paled.

After a moment, Gwen said, "Yes, I know how he was." She took a deep, shuddering breath. "He was probably drunk when you picked him up, right?" Without waiting for an answer, she continued, "I imagine he fell asleep at some point on the trip. When was he 'talking and talking'?"

"He woke up when we were almost at the airstrip. He wanted to take the controls. I had to be pretty firm to get him to let go. Not that it made a difference."

"How firm did you have to be?"

"Pretty freaking firm." He gave a harsh laugh. "He was a persistent bastard when he was alive."

Gwen looked down at her hands and they were both silent for a long moment.

Ann fidgeted, trying to resist filling the pause with questions of her own. When she mediated a conversation for a client—Mike had termed it "mediation" although she herself thought of it as "whisper down the lane"—she made an effort not to interject herself into the exchange. But what was the etiquette of a situation like the current one, where neither participant was a client?

Before she could justify another interjection, Gwen spoke. "The NTSB report isn't out yet, but I imagine they'll rule it loss of control in flight."

Bryan tilted his head back and looked up into the moonlit sky. "Loss of control. That pretty much sums it up."

Gwen's lips tightened, then she glanced at Ann and her features resumed an expressionless sangfroid. She turned back to Bryan. "I suppose I shouldn't pass up the opportunity to ask a dead man what happens once you've *slipped the surly bonds of earth*."

He shrugged. "I don't have much to tell. I don't remember the crash itself, or what happened immediately afterwards—" He glanced in the direction of the fire-blackened trees. "—which must have been pretty horrific, although I'm sure I was already dead. I just remember being in the air and heading for the ground and then later kind of ... waking up here. Alone."

They discussed what Gwen was doing these days (flying), what Bryan was doing (not much—passing the time didn't seem like a relevant concept anymore), and a persistent issue with the smoke injectors on the Extra.

"Is it ..." Gwen glanced again at Ann, uncharacteristically uncertain. "... lonely?"

"Not lonely," Bryan replied. "I just feel like I'm waiting for something."

"Waiting for what?" Then, as if sorry she had asked the question, she hurried on. "Never mind. It doesn't matter." Gwen looked toward Ann. "I don't have anything else to ask." She turned back to Bryan. "Do you have anything else to ask? Or to tell me?"

When Ann had conveyed Gwen's question, he shook his head. "Nope." He stood up, and Ann and then Gwen followed suit. "Will you be coming back?"

"Do you need me to?" asked Gwen.

Bryan thought for a moment, then shook his head—not sadly, not angrily, but with an air of resignation. "No, I don't think so. Best of luck to you, Gwen."

"Best of luck to you, Bryan," she replied. After a moment, she added, "Although I suppose luck doesn't have much to do with it at this point."

Bryan nodded to Gwen—although Ann didn't try to convey his gesture to her—nodded to Ann, then turned to climb toward the crash site. Ann watched as his flickering figure disappeared over the crest of the hill.

"He's gone," said Ann.

"So," said Gwen, "this is what you do for a living."

"Pretty much."

Gwen resumed her seat on the log and crossed her arms. "I thought it had started to cool off, but it must have been wishful thinking."

Ann didn't bother to point out to Gwen that the drop and rise in temperature had coincided with Bryan's arrival and departure.

"Why is Bryan here and Hal isn't?" Gwen asked.

"Like Bryan said, maybe he's waiting for something."

"Like what?"

"I don't know. Maybe he doesn't even know."

"In limbo," said Gwen.

"Yes—not condemned to the punishments of hell, but not enjoying eternal life in heaven either." Ann noted Gwen's surprised look. "That's what *in limbo* means." She shrugged. "You get to know these things in this profession."

Gwen looked around again at the surrounding woods. "Is it possible that Hal is here but you can't see him?"

"It's possible."

"Is he dangerous?"

"Hal or Bryan?"

Gwen shrugged. "Either one."

"A dead person is likely to be no more or less dangerous than he was when he was alive."

Gwen turned her gaze back toward the crash site.

"I guess I should have given Ellis a sense of how long we might be," said Ann, "and when he could come back." She cupped her hands around her mouth. "Ellis!" she yelled.

Half a minute passed, and Ann was about to yell again when she heard Ellis's return call.

"Coming!"

A few moments later, he appeared in the circle of illumination cast by the campfire, his book under his arm.

"Get some reading done?" asked Ann.

"Yup," he said. "Found a nice place far enough away that I couldn't overhear all the top-secret stuff you guys are talking about. I read by the flashlight."

"If you had it on your phone," said Ann, "you wouldn't need a flashlight to read it."

Ellis settled back into his place next to the fire. "I don't think you can get *Stick and Rudder* as an ebook. Plus," he added, "it seems wrong to read such a classic in anything except hardback. You should get a copy. It's super helpful."

"Maybe I will."

Ann sat down on a log and gazed into the flames, playing over in her mind the conversation between Gwen and Bryan. Her thoughts were interrupted by Gwen.

"So, did you leave the key fob at the crash site?" asked Gwen.

Ann was aware of the weight of the brass oval in her pocket. Gwen's recognition of Ann likely meant that Arno's cover story was blown, but it might be convenient for Gwen to have some doubt about whether the story of leaving the memento was completely fabricated.

"Yup," she said, fingering the brass oval in her pocket. "Just like Arno asked me to."

Gwen raised an eyebrow. "Touching."

25

In the morning, they packed up and headed back to the road, Ellis removing the strips of yellow plastic from the trees as they went.

"Why don't you leave them up?" asked Ann.

"I don't want to make it easy for curiosity seekers to find the site," he replied. "Some people get off on that kind of thing."

Except when the route required them to walk single-file, Ellis again walked next to Gwen. Snatches of their conversation —more accurately, *his* conversation—drifted back to Ann. When they stopped for a break, Ellis continued what must have been an ongoing topic.

"I know I wouldn't be qualified to take on Bryan's activities, but I could help a more experienced A&P, and I'd love to learn more about the Extra and the Lancair. I could help out around the airport, too. Manning the desk at the FBO, whatever—I'm not picky."

"I'll think about it," said Gwen, in a tone of voice that suggested that she had already thought about it and made a decision.

Ellis was at least savvy enough not to press the issue.

When they reached the place where Arno had left his backpack, Ellis shouldered it as well as his own. Once they picked up a cell signal, Ann called Arno to let him know they were nearing the pickup point.

Arno was waiting for them in Ellis's Tahoe when they reached the road. He climbed out of the driver's seat and pulled a pair of crutches out of the back seat.

"You can update me on the way back to Avondale," he said to Ann by way of greeting.

"Arno Scanlan, ever the gracious boss," said Gwen.

"I don't feel like hanging around here for a debrief," he growled. "I have business—*two* businesses—to take care of."

"I could help out around the airport," said Ellis, perhaps having given up on Gwen as a possible sponsor. "Whatever needs doing. I come cheap."

Arno, taken off-guard, rubbed his neck. "I don't know. Things are a little up in the air ..." He glanced at Gwen. "... what with Hal and Bryan's deaths. I'm not sure what kind of help we're going to need."

"I think it's a great idea," said Gwen. "He said he'll do anything. I'm sure we can find *anything* for him to do." She turned to Ellis. "You're hired—let me know when you can start."

Ellis beamed.

Arno glowered.

Ellis loaded the packs into the back of the Tahoe and they climbed in, Arno in the passenger seat and Gwen and Ann in back. They were quiet on the way back to the airport, Gwen tapping her fingers impatiently on the armrest, Arno tapping his phone.

They climbed out of the Tahoe near the gate to the ramp and Ellis extracted Ann and Arno's small overnight bags from their packs.

"Thanks for the loan of the equipment, Ellis," said Gwen. "See you soon at Avondale."

"Sure thing, Ms. Burridge."

Gwen turned to Arno. "See you back in Chester County, Arno. We'll have to see if we can't rustle you up a replacement keychain."

Arno pointedly ignored her.

Gwen looked toward Ann, then gave her a slight nod. "And I'm sure I'll be seeing you around Avondale as well, Ann."

She turned and strode toward the FBO.

Arno and Ann took their leave of Ellis, who lingered at the gate as they walked toward the tie-down area where the Bonanza had spent the night. He was no doubt waiting to see the Lancair's departure.

They started across the ramp, Arno struggling to keep hold of his overnight bag and maneuver the crutches at the same time.

"I can get that," said Ann, taking the bag from him.

"Thanks," he said, relinquishing the bag with some relief.

"Get your leg checked up?" she asked.

"Yeah. Nothing serious, just told me to keep off it for a week or so." He swung himself across the ramp toward the Bonanza and Ann followed.

"The walk back to the road can't have been fun."

"I took my time."

"You can fly okay?"

"Yeah, no problem. I just can't put my full weight on it." He grimaced. "My *considerable* full weight, as the doctor pointed out."

Arno was already puffing, so Ann decided to postpone further conversation until Arno had the breath to spare. When they reached the plane, she unfastened the tie-down ropes, then removed the plane's canvas cover and cowl plugs. Arno stowed them in back, then turned to her.

"So? How'd it go?"

"No sign of Hal," she said.

He sighed. "Damn."

"But I did speak with Bryan."

"Calvert? No kidding. What did he say?"

"Mostly just that he didn't know where the contract was, or anything about Hal's business dealings. After that, he wanted to talk with Gwen and since I couldn't get in touch with you, I decided that there wasn't any harm in mediating a conversation between the two of them."

"What did they talk about?"

"The fact that Hal was drunk when Bryan found him at the quarry. The fact that he was chatty during the flight. The fact that he was acting up."

"Acting up?"

"Evidently he tried to grab the controls."

"That's a dumb move. Anything else?"

"How to fix the smoke injector on the Extra. How much weight the tail of the Extra can hold."

"Why in the hell did that come up?"

"Bryan was feeding me information I could use to convince Gwen that he was really there."

"Huh." Arno shifted on his crutches. "Why isn't Hal there if Bryan is there?"

"It's different for each person. Unless someone feels like they have unfinished business, they usually don't hang around."

"That contract is unfinished business for me, even if Hal isn't in a position to care about it anymore. What's Calvert's unfinished business?"

"It could be anything—obviously not necessarily 'business' in the sense of contracts. Sometimes people have things they feel like they should have done before they died, things they should have said. Sometimes they just aren't ready to move on."

Arno turned to watch a small jet streak down the runway then lift into the already warm air and turn north. "I'd like you to go back to the crash site, without Gwen this time. Maybe Calvert has some information that would help." He glanced back to where Ellis leaned on the fence next to the gate. "Should we ask him if he can take you back now?"

"I suspect Gwen isn't going to leave until she sees your plane in the air, with me in it. Let's go back to Chester County and have Mike arrange a follow-up trip with Ellis."

He nodded. "That sounds good. Maybe Hal will show up if there's less of a crowd."

"You think Hal wouldn't want to see Gwen?"

"Who knows what was going on with those two, especially over the last year. Whatever it was, it was clear the honeymoon was over."

"Oh, by the way, I brought your key fob back ... although I wouldn't flash it around since Gwen thinks it's at the crash site."

She pulled it out of her pocket and dropped it into Arno's hand.

"Thanks, I'm glad to get that back."

As Arno struggled into the cockpit, the Lancair appeared from the hangar row and stopped, prop turning.

Arno powered up the Bonanza, listened through the automated weather briefing, turned the transponder to GND in preparation for taxiing, then looked across the ramp at the Lancair.

"I can't believe she's just sitting there," he said angrily. "Isn't she worried about overheating?"

"Speaking of overheating," said Ann, "do you think Gwen and Bryan might have been having an affair?"

He looked over at her. "Why do you ask that?"

"At the crash site, they talked about things that seemed normal on the surface, but there was a strange undercurrent, like they were talking in code."

Arno sat back. "Maybe. Considering the sorry state Hal was in, I wouldn't be entirely surprised if she had taken up with Calvert."

"You've said before that he was in a sorry state. What was the matter with him?"

Arno keyed the radio. "Lancair, you planning on taxiing?"

"After you, Bonanza," came the reply.

"God almighty," he muttered. Not taking his eyes off the Lancair, he said to Ann, "He never told me what the matter was. I'd taken the Bonanza to a transportation conference and got back to Avondale late. I found Hal in his office in the FBO. I'll tell you about it when we're in the air." He keyed the radio again. "Lock Haven, Bonanza taxiing to Runway Two Seven Right ..."

ARNO PULLED the Bonanza into the hangar and activated the switch that lowered the door. The conference had been worth the trip, especially the talks on the future of less-than-truckload transport, and he had made some valuable contacts. Now, however, he was glad to be home and was looking forward to hitting the sack. As the door rumbled down, he saw that a light was on in the FBO—in Hal's office, as far as he could tell. He locked up the hangar and climbed into his Lexus. He headed for the exit, then curiosity made him detour back to the FBO. If Hal had extra work to do, he usually did it at home, not at the airport.

Arno slid his key into the lock on the entrance door, but it was unlocked. He pushed it open and went in. The small main office area was dark, but the light cast by the open door to Hal's office was enough to see the worn strip that led from the front door to the desk. He had been meaning to get the carpet replaced with something more durable ever since they had bought Avondale, but there was always something more pressing to spend money on. He crossed to the office door.

Hal's chair was turned away from the door and toward the window that gave a view of Gwen's darkened hangar. In fact, this had originally been Arno's office, but when Hal and Gwen had chosen the site for the hangar for the Extra and the Lancair, Hal had asked if they could swap since he couldn't see the hangar from his office.

Arno rapped lightly on the doorframe with a knuckle. "Working late?"

There was no response for a moment, then a dull answer. "No. Just sitting."

Arno stepped into the room. "Hey, you okay?"

The chair rotated slowly to reveal Hal, a bottle of bourbon propped between his legs, a half-full glass dangling from his hand.

"I don't know."

Arno had seen Hal Burridge drunk before—hell, they had spent four years as undergrads at Penn together—but never like this, never with such a look of desolation on his face.

Arno lowered himself into one of the two guest chairs.

"Jesus, Hal, what's wrong? Is it Gwen? Did something happen to her?" It was the only thing he could think of that could have caused such a change from the cheerful man he had seen just a few days before.

Hal paused, as if considering Arno's question. Finally, he said, "Gwen's safe at home."

Arno waited for more, but Hal rotated the chair partially back toward the window so that his face was visible only in profile.

"Did you ... did she ...?" Arno tried to formulate the right question.

"She's twenty years younger than I am. I never thought that she might die first."

Arno leaned forward. "Jesus Christ, Hal, is Gwen sick?"

"No. Healthy as a horse." He laughed, a sad, choking sound. "A horse with blinders."

"Blinders?"

"She can't see what's coming."

"Is it ..." Arno cast about for what Hal could be referring to. "... her career? I know she's always been a little OCD about her flying. Is it something to do with that?"

Hal shook his head and squeezed the bridge of his nose with shaking fingers. "She'll protect her career to the bitter end." He turned his gaze back out the window. "The bitter end."

"Hal, for God's sake, don't make me keep guessing."

Hal waved the glass, sloshing a bit of bourbon onto the arm of the chair. "I went out to Octoraro Lake to watch her practice. Bryan was videoing her."

Arno noticed the small video camera sitting on Hal's desk.

"She was doing an outside half Cuban 8. She ..." Hal's voice caught. "She was so close to the ground." He took a swallow of bourbon.

"She always does that maneuver close to the ground," said Arno. "That's why the crowd loves it."

Hal stared into his now-empty glass.

"She's in a dangerous profession, Hal—you know that. You helped her get into it. But she's a good pilot. A very good pilot. She can take care of herself."

Hal nodded slowly. "I hope so." He roused himself, as if noticing for the first time that there was another person in the office, and raised the bottle toward Arno. "Want some? You'll need to find a glass. I only have one."

Arno stood. "I think we need to get you home, buddy."

Hal lowered the bottle and turned back to the window. "I think I'll stay here tonight."

"You want to come stay at my place?"

"No. Thanks."

Arno glanced around the office. There was a couch where Hal could sleep, a souvenir blanket from Sun 'n Fun draped over its back.

"Okay, but you need to give me your keys." He held out his hand to Hal. "If you change your mind you can make it home on foot."

Hal's lips twitched up in a momentary smile. "Just like college."

Although no college girl ever did a number on you like this, thought Arno.

Hal drew his keyring out of his pocket and handed it to Arno. Arno dropped it into his pocket, the two brass key fobs clicking together.

"Hal, is there something you want to talk about?"

Hal turned the chair back to Arno and studied him for a moment.

"No, thanks. You're a good friend, Arno, but this is between me and Gwen."

THEY WERE NEARING Avondale as Arno wrapped up the story.

"Hal was that upset by Gwen having a close call?" Ann asked.

"I felt like it had to be something else. He had watched her do plenty of hair-raising maneuvers and never come unglued like that. I came up with plenty of theories, but none that I could ever confirm. The only thing I could think of is that Hal caught Bryan and Gwen up to something."

"In the air?" she asked, trying to picture it.

He shrugged. "Maybe he made that part up. Maybe what he said about Gwen being close to the ground was some ... metaphor for their marriage. Maybe he thought she was blind to what she was doing to him."

"But why would he say that he never thought about Gwen dying first?"

Arno quirked his mouth. "Maybe he was thinking about killing her." He glanced over at Ann. "Sorry, not funny. Like I said, I really have no idea."

"If there really was a video, I wonder what was on it."

"I wondered that myself. I stopped back in the morning and Hal was passed out on the couch. I was going to take the memory card out and look, but the card wasn't in the camera."

"You think it was a video of Gwen and Bryan?"

"I wouldn't have thought that Hal would be going with Bryan to his cabin in Clinton County if he had found a blue movie of him with his wife, but who knows." He glanced down at the panel. "Can you believe it? She's following us. That Lancair is twice as fast as we are, and she's goddamn following us."

26

"So Arno wants me to go back," said Ann to Mike and Scott, wrapping up her report on the trip to Clinton County. She took a sip of the evening's offering: a pineapple basil cocktail, which Mike had paired with mozzarella toasts.

"I'll get in touch with Tapscott and line up his guide services again," said Mike.

"Better do it fast. Gwen Burridge offered him a job at Avondale and for all I know he might be headed down to Chester County already."

"If he's already at Avondale, maybe he could fly you back to Clinton County. Save you the drive."

"Much as I would like that, I think it's best that I drive up. Arno doesn't want Gwen tagging along again, and if she had Arno's plane plugged into FlightAware, it's not out of the question that she has Ellis's plane plugged in, too. He even mentioned its tail number to her."

"What was she like?" asked Scott.

After a long pause, Ann said, "Bigger than life."

Mike laughed. "I could track every statement you formulated and discarded before you came up with that one."

She grimaced. "Well, I have to admit that it's kind of hard to warm up to someone who was as obnoxiously disbelieving of what I do as she was, but she changed her tune once I mediated a conversation between her and Bryan. Plus, I can't blame her for being angry that Arno was trying to contact her husband and leaving her out of the loop."

"Maybe Corey can bake Gwen Burridge into your documentary," said Mike. "The perspective of a skeptic who was convinced of your skills by her own experience."

"I'm sure she'd be happy to be in the documentary." Ann took a sip of her cocktail. "She has this whole theory about how every professional is a performer. That's why she'd be a good topic for a documentary—she wants to perform. I don't consider myself a performer. And Garrick certainly wouldn't consider himself a performer."

Mike raised his eyebrows. "Are you kidding me? Think about the persona he's created for himself—the un-modernized house, the vintage car, his unwillingness to drink anything other than water or eat anything other than bread in public. He could give Gwen Burridge lessons in performance."

Ann sucked in a breath to launch into an automatic defense of Garrick, but then she realized that Mike was right—everything Garrick did was aimed at creating and maintaining the Garrick Masser brand. Did she have a brand? Maybe she needed a brand. She stuffed a mozzarella toast into her mouth.

"They're in control of their performances in their professional lives," said Scott. "I'm not sure that that would be true in a documentary, no matter how nice a guy Corey Duff seems to be. It might be more like the unofficial YouTube channel—you'd be at the mercy of the picture someone else wanted to paint of you."

"Corey treated my ability respectfully in the first documentary," said Ann, a bit uncertainly. "I don't think he'd have a reason not to do that in this new project."

"My feeling exactly," said Mike.

"Well, Annie knows Mr. Masser better than I do," said Scott. "You need to do what you think is right, sweetie."

"By the way, how did Tapscott work out?" asked Mike.

"Good," said Ann. "Knows his way around those woods, obviously fascinated by aviation topics."

"Do you think you'll be able to get anything useful from a second trip?"

"Maybe. On one hand, it makes sense that the airport A&P wouldn't know about the business dealings of the owners. On the other hand, if Bryan was more than just Gwen's mechanic, maybe he learned something he wouldn't have otherwise."

"You think Gwen and Bryan were having an affair?" asked Scott.

"Maybe. Arno seemed to think it was possible. Their whole conversation seemed a little off, like they had something they needed to communicate but they didn't want me to know what it was. Gwen also knew about Hal's truck being at the quarry, which seems weird."

"How do you know that?"

"Corey was talking with Officer Morelli, who was on the notification team that told Gwen about the plane crash. Morelli mentioned it."

"Why would Bryan invite Hal to go with him to his cabin if he was having an affair with Hal's wife?" asked Scott.

"Maybe they were planning to do away with him in Clinton County," said Mike, waggling his eyebrows. "Tragic hunting accident."

Ann took another sip of her drink. "There is a lot of space up there where you could hide a body."

Scott looked from Ann to Mike and back. "Are you guys serious?"

"I wasn't," said Mike, surprised. He looked at Ann. "Are you?"

She shrugged. "Just playing around with ideas." She sat forward. "But it kind of makes sense with what Morelli said about Gwen's reaction to finding out about Hal's death. It sounds like she was more shocked to hear about Bryan dying than about her husband. He said she was oddly stoic about the news of Hal's death."

"That's how he described her?" asked Mike. "'Oddly stoic'?"

"I believe 'nerves of steel' was the phrase he used."

"Arno did say that Hal was kind of a wreck," said Mike. "Maybe his wife got fed up with him."

Scott threw up his hands. "Whatever happened to 'for better or worse'?"

"Scott," said Mike with a shake of his head, "you're such a romantic."

27

The mid-afternoon sun beat down on the asphalt and shot daggers of light off the polished surface of the Lancair as the make-up artist, Tanny, wielded a powder puff over Gwen's cheeks to remove the sheen of sweat. When she was done with Gwen, she moved on to the photo shoot's other subject, Jeff Bucholtz.

"Places, everyone!" called Art, the director, from behind the camera.

Tanny stepped out of range of the camera and Gwen and Jeff resumed their places next to the Lancair, Gwen's elbow resting on the plane's fuselage, Jeff's arms crossed.

"Gwen, turn your wrist a little more so I can see the face of the watch."

Gwen turned her wrist.

"Jeff, lean toward Gwen a little bit more."

Jeff leaned toward Gwen. Jeff's wife, Jessica, standing behind the small crew grouped around the camera, crossed her arms and scowled.

The photo shoot had been scheduled months ago, originally planned to take place at Jeff's home airport in Texas, but Gwen had been loath to leave Avondale while the contract was still missing and had asked that the shoot be moved there. Her contact at Jura Bernois had acquiesced, probably because they were grateful that she had agreed to go ahead with the shoot despite the fact that she had buried her husband a week earlier. It meant not only that Jeff and Jessica Bucholtz had to fly to Pennsylvania—commercial, although first class—but also that Gwen's Lancair rather than Jeff's Glasair was serving as the backdrop to the hundred-thousand-dollar Jura Bernois watches they were modelling. Jeff was not happy. Jessica was even unhappier.

The day had started a little more auspiciously, with Gwen hosting the Bucholtzes in her hangar as the crew set up. Dottie had lined up a caterer to provide finger food and drinks. Tanny, who sported spiked hair and goth make-up, had arrived with a small foldable table and what looked like an overnight case to give Gwen and Jeff manicures in preparation for the close-up shots of their hands.

She looked critically at Gwen's nails. "Too short for me to do much shaping."

Gwen took a sip of Perrier.

Tanny sorted through her case, pulled out a bottle of bright red polish, and shook it vigorously. "A little polish and no one will notice how short they are."

"No polish."

Tanny stopped shaking. "A lighter color?"

"No polish."

Tanny sighed and replaced the bottle in the case. "Any objection to a little buffing?"

"Buffing's fine."

Gwen was alarmed to learn that Tanny was the make-up artist in addition to the manicurist. She expected to emerge from the chair with whitened skin and black-rimmed eyes, but she couldn't fault the subtle job the young woman did on her as well as on Jeff.

By the time their manicures and makeup were complete, the hors d'oeuvres and drinks had done their work, the atmosphere had lightened, and even Jessica seemed to be thawing a bit.

"I'll tell them we're done in here," said Tanny, snapping her case closed.

She stepped out of the hangar and a few minutes later the representative from Jura Bernois entered. He set an aluminum briefcase on the desk, unfastened its locks, and raised the lid, revealing a dozen watches arranged in two rows, each watch lying in a custom-shaped nest of foam.

Jessica leaned forward and made appreciative noises.

The rep took the watches Gwen and Jeff were wearing—their signing bonuses from Jura Bernois—and slipped them into two pockets in the lid of the case.

"Let's start with the Chronair models," said the rep, reverently lifting one of the watches out of its nest. The watch's face was festooned with tiny dials, its perimeter dotted with minuscule knobs. A sizable diamond sparkled at twelve o'clock.

The rep fastened the watch on Gwen's wrist—all the women's watches in the case had already been sized for her—and fastened the men's version on Jeff's wrist. He stepped back, admiring the effect.

"Very nice indeed." He swept his hand toward the door. "I believe they're ready for you."

Gwen retrieved her sunglasses from her desk and followed Jeff and Jessica outside.

The Lancair was staged in front of the hangar's steel doors, the brilliant sun glinting off its silver wings. Art stood by the plane, iPad in hand.

"Gwen and Jeff in the house!" he called cheerfully. "You two look gorgeous. We'll start out with you next to the plane," he said, herding them toward the Lancair, followed by a production assistant. Art held his hand out to Gwen. "Glasses."

"Pardon?"

"Sunglasses. We don't want that pretty face hidden behind a pair of sunglasses."

She removed the glasses and handed them to Art who in turn passed them to the PA.

"Okay, you two," said Art. "Step a little closer together—"

Gwen raised her arm to shield her eyes from the sun.

"Gwen, you'll need to keep your arm down so we can compose the shot."

"Do we have to be facing right into the sun?"

"It's a great effect—reminiscent of that desert light at White Lake."

"Okay, fine." She dropped her arm.

"Look straight at the camera, Gwen."

Gwen adjusted her gaze to what she guessed Art was looking for.

"Try not to squint."

"I'm not doing it on purpose, Art."

Art called a break, assigning one of the crew to hold an umbrella to keep the sun out of Gwen's eyes. There was some consultation among the crew, then another assistant began assembling an extra stand, to which he attached a piece of cloth to diffuse the light. Jessica went into the hangar and emerged a few minutes later with a glass of Sauvignon Blanc.

When they started again with the new set-up, Art arranged Gwen and Jeff in various poses next to the plane, calling out instructions that always seemed to include having them move closer together. Jessica disappeared into the hangar and didn't come out.

"Jeff, put your foot on the wing," said Art, "and then rest your arm on your leg so we can see the watch."

"No foot on the wing," said Gwen.

"Jesus, Gwen," said Jeff with a tight laugh, "get over yourself."

"Okay, fine," said Art. "Gwen, why don't you sit in the plane and, Jeff, you stand next to the wing."

"I'll look like I'm a member of her race crew," said Jeff.

Gwen smiled. "Get over yourself, Jeff."

"We'll take this sequence and then you guys can swap places," said Art.

"If she doesn't want my foot on the wing," said Jeff, "I'm guessing she *really* doesn't want my ass in the seat."

"If we were at your airport, I wouldn't expect to pose sitting in your Glasair," said Gwen.

Art threw up his hands. "The whole point of this campaign is to portray the two of you as friendly competitors. Can you at least *pretend* you like each other?"

"Maybe you can play up the competitors part," said Gwen.

When Art had all the photos he wanted with the Lancair— with plenty of breaks for Tanny to blot the perspiration from Gwen and Jeff's faces—Gwen pushed the plane into the hangar, and they did it all over with the Extra.

Two hours later, the Jura Bernois representative unfastened the last set of watches and lowered them into their designated spaces in the aluminum case, then fastened Gwen and Jeff's own watches on their wrists. The two pilots retired to the hangar, where Jessica was seated in the desk chair examining her phone, legs hanging over one arm of the chair, a lipstick-smeared glass of wine on the desk beside her. Jeff stepped into the hangar's small bathroom to change out of his flight suit. The caterer had cleaned up the spread and was standing to one side—Gwen guessed until she could retrieve the glass that Jessica was still nursing. Gwen noticed a Jessica-sized handprint on the canopy of the Lancair and buffed it away with a fiber cloth.

In a few minutes, Jeff emerged in jeans and a Hawaiian shirt, duffle bag in hand.

"Gwen," he said, "should have said before, sorry to hear about Hal."

Jessica stood, swaying a little. "Yeah. Condolences."

The caterer edged toward Jessica's unattended glass.

"You're too kind," said Gwen.

"So, you're planning to race at White Lake?" asked Jeff.

"I wouldn't miss it for the world."

"I hear there will only be one other girl there this year."

"Jeff, I haven't been a 'girl' since I got my instrument rating when I was eighteen."

The production assistant popped her head in the hangar door. "Ms. Burridge, could I ask a favor? One of the grips is a big fan of yours and I think he'd be pretty excited if he could get his picture taken with you—just a quick cell phone shot. Would that be okay?"

"Of course," said Gwen. She turned back to the Bucholtzes just as the caterer slid Jessica's glass off the desk. "I'll be right back."

She posed in front of the Extra with the photo crew member, a painfully thin young man with a prominent Adam's apple.

As she approached the open hangar door, she heard Jessica's slightly slurred words. "Yeah, I'm sure it's a big sacrifice for you to be posing wearing a million-dollar watch and a girl who looks like that."

Gwen stepped into the hangar and Jeff caught her eye over his wife's head. He grinned. "*Woman*, sweetheart. She's all grown up now."

WHEN THE BUCHOLTZES had departed in their rental Hummer and the photo crew had packed up and left, Gwen changed out of the flight suit she had worn for the shoot into a T-shirt and shorts, then pushed the Extra back into the hangar.

She spent an hour fiddling with the smoke system. She had already cleaned the injectors once but at this point she was mainly using it as an excuse not to go back to the house, which now seemed even more like Hal's than it had when he was alive.

She was still mentally sorting through the experience at the crash site. There was no way Kinnear could have faked that conversation with Bryan. He would never have discussed technical details about Gwen's planes with someone else, least of all some random flight school student. He would have been even less likely to share the other situation Kinnear had referenced, when Gwen and Bryan had tested the ability of the Extra's tail to support her weight.

As Gwen, Ellis, and Ann had hiked back to the road the morning after the conversation with Bryan, Gwen had wondered if there were other things she should have asked him. How often did one have the opportunity to talk with a dead man? Even having had more time to consider, she still couldn't think of what she should have asked him. As far as she could tell, Bryan's experience of the afterlife wasn't much different from his experience of his fishing weekends at the cabin. *Maybe*, she thought with a twist of her mouth, *that was his idea of heaven.*

But now her thoughts were turning from the question of what she could have learned from him to the question of what others could learn if they availed themselves of Ann Kinnear's abilities.

She knew Arno Scanlan not to be the kind of man to invest the time and effort of the trip to Clinton County just to drop a key fob where his partner had died. It was obvious that he was trying to find out where the signed contract was.

What if Kinnear went back to the site without Gwen and talked with Bryan again? Might Bryan eventually share the real story of what happened? What would he have to gain? On the other hand, what would he have to lose?

Even if Bryan did reveal what had happened that night, Gwen couldn't imagine that Kinnear could go to the police with evidence given to her by a dead man.

However, if Kinnear talked to the right people, might they look at the other events of that night more closely? Might they take a second look at other crashes tied to Avondale Airport?

Only if they took Ann Kinnear seriously.

Gwen had to make sure that if Kinnear did talk to anyone, there would be plenty of reason for them to chalk up any claims she made to the rantings of an unbalanced mind, or of a scam artist.

28

Gwen watched from the hangar as Russo and a dejected-looking student made their way from the flight school tie-down area to the FBO, where the flight school office was housed. They disappeared into the building, then the student emerged alone a few minutes later and plodded off toward the parking lot. Gwen lowered the hangar door and crossed the ramp to the FBO.

She entered to Russo recounting the lesson to Dottie, who was staffing the desk.

"... I said, 'We're landing on a runway, not a carrier deck.'" He turned. "Hey, Gwen, how are you doing?"

"Fine. Thanks. I was wondering, is Ann Kinnear coming in for a lesson anytime soon?"

Russo turned to Dottie, who pulled up the schedule on the computer.

"This afternoon, actually. Three o'clock."

"Thanks." She turned to Russo. "Can you ask her to stop by the hangar after her lesson?"

"Sure. Why? You want to hire—"

He had obviously been about to make a joke about Ann

Kinnear's occupation before realizing that it was in bad taste, even for him, to joke about it with someone so recently bereaved.

"I don't need her services myself," she said icily, "but evidently Arno felt he did. He hired her to go up to Clinton County and try to," she twisted her mouth in distaste, "contact Hal."

"He did?" asked Russo, surprised. "I mentioned to Arno what Ann does for a living, but I didn't really think he'd go through with it. He doesn't seem like the type to go in for that kind of thing."

"I followed him up there—I got curious about what was going on—and actually went to the crash site with Kinnear and her guide. She claimed not to be able to contact Hal—no doubt since with me there it would have been harder to fake a communication—but she did claim to talk with Bryan Calvert. It was all pretty seamy."

"Really?" said Russo, looking uncomfortable. "I can't say whether I believe in that stuff or not, but I always figured Ann was on the up-and-up—you know, that at least *she* believed she was really doing it."

Gwen shrugged. "Perhaps she does. Either way, I wanted to suggest to her that she drum up her business somewhere other than Avondale. She's taking advantage of a man who just lost a good friend."

"Sure," said Russo reluctantly. "I'll tell her to see you. Or ... do you want me to warn her off?"

She gave it a few moments for consideration, then allowed her face to relax into a look of relief. "Why, yes, I'd appreciate that. She might take it better from you than she would from me." She turned toward the door, then turned back. "Tell her at the end of her lesson. I wouldn't want you to fluster her before she flies."

"Oh, Gwen," said Dottie, "message for you." She passed a pink slip of paper across the desk. "Someone named Corey Duff called from L.A. I looked him up—he makes documentaries."

Gwen took the slip. "Did he say why he was calling?"

Dottie smiled. "He was at the airshow and was evidently quite taken with the Peregrine Falcon. I think he might be looking for the topic for his next project."

Gwen smiled back. "Interesting."

"If he calls back, do you want me to give him your cell number?"

"Sure, that would be fine. Thanks, Dottie."

Gwen walked back to her hangar, pleased to have taken some steps to safeguard her position. She knew that Russo's loyalties were torn: Gwen was paying half his wages as an instructor, but he was obviously fond of Kinnear. Gwen had time to win him over to her side. She knew she could count on Dottie to spread word of her conversation with Russo.

She needed to consider Ellis Tapscott as well. Ellis had arrived the previous day, just as the photo shoot was wrapping up, much to his chagrin. Now he was settling his Stinson—and himself—into an Avondale hangar.

She had originally agreed to hire Ellis as airport gofer mainly to annoy Arno, but she realized that he might prove helpful to her plan as well. Considering the story he had told of his father's ghostly appearance at his graduation, she didn't plan to involve him in her campaign against Kinnear. However, since Ellis and Kinnear seemed to be buddies—although obviously not boyfriend and girlfriend—he might prove useful in keeping tabs on what Kinnear got up to.

That should take care of Avondale, but she didn't plan to limit her campaign to discredit Kinnear to the airport.

She pulled up a chair to the computer on the hangar's desk and went to the website of the *Philadelphia Chronicle*. She scanned the various articles, looking for someone who focused on human interest stories in the Philadelphia metro area—she doubted she'd be able to convince a business or science reporter to handle the story she wanted to tell.

After some time, she found the person she was looking for: Lincoln Abbott. She opened another tab in her browser and typed in his name. Her eye was drawn in the list of his articles to a recent headline in the search results:

Firth Investments Scion Implicated in Death of Wife and Attack on Psychic

She clicked the link and, as she read, her lips curved up in a smile. She wouldn't even need to educate Mr. Abbott on Ann Kinnear's profession—he knew all about it already.

29

Ann completed a circle around a silo in the practice area with that little bump of turbulence that indicated that she had completed it at exactly the point she had started it.

"That was pretty good, right?" she asked, not expecting anything more than Russo's usual underwhelmed response.

"Excellent!"

She glanced over at him, anticipating a snarky follow-up. When none was forthcoming, she said, "Really?"

"Yes, really. Excellent!"

"You're acting weird."

"Just offering some words of praise," he said, sounding vaguely offended. "However, speaking of unusual attitudes, let's work on our unusual attitude recovery."

After a few more exercises, they turned back toward Avondale. As they approached the airport, she caught a glimpse of the quarry that adjoined the airport property.

"Hey," she said, "I understand that Gwen told the police that Hal sometimes went to the quarry, and that his pickup was there the morning after the crash. Do you know where he went? Where the pickup would have been?"

"Not specifically. Want to check it out?"

"Yeah."

Russo took over the controls and made the appropriate radio calls to alert other pilots in the area that they'd be circling the quarry.

Relieved of the responsibility of flying, Ann looked around, enjoying the view. "Why would someone go to a quarry to hang out? It can't be very picturesque."

"Unless you're right on top of the pit, you probably can't see it. The property's pretty big and most of it's wooded. It's probably nice and quiet on the side with the idle pit." He banked the plane and pointed toward a grassy field. "I'll bet that's where he went."

From two-hundred feet above the ground, the details were quite clear. Ann could see a dirt road leading from a gate in the chain link fence that surrounded the property, disappearing into a wooded area, then emerging into a field. On the opposite side of the field from the dirt road was a pit that appeared to be absent of any machinery or activity. The idle pit bisected the quarry property, with the nearer portion consisting of the woods, a grassy field, and what looked like a small clearing near the fence that separated the quarry from the airport. At the edge of the field she could see two small constructions—maybe benches.

"Could you see that area coming into the airport?" she asked, pointing at the area near the benches.

Russo craned his neck to looked back toward the airport. "I doubt it—not if you were on a normal approach course or in the pattern. I think the trees would hide it. Why?"

Ann shrugged. "Just curious."

Russo turned the controls back to her and she entered the

pattern—downwind, base, final—and brought the plane in for a landing. Her distraction with the question of whether Gwen Burridge could have seen her husband's pickup from the air didn't improve her performance.

"A good landing is any landing you walk away from," said Russo as Ann steered the plane off the runway onto a taxiway. "A great landing is one where you can use the plane again."

Ann steeled herself for the rejoinder.

"I *think* that was a great landing, but we'll confirm with an inspection of the undercarriage."

Russo was back to his usual attitude.

She taxied to the tie-down area and went through the shut-down procedure. As she was chocking the wheels, she said, "You knew Hal Burridge pretty well, right?"

"Just from around the airport. I didn't socialize with him."

"Would you describe him as someone who 'talked and talked'?"

Russo laughed. "Hardly. He was more the strong, silent type. Why?"

"I heard—" She almost said 'Bryan,' but changed her mind. She wasn't in the mood for Russo's ribbing. "I heard Gwen refer to him that way."

Russo shrugged. "Maybe he was more chatty around her." He took Ann's logbook from her and jotted in the details of the flight. As he handed it back, he said with what seemed like forced casualness, "Speaking of Gwen Burridge, I hear you went up to Clinton County with Gwen and Arno."

Ann tucked the logbook into her knapsack. "Who did you hear that from?"

"Gwen."

Ann raised her eyebrows. "Really? I didn't expect her to be talking it up around the airport."

"I don't think she wants you doing any more work for Arno."

"That's not a surprise. Seems like there's no love lost between those two." She pulled the elastic out of her hair, preparatory to smoothing the frizz back into place.

"She thinks ..." said Russo.

"She thinks what?"

"She thinks that you're faking."

Ann's hands dropped from her partially formed ponytail, allowing her hair to fall in tangles around her shoulders. "Faking?"

Russo shrugged.

"She told you that?"

"Yeah."

"Does she know you're telling me that she told you that?"

"She asked me to tell you. She was going to tell you, but I thought you'd rather hear it from me."

Ann glared at him.

"But what do I know," he said sheepishly.

"Where is she?" asked Ann through gritted teeth.

"Now?"

"Yes."

"Probably in her hangar. She's always in her hangar these days—"

Ann turned and strode toward Gwen Burridge's hangar.

"I don't think she was expecting a personal visit," he called after her.

The hangar doors were closed: both the large raisable door through which the plane passed and the small inset door which was generally referred to as "the man door." Ann knocked loudly on the smaller door.

"Come in."

She opened the door and stepped in.

She had never been in a hangar as fastidiously kept as this one. The concrete floor was pristine—not an errant leaf or drip of grease marred its polished surface. A workbench ran along one side of the hangar, tools hung with military precision on a pegboard above it. The light filtering through the hangar's skylights was dim, but Gwen's planes—the Extra 330 she had flown at the airshow and the Lancair in which she had followed Ann and Arno to Clinton County—were lit by spotlights, stars on a stage. Ann had done some research on Gwen Burridge's planes and knew that a million dollars' worth of equipment was housed in the hangar.

Gwen sat at an equally tidy desk that faced the wall opposite the workbench. She turned her swivel chair toward Ann.

"Can I help you?" she asked blandly.

"You told Russo that I was faking talking to Bryan?"

"I told Russo that I didn't want you taking advantage of Arno at what is a difficult time for him."

"I would think it would be a difficult time for you, too, but you seem to be bouncing back all right."

Gwen's face went red and she stood abruptly, then took a deep breath. "We all have our own ways of dealing with loss. I believe Arno would be better served by you not feeding him information about your claimed conversations with the dead."

"*Claimed?* You were there! I mediated a whole conversation between you and Bryan, and it was pretty clear that you believed it was really him."

"I was swept up in the moment. In retrospect, I realize that you didn't say anything that you couldn't have made up or gleaned online or from airport gossip."

Ann opened her mouth, clamped it closed, then burst out, "Are you kidding me? That thing about fixing the plane so it handles like you want it to?"

"As I said, Bryan might have mentioned it to you."

"The thing about the tail of the Extra being able to support a hundred and forty pounds?"

"You could probably find that in the plane's technical specs."

"Why in God's name would I be reading the technical specs for the Extra to find out how much weight the tail can support?"

"Because you wanted to convince me that you were communicating with Bryan."

Ann's voice climbed to an even higher register. "This is ridiculous!"

Gwen waved her hand. "I'm not going to argue with you about this. I'd just ask that you not spread around information about what you claim to have learned from a pair of dead men in Clinton County."

"One dead man."

"*Any* dead men—*dead* being the operative word."

"Or else ...?"

"At the moment, only Russo and Dottie know about my reservations—"

"Only Russo and Dottie? You might as well get on the airport PA system and make an announcement!"

"Fine. Then I'll amend my comment to say that only people at the airport will know of my reservations—at least from me. However, I don't want you leading Arno on, so I'll take my concern to a wider audience if necessary. I'm determined to make sure you don't make a difficult situation more difficult."

"And who do you propose to tell?"

"Lincoln Abbott at the *Chronicle*."

Ann's mouth dropped open. "That—?" She groped for the right word.

"It seems like you're already familiar with him. And that he is already familiar with you."

"He stuck his nose in where it didn't belong."

"He's a reporter."

"There are some things that should be kept private."

"My feeling exactly."

Ann clamped her lips together, then said, "Were you having an affair with Bryan?"

Gwen crossed her arms. "No."

"The conversation you had with him—that you and I both know you had with him—sounded a lot chummier than I'd expect between a pilot and her mechanic."

"He wasn't just a mechanic, he was a member of my team, and a friend."

"I think the Russos and Dotties of the world would be just as interested to hear my side of the story—and what you talked about with Bryan—as they will be about the fact that you engaged in a conversation that you now claim was bogus."

"I don't recall any conversation. And who do you think they'll believe? Who do you think Lincoln Abbott—and others like him—will believe?"

Ann stared at her for a moment, then she spun and stalked toward the door.

"Do I have your assurance that you will discontinue your work for Arno?" Gwen called after her.

"Fuck off," said Ann, and slammed the hangar door behind her.

30

Ann stomped into Mike and Scott's townhouse, slammed the door, and threw herself onto the couch. A second later, Scott's head popped out of the kitchen door.

"Sweetie, what's the matter?"

"I hate my job."

She heard footsteps on the stairs. "What's going on down there?" called Mike.

"Annie hates her job," said Scott. "Do you want some tea?" he asked Ann.

"No. Sure. Thanks."

Scott disappeared back into the kitchen and Mike sat down on the couch next to her.

"What now?" he asked.

"Wait for me!" yelled Scott from the kitchen.

Ann sulked and Mike scrolled through Twitter on his phone until Scott returned to the living room with a tray holding a teapot, three china cups, and a creamer and sugar bowl.

"Okay, what's up?" Scott asked as he poured the tea.

"Gwen Burridge is now claiming that I never mediated a

conversation between her and Bryan Calvert at the crash site. She's telling people at the airport I'm a fraud, she's warning me away from doing any more work for Arno, and she's saying if I don't cease and desist, she'll call Lincoln Abbott."

"Why would she claim that you didn't help her talk with Bryan Calvert?" asked Scott, shocked.

"Because she and Bryan were having an affair and planned to kill Hal in Clinton County."

Mike's eyebrows shot up. "She said that?"

"No, she didn't say that," said Ann in an aggrieved manner, "but why else would she decide she wants to discredit me when she obviously believed she was talking to Bryan when we were at the site?"

"Well, they say there's no such thing as bad publicity," said Mike uncertainly.

"I'm not worried about the publicity," said Ann. "She's claiming she doesn't believe I can do what I do—what I did for her! It's ... *wrong!*"

Scott patted her knee. "It certainly is."

"What are we going to do if Abbott gets involved?" asked Mike.

"I don't know, Mike," said Ann, exasperated. "What do you think he's going to do—write some kind of consumer watchdog exposé in the *Chronicle* about how I'm scamming money out of our clients?"

"Well, if that's his plan, we should decide what we're going to do—"

"I don't know what you're going to do," said Ann, "but I'm going back to Clinton County like our client is paying me to do."

"I'm not questioning that. I'm saying that we have a client that seems pretty hung up about confidentiality and Gwen Burridge is threatening to call a reporter at the *Chronicle*."

"It's not my plane she followed to Clinton County," she

retorted. "Arno should have guessed that someone as used to controlling every little thing as Gwen Burridge is would be tracking the planes leaving Avondale. If he hadn't fallen and hurt his leg—and then dumped the whole issue of dealing with her in my lap—he could have decided what to do about her once we got to the crash site. He shouldn't complain about the outcome."

"Calm down," said Mike. "I'll deal with Arno."

She took a swallow of tea and winced as the hot liquid scalded her lip. She plunked the cup down, sloshing some tea into the saucer. "He probably doesn't even know this is going on."

"Maybe not yet, but I don't want him to find out when he cracks open the *Chronicle* over his morning coffee. I'll give him a call."

"Fine."

He pinched the bridge of his nose. "But there's still the issue of how this will reflect on us. I was sort of kidding when I said that there's no such thing as bad publicity. If someone like Gwen Burridge, with a public following and devoted fans—fans who show up at her wedding, for God's sake—starts saying that you're lying about your ability, it's not going to be good for the business."

"Screw the business."

"That's easy for you to say—"

"It's not easy for me to say," she burst out. "It's my face on the metaphorical billboard! *Plus*, I'm trying to protect the business by avoiding having to tell a client that we can't accept any more work from him because someone is trying to bully us."

Mike fell back against the sofa cushions. "Maybe there's a way to spin this to emphasize that you will continue to practice your craft even in the face of disbelief."

"Yeah, do that," she said grumpily.

"The other thing we have going for us is that all of Abbott's articles about you have been fair and non-judgmental."

"Yeah. Is it too early for a glass of wine?"

"It's never too early for a glass of wine," said Scott, "but it's better if you're drinking it in a celebratory mood, not a depressed mood. Have some more tea. It's probably cooled down enough by now."

She took a cautious sip of tea and made a face. "It's just not the same."

"Maybe Mr. Masser would have some helpful advice," said Scott. Mike opened his mouth and Scott held up a hand. "I know you don't like to give him any credit, but he's been in the sensing business a long time and he must have had to deal with this type of situation over and over again."

Ann sighed. "I doubt he cares what people say about him—" Mike opened his mouth again, and she hastily added, "—despite what you think about his business being a performance. He'd just tell me to toughen up."

Mike leaned forward. "You're plenty tough. And if Gwen Burridge decides to start mudslinging, she'll find that the slinging can work both ways."

31

G wen lowered the barbell into its rack and sat up,
shaking her arms and rolling her head to loosen the
muscles in her neck. Hal had surprised her with the
basement gym for her birthday several years before, teasing her
about the fact that he could have an entire professional-grade
gym installed and not worry about having her ruin the surprise
by returning home from the airport early.

She appreciated the difference weightlifting had made in her
ability to sustain Gs—the seconds-long spikes of aerobatic
flying, the minutes-long press of an air race. She took a drink
from the water bottle at her side and redirected her thoughts
from the air race to more immediate concerns.

The conversation with Kinnear had not gone exactly as
Gwen had intended. She should never have let Russo be the one
to convey the message.

She had to admit that she had not anticipated Kinnear's
response. How could the woman not care if her public persona
was discredited, especially considering that her business must
be entirely dependent on her reputation for trustworthiness? On
the other hand, it was clear that Kinnear had some professional

pride, and Gwen intended to use it to her advantage. Kinnear might be able to discount the impact—professional and personal—of losing the respect of the people at the airport, but it would be harder for her to ignore an article in the *Chronicle*.

Gwen planned to call Lincoln Abbott in the morning.

And in the end, Kinnear's reaction to the hit to her reputation was not the point. The goal was to make sure that if Kinnear went to the police or other authority with any suspicions or accusations, they would be primed to disbelieve her.

Gwen pulled a towel off the back of a nearby chair and patted some beads of sweat off her neck. Her thoughts turned to the trip to the crash site.

Just because Hal hadn't been there during the first visit didn't necessarily mean that he wouldn't be there at another time. Or maybe he had been there, and Kinnear wasn't letting on—maybe Arno had warned Kinnear against acknowledging Hal's presence once Gwen joined the party. On the other hand, Bryan had said that even he had not seen Hal, and who would be in a better position to see Hal than another dead man. But here, too, she was relying on Kinnear's mediation of the conversation. The reference to the weight the Extra's tail could support —her own weight, not coincidentally—had convinced Gwen that Kinnear was, in fact, in contact with Bryan. However, it didn't mean she was conveying everything he said faithfully.

Gwen wadded up the towel and threw it back on the chair. How could she put a reasonable plan in place when there were so many variables—and so much information she had to rely on others for.

Another trip to Clinton County seemed inevitable. But Gwen couldn't make the trip on her own—she'd need help to get back to the crash site. It wasn't out of the question that she could enlist Ellis as her guide, especially since she had given him the airport job he was so desperate for. If Ellis wasn't available, or if he felt as committed to Arno's side as Kinnear did, Gwen was sure she could find someone else who could take her to the site.

But, more importantly, who could she get to play Ann Kinnear's part in her party? Once Gwen was back at the crash site, she would need someone who was not on contract to Arno Scanlan to mediate any conversation she might have with Hal or Bryan.

With a sigh, she draped the towel around her neck, strapped on her Jura Bernois watch, grabbed her phone and water bottle, and headed upstairs.

As she reached the top of the stairs, her phone rang. She didn't recognize the number, but the call was from Los Angeles. She hit *Accept*.

"Yes?"

"Hi, this is Corey Duff. Is this Gwen Burridge?"

"Yes, this is Gwen."

"Hi, Gwen—thanks for letting Dottie pass your phone number on to me."

"Sure. How can I help you?"

"As Dottie may have mentioned, I'm a documentary filmmaker, and my projects focus on people who have an unusual or highly specialized skill, especially if they're at the top of their profession. I saw your aerobatic performance at Avondale Airport, and I believe you qualify. Very impressive."

Gwen reached the sunroom and sank into a chair. "Thank you. What were you doing at the airport? Are you local?"

"No. I grew up in Pittsburgh, but I live in L.A. now."

"What brought you to Chester County?"

"I was there with Ann Kinnear—maybe you know her. She's taking flying lessons at Avondale."

Gwen scowled. "Yes, I know her," she said, trying to keep her tone neutral.

Corey continued in the same cheerful tone. "I produced and directed a documentary Ann appeared in called *The Sense of Death*. Very well received, favorably reviewed. I was in Chester County talking to her about another project, but I was fascinated by what I saw at the airshow: the interesting juxtaposition of high tech and country fair, the sense of community. And, of course, your impressive performance. I'd love to do a documentary profile of you. How did you get where you are today? What challenges have you encountered along the way, especially as a woman in a male-dominated field, and how have you overcome them? What does your future hold?"

She held back a derisive snort. At the moment, her future depended on the outcome of a race to find a document only a dead man knew the location of. However, she realized that even if Arno found the contract before she did, having Corey Duff as an ally could prove useful. She had staked out her position on the sale of the airport at the Dover Aero Club dinner—a professionally produced documentary would be an even more effective platform.

"I'd be interested to hear more," she said. "Just so long as you promise not to call it *The Sense of Community*."

He laughed. "That's a deal. I'm probably going to be out your way in the next week or two and I'd be happy to swing by Avondale."

"That would be fine."

"I'll text you a link where you can watch *The Sense of Death*, just to get an idea of what my work is like."

"I'll take a look at it."

Corey promised to check back with her once his travel plans firmed up and they ended the call.

She stopped in the kitchen to refill her water bottle, then went to Hal's office. She booted up the computer and went to the link that Corey had sent her, then settled back in the desk chair.

An hour later, she watched Corey Duff's name roll past in the end credits. She sat back, fingers laced over her stomach. Kinnear had been convincing in the show, but the subject who had held her attention was Garrick Masser. The documentary, and even the documentary's other subjects, seemed to acknowledge him as at the top of the esoteric field of spirit sensing. She thought back to the conversation around the campfire in Clinton County—Kinnear herself had said Masser was the best in the country.

He certainly looked the part—the untamed black eyebrows over the deep-set black eyes, the gray-shot black hair allowed to grow over the collar of his black shirt, the monochromatic wardrobe that drew the viewer's eye rather than camouflaged the wearer. She appreciated a person who committed fully to a look. Granted, this particular look was easier for a man to pull off than a woman, but Kinnear wasn't doing herself any favors with a wardrobe seemingly sourced exclusively from L.L. Bean.

She sat forward and tapped *garrick masser* into the browser and clicked on the link for garrickmasser.com. She scanned the page for tabs, but it appeared that everything Masser had to say, he said on the home page.

She glanced at the time: eight o'clock. Not too late for a phone call to someone who no doubt worked from home.

She tapped in the number listed on the website.

There was a slight click, suggesting the handset of an old-fashioned land line phone being removed from the cradle, then a rumbled "Yes."

"Is this ..." She glanced back at the webpage. "... Garrick Masser Consulting?"

"It is."

After a beat, she asked, "And is this Garrick Masser?"

"It is."

"My name is Gwen Burridge. Did I catch you at a bad time?"

After a pause, the voice on the other end replied, "Not particularly."

"I'm calling to ask about hiring you for a job."

"A consult."

"Pardon?"

"I refer to the services I provide as consults, not jobs."

"Okay, fine, I'm calling to ask about hiring you for a *consult*."

"Please provide me with some details."

"My husband was killed in a small plane crash two-and-a-half weeks ago and I need to contact him."

"Where did this plane crash take place?"

"Clinton County, Pennsylvania. It's in the north-central part of the state."

There was some indistinct noise and some shuffling sounds.

After half a minute, she said, "Hello?"

"Yes. I'm ascertaining the location of Clinton County."

"Are you looking at Google Maps?"

"No. I'm looking at an atlas." More shuffling, which she now recognized as pages turning. "Clinton County appears to be somewhat remote."

"That's no problem. I'm a pilot. I can pick you up in Maine and fly you to an airport that's only a few miles away from the site."

"You'd fly me to the site of the crash?"

"Yes."

"The small plane crash."

"Yes," she said, exasperated. "It's not like we're flying into the Bermuda Triangle."

"How does one access the crash site?"

"We'd need to hike in."

"And how long a hike would it be."

"About three miles."

"Good heavens."

Evidently Kinnear hadn't been joking when she said that her competitors would balk at making the trip to the crash site.

"Do I take it that will be a problem?" she asked.

"I don't believe that I am the appropriate professional for this engagement. However, I can give you the name of another spirit senser who in all probability would be willing to fly in a small plane to north-central Pennsylvania and then hike three miles to an aircraft crash site. Ann Kinnear. I believe her contact information is available on the internet. You would no doubt be required initially to contact her brother and general factotum, Mike Kinnear."

"General factotum?"

"Her business manager."

A business manager? That was good news for Gwen's smear campaign. Even if Kinnear didn't care about her reputation, perhaps her brother would.

In the sweetest voice she could muster, she said, "There's nothing I can do to persuade you to change your mind?"

"I think not. Good evening."

And the handset clicked into the cradle on the other end of the line.

32

Ann pulled up in front of Ellis's hangar at Avondale, having gotten a call from Arno that Gwen had left in the Extra for a practice session. Ellis had enthusiastically agreed to Mike's request that he accompany Ann on a return trip to Clinton County, although he was less enthusiastic about the plan to drive up, in case Gwen was tracking Ellis's plane as well as Arno's. By the time Gwen returned from the practice area near Octoraro Lake, Ann and Ellis would be on the road.

Although not nearly as elegant as Gwen's hangar, Ellis's was nearly as shipshape, the floor swept, his supplies housed in a stack of plastic totes. A collapsible privacy tent was deployed in one corner, a college dorm-sized fridge in the other.

"Do you sleep on the floor?" Ann asked.

"No, I have a cot."

Ann looked around the hangar.

"I keep it in the privacy tent when I'm not using it. I figure I'm probably not actually supposed to be sleeping here and I don't want to get Gwen and Arno in trouble."

"I've seen plenty of hangars that look like the inside of an RV."

Ellis laughed. "Yeah. I don't need that much stuff."

She did a mental calculation of the cubic yardage of the hangar's contents. "You didn't bring all this in your plane, did you?"

"No, Russo drove me to the Walmart to buy some of the stuff I needed."

"And the tent is ... the head?"

"I have a camp toilet in there, but I have a key to the FBO so I can use the restroom there. I have a shower hooked up in the tent—there's a spigot right at the end of the hangar row where I can get water."

"That tent must be a lot bigger than it looks from the outside."

Ellis grinned. "I have to move stuff in and out of it depending on what I need to use it for."

"Where do you cook?"

"There's a really good Italian restaurant nearby that delivers."

"What do you eat for breakfast?"

"Italian leftovers."

"Man, it's been a decade since I could stomach cold pizza for breakfast," said Ann.

Ellis locked up the hangar and they climbed into Ann's Forester and headed for Clinton County.

Ellis had not only the stomach of a young man barely out of his teens, but also the nervous energy and need for distraction. They were only a few minutes into the drive when he asked if he could turn on the radio. He scanned through the dial until he found a country station.

"This okay?" he asked.

"Sure."

He settled back in his seat, tapping out the rhythms on his thighs, humming along with the choruses.

After the third song about girls, guns, and God, Ellis reached over and turned down the volume.

"Hey, you think it would be okay if I drove my Tahoe back from Clinton County? I hate to have to ask Russo or Dottie for a ride every time I need to go somewhere, and even I'm going to get tired of Italian after a while. It would be nice to be able to run to the store on my own."

"I don't see why not."

"Gwen might wonder how I got it to Avondale from Clinton County."

"I don't think it matters. I'm not so worried about keeping the trip a secret long-term as I am about making sure we can get to the crash site without her tagging along. I'm hoping not to have to keep making trips to the site, but if I do, I can always sneak up there again ... assuming she doesn't decide to put a tracker on the Forester."

After a pause, he said, somewhat reluctantly, "I heard what Gwen was saying about the trip to the crash site ... and about you."

Ann grimaced. "Yeah."

"But she had a conversation with Bryan Calvert through you, right?"

"Yup."

"Why would she say that she didn't?"

Ann briefly thought about turning this into a teachable moment to imbue Ellis with a bit of her cynicism about human nature but decided she didn't want to be the one to tarnish his youthful naïveté.

"People don't always feel comfortable with the idea of communicating with the dead. Sometimes they deny it's happening in the moment. Sometimes they believe it in the moment but later talk themselves out of believing it."

"Maybe sometimes they still believe it but don't want to admit it to other people."

So, not so naive after all.

"Yeah, sometimes. Maybe it doesn't jibe with her Woman of Steel image."

Ellis nodded sadly. "Yeah, maybe not."

After a moment, Ann asked, "Have you seen your father since he died other than at your graduation?"

Ellis laughed. "It's funny to hear you ask the question so straightforward like that, like you were asking me if I had ever seen a beaver other than at the pond."

Ann laughed, too. "For me, it is sort of like that."

He shook his head, his smile dimming. "No, it was just that once. Why do you think that was? Do you think it was because I needed to see my dad because it was a big moment in my life?"

"Maybe your dad needed to see you because it was a big moment in his son's life."

A smile crept back onto Ellis's lips. "Yeah." He cleared his throat and swiped at an eye. "Yeah, maybe that was the reason."

They drove northwest, through Lancaster and Harrisburg, then turned north to follow the Susquehanna River. As they drove, the land transitioned from rolling farmland to hills to more mountainous terrain, the highway periodically traversing cut-throughs striped with the striations of eons of sediment deposits. The national chain restaurants and convenience stores gave way to local mom-and-pop businesses and diners.

When they reached Clinton County, they stopped at Ellis's mother's house—which, Ann supposed, was still Ellis's house when he wasn't at college or summering in an airport hangar—so that Ellis could assemble two packs for their trip to the crash site. The house was a trim Cape Cod with flowers in the window boxes and a *Welcome!* flag hanging from a pole off the porch.

Well-tended flower beds surrounded the house and lined the walk, although the grass in the expansive yard was shaggy.

"I should probably stay around long enough to mow the grass," said Ellis as they climbed out of the Forester. "If you can drop me off back here tomorrow morning, I'll take care of it and then drive back to Avondale the day after."

Ellis's mother was plump and pretty, blonde hair tied back in a ponytail highlighting a lovely peaches-and-cream complexion. She had made up a small cooler of food for their dinner that evening and breakfast the next morning. She served Ann lemonade while Ellis collected the supplies. She appeared more concerned that her son refused to pack an extra can of bug repellent than that he was leaving for an overnight camping trip with a woman whose age teetered precariously between her son's and her own.

When the packs were ready, Ellis loaded them into the Forester, and they headed to the pull-off from which they would start their hike. When they arrived, they hoisted their packs onto their backs and set off through the woods. After a few dozen yards, Ellis pulled one of the yellow plastic strips out of his pocket and tied it to a tree.

When they reached the campsite, they followed the pattern of the first visit, minus Gwen. Ann paid an unproductive trip to the crash site while Ellis set up camp, then they lounged around the campsite until it was time for a second try. They ate the dinner Ellis's mother had packed and read until the light became too dim for Ellis to read *Stick and Rudder*, then they switched to chatting, mainly about Ellis's college courses and post-college plans.

"It sounds like you really enjoyed working with the NTSB—maybe you could get a job there," said Ann.

"It was interesting, but I imagine that outside of the actual investigations it's just a big corporate entity, with all that bureaucracy and red tape. Everyone *leaning into stretch goals* and *pivoting to meet market demands*."

Ann laughed. "Where did you come up with that?"

"My roommate interned at one of those companies. He kept a dictionary of that kind of stuff."

"What would suit you better?"

"I really love Avondale—it would be fun to manage a place like that someday. Big enough to be interesting, small enough to be personal, and none of that corporate bull. Can you imagine Russo talking about *creating stretch goals*?"

Ann laughed again. "No, but I can imagine him talking about *busting your ass*."

"Yeah. I'd love to hear Dottie's take on *the customer is always right*."

At around eleven, Ann stood and stretched. "I'm going to the crash site. I'm going to ask you to stay here."

He sighed. "Yeah, I figured."

Taking a flashlight, she made her way up the hill.

33

As Ann topped the rise leading to the crash site, she saw that Bryan was already there, seated on one of the charred logs. He was easily visible in the dark, although as she neared, she could see that his form was slightly more amorphous than it had been on their first encounter. She made her way toward the crater, noting the same slight drop in temperature that she had noticed during her first visit, although the difference this time was less marked.

"Have you been waiting for me?" she asked.

"Waiting for something," he replied, his voice a fraction less clear than it had been. "Is Gwen with you?"

"No, this time it's just me and the guide."

Bryan looked toward where the light from the campfire flickered in the trees. "I could check, you know."

"Be my guest."

He gazed toward the light for a moment more, then shook his head. "Not sure what we'd talk about even if she were here. Why are you back?

Ann took a seat on the log a few feet away from Bryan. "Arno wanted me to check again to see if Hal was here. Any sign of him?"

"Nope."

"Last time I was here, I asked if you knew anything about Hal's plan for Scanridge and you said you didn't. But even if he didn't confide in you, maybe you would have an idea of where he might have put the contract for safekeeping." She paused hopefully. When Bryan didn't respond, she asked, "Do you?"

"Nope."

"Can you think of why he might have hidden it? That might help Arno figure out where it is. For example, if he was hiding it from the competition, he might hide it in his house, but if he was hiding it from Gwen, he might hide it somewhere else."

"I have no idea," he said, obviously irritated.

"Sorry to be a pest, I'm just trying to get this thing resolved for my client." She dug the toe of her boot into the charred earth. "I went to the airshow at Avondale a couple of weeks after the crash, right before I ended up here with Gwen. A friend of mine was talking to one of the police officers who notified Gwen about the crash. He said that she seemed more surprised to hear about your death than to hear about her husband's death."

Bryan raised an eyebrow. "Should I be flattered?"

"Did she have reason to be more affected by your death than Hal's?"

"Affected? I couldn't say. Surprised? I can imagine she might have been more surprised to hear I had died than that Hal had died."

"Why's that?"

"He was drinking a lot. Wasn't being too careful about what he did while under the influence. If I were Gwen and saw a cop show up at the house or the airport, the first thing that would have jumped to my mind was Hal in a wrecked car."

"She also knew that Hal's truck was at the quarry."

He shrugged. "I knew he'd be at the quarry. It's where he went."

"She said she had seen his truck from the air. You can't see the parking area from the normal approach or in the pattern."

"Maybe she was just overflying the airport."

Ann regarded Bryan. She wondered if he had been as deadpan when he was alive as he was now.

"The conversation you and Gwen had during the last visit seemed ... odd."

"Odd?"

"Like you were talking in code."

He was silent.

"What's the deal with how much weight the tail of the Extra can hold?"

His deadpan expression lifted. "Now that I can't share—it wouldn't be gentlemanly," he said with a grin.

After a moment, she blushed. "Oh."

He sat forward, his grin fading. "What are you getting at?"

"Gwen's launched a smear campaign to discredit me, and I want to know what's behind it. She's claiming that I never mediated a conversation between the two of you. She's spreading the word at the airport that I'm scamming Arno, and she's threatening to call a reporter from the *Philadelphia Chronicle*."

He sat back. "Interesting."

"Why would she do that?"

He didn't respond.

"What is she hiding?"

"I have no idea what she might be hiding, assuming she's hiding anything."

"Are you sticking with the story you told me last time I was here?"

Almost a minute had ticked by when he finally spoke. "Why

do you think I'm still here?" The words could have been challenging, but his tone was questioning.

"What?"

"Why am I here when Hal isn't? Why am I anywhere when, I assume, you're not seeing every person who ever died wandering around?"

Ann gave her usual answer. "Unfinished business."

"Secrets?"

Ann felt her heartbeat speed up. "Yes, sometimes secrets keep a person here."

He sat forward and took a deep breath. "For a while, I didn't mind being here. It's beautiful. It's peaceful. But I've started to feel … antsy. Like I should be going somewhere but can't."

She nodded.

"If I tell you what happened, can we keep it confidential? Just between the two of us?"

She hesitated. "I can't promise that. It depends on what you tell me."

"Just stuff that would only make life difficult for the people who are still alive if you told them."

"I'd have to be the judge of that."

He examined her for a moment, then sighed. "Fair enough." He looked toward where the light from the campfire flickered in the treetops on the other side of the rise. "Hal showed up at the hangar that night, while I was getting the plane ready to go to the cabin. He accused me of having an affair with Gwen. He grabbed a wing jack leg off the workbench and came after me with it. We struggled, and I accidentally hit him in the head with it. I checked for breathing and a pulse—nothing. I gave him CPR for a while, but he didn't come around. By that time, I felt like too much time had gone by to call 911. Even if they could have revived him, he would have been a vegetable, and I knew he wouldn't want that." He took a deep breath. "And, to be perfectly honest, I knew I didn't want to try to explain what had happened, and I *definitely* didn't want to risk going to prison. So I loaded him into the plane, intending to bring him to Clinton County and bury him up here. Then the plane crashed." He spread his arms to take in their surroundings. "And here we are."

Even though this wasn't far from what she had thought might have happened, it was still a shock to hear her suspicions confirmed. She resisted the urge to rise from the log seat she shared with Bryan and move away from him.

"You were willing to just have Hal disappear?" she asked. "To leave Gwen wondering what had happened to him?"

"I hadn't thought that far ahead. Maybe I would have eventually told her, but I don't think she would have blamed me for—" She thought he wasn't going to continue, but then he said, "—something that was an accident."

"You had killed her husband, whether it was an accident or not. You think she wouldn't have cared?"

"Of course she would have cared," he said, his voice tight. "I just think she would have understood what I did."

"You said that Hal accused you of having an affair with Gwen."

"Yes."

"And I'm guessing based on your gentlemanly reluctance to talk about what you and Gwen were up to on the tail of the Extra, he was right."

He rubbed the back of his neck. "Yes."

"How did he find out?"

"Who knows. Sneaking a look at her text messages when her phone was unattended? An ill-timed visit to my hangar?"

She considered what Bryan had told her. If Bryan had made it to Clinton County and later told Gwen about the altercation at the hangar, and that Hal was buried in an unmarked grave in the Pennsylvania Wilds, would Gwen have understood why Bryan did what he had done? Would she have kept his secret? Maybe —especially since the public would have a lot more sympathy for the worried wife of a missing husband than for the woman who had cheated on that husband with the man who had ended up killing him.

"What time did the fight at the hangar take place?"

"A little before ten o'clock. Why do you want to know?"

"Because I might be able to contact Hal at the hangar and find out the information that Arno is looking for."

He sat forward. "How do you plan to explain to Arno how you know that Hal died in the hangar?"

"I don't need to tell him I know that for sure, I'll just tell him I'm covering all my bases."

"It's up to you. It won't make any difference to me one way or the other."

Ann finally gave in to her compulsion to rise from her seat. "You've explained why Gwen would be less surprised to hear that Hal was dead than that you were dead: because he was a basket case who drove drunk. You've explained why she might have seen Hal's truck at the quarry: because she was flying some non-standard pattern over the airport. You've explained why the conversation between the two of you sounded weird: because you were referring to your extracurricular activities in the hangar. So why is she going out of her way to deny that I mediated a conversation between the two of you?"

He shrugged. "She's got a reputation to protect, and it doesn't involve holding conversations with dead people."

"I can't see how it would make a difference. It's not like people come to the airshows to chat with her about her beliefs about life after death. They come to watch her fly."

"It's not just the airshows themselves that she's worried about. It's the sponsorships. She was able to stop relying on Hal to foot the bill when she started finding companies like Jura

Bernois that were willing to pay handsomely to have their brand associated with the Peregrine Falcon. They might change their minds about that if they thought she was going off the deep end." After a pause, he continued. "I think you can see why I said that if you passed on the information I gave you, it would only make life difficult for the people who are still around."

She tilted her head back and gazed up at the star-flecked sky. Who would she tell? The police? She knew how that would go. They would dismiss her accusations with anything from sympathy to anger. Arno? What good would it do him to know that his friend and partner had been struck down when he had attacked Gwen's lover in a drunken rage? Gwen? Wouldn't it be better for her not to know that her unfaithfulness to her husband had ultimately led to his death?

Eventually, she nodded. "Yes, I agree with that."

He stood up. "So, do you think this will let me move on?" he asked, a joking tone not quite masking his concern.

"In my experience, unburdening yourself of those types of secrets does help."

"Well, Ann, I'm hoping you don't have a reason to come to Clinton County again, but if you do, I hope you don't find me still here."

"Me too."

She turned back toward the light of the campfire and made her way up the slope. When she reached the top of the rise, she turned and looked back toward the crash site. At first, she thought Bryan had left, but then she saw the flicker of his presence where she had left him, noticeably fainter than it had been less than an hour ago.

34

The next morning, Ann and Ellis packed up and started the hike out. When they reached the first strip of yellow plastic fluttering in the slight breeze, Ellis reached up to untie it.

"Can you leave those up?" she asked.

"I could, but like I said, I hate to mark the trail to the crash site for people who want to go there just to satisfy their morbid curiosity."

"It would be handy for me, just in case I need to come back at a time you're not available."

Ellis crossed his arms. "Now you're leaving me out of the trips altogether?"

"I'm not trying to leave you out, I'm just trying to set it up so I can be at least a little self-sufficient if another visit is needed."

"Why would you need another visit?"

She smiled wanly. "Morbid curiosity?"

She had spent a good part of the night thinking through the conversation she had had with Bryan. There were no obvious anomalies, but something about it didn't seem right. If she needed to have another chat with him—assuming he was still around—she wanted to be able to do it on her own schedule, and by herself.

When they got back to the road, they loaded their packs into the Forester and Ann drove Ellis back to his house.

"See you tomorrow at Avondale?" he asked as got the packs out of the back.

"No doubt. Thanks for the help, Ellis."

"No problem."

Ann set the GPS for West Chester and then called Arno.

"How did it go?" he asked.

She had a momentary desire to renege on the promise she had made to Bryan and tell Arno what she had learned about the circumstances of Hal's death, but her opinion hadn't changed about the uselessness of sharing that information. And she didn't feel like feeding Arno's dislike of Gwen by confirming that Gwen had been having an affair with Bryan. She took a deep breath.

"I asked him about the contract, but he didn't know anything."

"Didn't know or wouldn't tell?"

"I don't know, Arno—telling if a spirit is lying isn't any easier than telling if a living person is lying."

"Damn. So, I guess that's the end of the road."

"Not necessarily. Although it's true that spirits usually appear where the person died, it's not always the case. I think it makes sense for me to check out some other places that were Hal's common haunts—no pun intended. Maybe around the airport."

"But you've been around the airport plenty since he died."

"But not at night. And I haven't been looking for him."

"It's all right with me if you think there's a possibility of contacting him there."

"I'll go there tonight. If I go at the time when Hal died, that will not only improve the chances of me contacting him but will also keep Gwen from interfering ... unless she's in the habit of spending the night at the airport."

Arno snorted. "It's not a common practice, as far as I know, but I wouldn't put it past her. By the way, now that she's planted the seed at the airport about what happened—or didn't happen —at the crash site, she's evidently casting her net wider. I got a call from some reporter named Lincoln Abbott. He's with the *Chronicle*.

Ann sighed. "Yeah, I know him."

"It won't do me any good with the people I work with through Scanridge if they hear I hired a psychic to contact my dead partner."

"Yeah, that would be a shame," she said sourly.

"Not that it's not worse for you," he added hastily.

"I hope that whatever the contract will let you do with Scanridge is worth it," she said.

Arno was silent for a beat, then said, "So, the airport tonight. Want me to be there? I have an early morning meeting tomorrow, but—"

"No, I think it's better if I'm on my own. Can I get keys to the buildings? The FBO, the hangars, Bryan's shop?"

"I can get you keys to the FBO and the shop. We have duplicate keys to the locks on the hangars, but those might take a while to get sorted out."

"That's fine—we can pursue that later if I come up empty tonight."

She reached the townhouse in West Chester in the late afternoon and had just dropped her bag on the floor of the entry when Mike emerged from his office.

"How did the trip go?" he asked. "Get any intel from Bryan about the Scanridge contract?"

"No, but I did contact Bryan again and the conversation was ... interesting. I need a drink." He followed her into the kitchen. He got a wine glass out of the cabinet and a bottle of Sauvignon Blanc out of the refrigerator and poured himself a glass. He held the bottle up in her direction with a questioning look.

"I'm going for the hard stuff," she said, taking the bottle of Macallan down from the shelf.

She poured herself a finger of Scotch.

"So ...?" he prompted.

"Where's Scott?" She glanced around the kitchen. "For that matter, where's Ursula?"

"He ran down to Baltimore overnight to visit his brother and brought her along. Should I try to get him on a call?"

"No. I'd rather tell you first and then we can decide what to tell Scott."

Mike raised an eyebrow. "I'm intrigued."

They sat at the kitchen island.

"According to Bryan Calvert," said Ann, "he killed Hal Burridge in self-defense when Hal attacked him because he found out that Bryan was having an affair with Gwen."

Mike sat back. "Holy shit."

"Yeah."

"How did Hal get in the plane?"

"Bryan tried to revive him and, when he couldn't, he decided he'd fly the body to Clinton County and bury it."

"Jesus, you were right."

"Yeah."

"Does Arno know?"

"No. I can't see any upside to telling anyone what Bryan said. Can you?"

Mike pushed his wine glass away. "Give me that," he said,

gesturing to the bottle of Scotch. She passed the bottle to him. He got a glass from the cabinet and poured for himself. He tossed back a swallow, then sat back down. "I agree that there's no upside to telling anyone what Bryan said. The police couldn't do anything with that information, and it's not going to help Arno or Gwen. Plus, Bryan got his comeuppance already."

"That's what I thought." She hesitated. "What about Scott?"

Mike grimaced. "I never have secrets from him, but if there could be some sort of accessory-after-the-fact thing to worry about, I'd just as soon he didn't know." He sighed. "Let me think about it."

"Okay."

He raised his glass. "Here's to my big sister—not only able to talk with the dead, but to think like a murderer."

She raised her glass. "Well, at least like a manslaughterer."

They clinked glasses and drank.

"So ... what now?" asked Mike.

"I'm going to Avondale Airport tonight and see if I can contact Hal at Bryan's hangar." She glanced at her watch. "I'm going to finish this and then see if I can get a nap. I'll be glad when this whole screwed-up engagement is done, and I can get back to a normal sleep routine."

"Don't hold your breath. I have another engagement lined up for you once this one is wrapped up and it's likely to be a nighttime gig."

She groaned and pushed herself to her feet.

"Oh, just to make your day even more special, guess who called," he said.

"Lincoln Abbott."

"How did you know?"

"He called Arno too. What did he want?"

"Wanted to get a response from you about what Gwen Burridge is saying about us scamming Arno Scanlan."

"What did you tell him?"

"That all statements from *Ann Kinnear Sensing* come through me and that we aren't scamming anyone, and he can read his own articles about the Philadelphia Socialite murder if he doubts it."

Ann smiled. "Thanks, Mike."

"It doesn't mean he isn't going to keep trying to get a statement from you."

"I know. I'll just point him to my PR department if he catches up with me."

35

In a continued effort to keep her activities off Gwen's radar, Ann swung by Arno's house to pick up the keys to the various Avondale buildings rather than meeting up with him at the airport.

When she arrived at her destination, she was surprised. She had pictured Arno living in a huge house in a gated community, or maybe in some glass box monstrosity, but the drive led to a rehabbed stone farmhouse with a stone barn in back, both meticulously restored.

There was no answer to her knock at the door, and no other cars in the driveway, so she wandered around the grounds, which were tastefully landscaped with native plants. A few minutes later, a Lexus SUV wheeled into the driveway and pulled up behind the Forester. Arno climbed out, grabbed his crutches from the passenger seat, and swung himself over to where Ann stood.

"Sorry," he said, already a little breathless. "Just as I was getting ready to leave Avondale, some muckety-muck stopped by to complain about the runway. Took me a couple of minutes to get rid of him."

"What's up with the runway?"

"Needs to be repaved," he said. "Come on in, I need to pull a couple of keys off the ring and explain what they are. Meant to write up some notes before I left the airport but didn't have time."

She followed him to the front door.

He got his keyring out of his pocket and unlocked the door. She noticed that there were two brass key fobs attached to the ring—one shiny from use, one dulled and slightly deformed, one Arno's, one Hal's. "Come on back to the kitchen."

She followed him down the home's central hallway, glancing into rooms as she passed. The furnishings and decor were compatible with the farmhouse ambiance—comfortable, over-stuffed chairs, rustic woodwork painted in subtle greens and blues—but not over-the-top. No decorative spinning wheels or faux butter churns.

"You have a lovely home," she said when they got to the kitchen.

"Thanks. It's all my wife. She's an attorney at one of the big banks in Wilmington, but she likes interior decorating."

Ann further adjusted her assumptions about Arno. She would have pictured him having a beautiful young trophy wife who spent her days at the country club swimming and playing tennis. She suppressed a smile. She supposed that Hal Burridge had been the one with the trophy wife, although she'd be inter-ested to see Gwen Burridge's reaction to being called one.

Arno's phone buzzed just as they got to the kitchen. He pulled out the phone and scowled. "Goddammit. Sorry, got to take this." He limped into the next room and it wasn't long before Ann could hear the volume of the conversation escalating.

She wandered back down the hall toward the front of the house and took a turn around the living room, both to admire the decor at closer range and to give Arno some privacy. She was paging through an aviation magazine she had found on an end table when he appeared at the door.

"Sorry," he said. "Still with the runway. These idiots are going to be the death of me. Two businesses is one too many businesses to run," he muttered, almost to himself.

She thought about the Scanridge contract Arno had hired her to find. "Are you planning to sell the trucking company to focus on the airport?"

He looked startled for a moment, then collected himself. "I'm speaking out of turn. These kinds of things need to stay confidential in the planning stages."

She held up her hands. "I promise not to call the competition as soon as I leave here."

He laughed and held out a set of keys. Rather than putting them on his spare Avondale key fob, he had fastened them together with a twist tie. "That's to the FBO," he said, separating one of the keys, and then worked his way around the ring, "I think that one's to Hal's office ... that one's to the maintenance shed—can't imagine he'd be there, but I figured I'd give you all the keys I could round up—and that one's to Bryan's shop. Those are all the places I could get keys to on short notice. If you need to get into other places like the hangars, I'll see what I can do on that front."

She pocketed the keys and Arno hobbled behind her to the front door.

"Just lock up when you're done and leave the keys in the key drop by the FBO," he said.

"Okay."

"Let me know how it goes," he said as she stepped outside. "I'll be up late—at least until midnight."

"I know—running two businesses."

He smiled bleakly. "Something like that."

36

Ann arrived at Avondale at nine o'clock, about an hour before the time when Bryan had reported that the altercation with Hal had taken place. The sun had set about a half hour earlier, and a waning quarter moon hung in the twilit sky.

The airport was quiet: the parking lot empty, buildings dark, no sound of activity from the hangars. Although it was possible to fly in and out of Avondale after dark, most of the pilots were daytimers, and it was convenient that Ellis was in Clinton County mowing his mom's lawn. The lack of traffic—human and aeronautical—suited her needs.

She decided she'd make a circuit of the other buildings Arno had given her keys to—and the airport in general—and then spend most of the night at Bryan's hangar. She wished she had been able to avail herself of Ursula's proven spirit-sensing abilities, but the dachshund was still in Baltimore with Scott.

Ann started with the FBO. She had never been further into the building than the desk where she paid Dottie for her last lesson and scheduled the next one, and she felt a bit like a teenager being given the keys to the school after hours and being able to peek into the teacher's lounge.

She guessed the FBO had been built in the sixties or seventies, and other than the elderly Dell on Dottie's desk, there was little other evidence of updates. The walls were knotty pine, the carpeting a worn orange-brown. Against one wall of the small reception area stood a vinyl-covered love seat, one of its orange cushions patched with orange duct tape, a stack of aviation magazines on a veneer table at its side.

There were three doors off the office area, one with Arno's name in a holder at its side, the second with Russo's name. The key that Arno had identified as the one to Hal's office fit the third, unlabeled door.

The room was neat, although whether because Hal himself had been neat or because someone, likely Dottie, had tidied it after he died, she didn't know. Its window overlooked Gwen's hangar, which was bathed in bright security lights.

She was unsurprised to get no sense of Hal in the FBO.

She looked briefly in the maintenance shed, although she had a hard time imagining encountering the spirit of the tuxedo-clad man from the wedding video there. She walked up and down the hangar rows, then headed for Bryan's hangar.

She unlocked the door, stepped in, and flipped a light switch beside the door, illuminating a single bulb hanging from the ceiling. She realized that she had no idea if the police had ever had reason to visit the hangar after Bryan's death. As far as they knew, it was just a piece of property owned in part by one of the victims of the crash and used as a place of business by the other. Scanning the interior, she could see no sign that anyone had searched the hangar, or even visited it.

There were no planes in the hangar, leaving the center of the space clear. Equipment, workbenches, and shelves of tools and supplies lined the walls. The single bulb was not enough to

penetrate the shadows that gathered in the corners. She experimentally flipped another switch and two banks of fluorescent
lights buzzed to life, lending the hangar an operating room vibe
—an operating room for airplanes, she supposed. She flipped
the fluorescents off—they would make Hal hard to spot if he
appeared in the form in which spirits normally manifested.
Even if he were here, perhaps he was gradually fading away, as
Bryan seemed to be doing, as he left the commitments and cares
of his life behind.

She made a circuit of the hangar. In a corner was a device
that she imagined could be used to jack a plane up by its wings,
and she recalled Bryan's comment that he had hit Hal in the
head with a wing jack leg. She examined the detachable legs
with some unease, wondering if brighter light would reveal a
streak of blood or a strand of Hal Burridge's hair. Glancing
around the confines of the hangar, she let her imagination play
out the scene based on the sketchy details Bryan had provided.
Her ability to speak with the dead didn't make her immune to
chills at the idea of standing in a place where a violent death
had taken place. She crossed to the door and flipped the lock.

She sat down on one of the stools next to the workbench, her
back to the uncurtained window, and scanned the hangar.
Maybe even the single lightbulb would interfere with her ability
to see Hal Burridge. She returned to the door and flipped off the
remaining light, used her flashlight app to guide her back to the
stool, then switched that off as well.

She was eager to wrap up Arno Scanlan's engagement, if for
no other reason than so she could get a good night's sleep. If
sitting in the dark would improve her chances of contacting Hal
Burridge, she'd sit in the dark.

The night had seemed quiet, but as she sat there, undis-
tracted by visual input, she became aware of a sound that was so

ubiquitous in the Pennsylvania summer that it had escaped her notice: the whir of cicadas.

She was calculating how much caffeine a thermos of espresso would contain when she became aware of a sound inside the hangar—a rustle in the corner. She switched on the flashlight app and shone it in the direction of the noise, then around the interior of the hangar. Nothing. She turned the light off again. Probably mice.

A minute of silence ticked by, the sound of the cicadas rising and falling, then there was another noise—this one from outside the hangar. A crunching noise.

A footstep on gravel?

She turned her head, trying to zero in on where the sound was coming from.

A moment later, she caught a movement outside the dirt-grimed window in her peripheral vision, but by the time she turned, it was gone. She heard another crunch.

Someone walking along the side of the hangar, headed for the hangar door.

Was it Hal Burridge approaching the hangar as he must have approached it the night he arrived to confront Bryan about his affair with Gwen? Ann spun through her mental index of the spirits she had encountered in her engagements. Had any of them made a sound with their footsteps?

She jumped off the stool. If it was Hal, would he arrive as a bereft man wandering a deserted airport in the middle of the night, or a man reliving his murderous anger—anger he planned to vent on the person he found in Bryan Calvert's hangar? Or was there a living visitor outside with his or her own reason for stealth?

Either way, she suddenly felt uncomfortably exposed sitting on the stool. She made her way as quietly as she could to the door, positioning herself so that she would be behind it if it opened.

She heard the footsteps stop just outside. She held her breath, listening for anything that would give her an idea of what was happening just a few feet away. All was silent. She leaned forward, her ear close to the door—then almost let out a yelp when the doorknob rattled.

Her heart thumping, she scanned the interior of the hangar, assessing her options. She knew from her conversation with Bryan that the leg of the wing jack made an effective weapon. However, her mind balked at that option, due in part to a general squeamishness and in part to the difficulty of explaining the presence of DNA from both Hal Burridge and the current intruder, should she need to deploy it as a weapon. She pulled her phone out of her pocket, ready to punch in 9-1-1, even as she realized that if someone meant her harm, the police couldn't possibly get to the airport in time. And if it was Hal Burridge, there would be little they could do to thwart whatever his intentions were.

She dropped her phone back into her pocket and grabbed a length of pipe that was leaning against the wall near the door. Gripping it with both hands and holding it over her shoulder like a bat, she strained her ears, trying to picture what was going on outside the hangar. All she could hear was the cicadas' song, which was reaching a buzzing crescendo.

The knob turned.

She had locked the door—who except Hal Burridge could open it so effortlessly?

The door swung open.

"Hello?" she heard an unsteady voice call. "Is someone in there?"

"Ellis?"

There was a startled squawk from the other side of the door, then Ellis's voice. "Ann?"

Ann lowered the pipe and stepped out from behind the door.

Ellis stood outside the door, his hair askew, a baseball bat in his hand.

"What are you doing here?" she asked. "I thought you were in Clinton County mowing your mom's lawn."

Ellis stepped into the hangar, the bat now hanging at his side. "Turns out Mom didn't need the yard mowed, just needed to have the spark plugs replaced so she could get the mower started. She actually likes to mow, so I left after I did that. Stopped to visit a buddy in State College. I got back a couple of minutes ago and saw a light like a flashlight moving around—I thought someone had broken in. What are you doing here?"

She flipped on the single bulb, then propped the metal pipe back behind the door, the pounding of her heart gradually subsiding. "Still looking for Hal Burridge."

Ellis dropped his bat on the workbench. "Jesus, would you guys please stop leaving me in the dark? I could have brained you before I realized who you were." He glanced over at the length of pipe. "You could have brained me."

"Sorry, Ellis ..." She sat down on one of the workbench stools. "Even if I had realized you were back at the airport, I'm not sure I would have thought to factor in your new role as Avondale night watchman."

Ellis sat down on the other stool. "I'm just keeping an eye on things. I like it here. I don't want people messing with airport stuff." He looked around the hangar. "Why did you have the lights turned off?"

"If Hal showed up, I thought I could see him better in the dark."

"How come you're looking for him here?"

"Just covering all the bases."

"I think you and Arno are handling this all wrong," he said, clearly still irritable from the shock of the encounter. "You should let Gwen go back to the crash site. I know you guys are on the outs because she's saying bad things about you, and I know that her husband didn't show up when she was there the first time, but I still think he'd be more likely to show up if there was someone there he was close to—like my dad showing up at my graduation."

Ann was silent for a few moments, then gave a groan. "I've been an idiot."

"What do you mean?"

She looked at him, then shook her head. "Nothing."

Ellis scowled. "I suppose you want me to leave."

Ann sighed. "I'm afraid so, Ellis, but trust me—I don't think you'll be missing anything."

By MIDNIGHT, Ann felt reasonably sure that Hal Burridge wouldn't be making an appearance, at least not that night. She tapped out a text to Arno.

No luck in hangar but I have another idea. Will tell you tomorrow.

After a moment, Arno's answer came through.

Can you stop by the house at 7am?

"Of course, why shouldn't I be able to stop by your house at seven o'clock," she muttered. She tapped and sent her response.

Ok

She locked up the hangar, dropped the keys in the FBO drop box, and headed back to West Chester.

As she drove, she mulled over the situation. Despite having heard Ellis's story of seeing his father at his graduation ceremony, despite the fact that it was unlikely that Ellis's dad had died in the high school gymnasium, despite her own statement to Ellis that she was just covering all the bases by visiting Bryan's hangar, she had gotten tunnel vision about looking for Hal at the location of his death—the crash site when she thought he had died there, the hangar when she learned from Bryan of the altercation there. She usually encountered spirits where they had died ... but not always. She needed to cast the net wider: the Burridge house, the quarry, even Hal's office at Scanridge. She'd ask Arno where else Hal had spent time when he was alive.

By the time she reached West Chester, she was beginning to question the wisdom of driving with so little sleep. If this schedule kept up, she'd have to press Mike or Scott into chauffeur duty.

37

The next morning, Ann crawled out of bed at six, having decided to buy herself an extra half hour of sleep by postponing her shower until later in the day. With Scott and Ursula not expected to return to West Chester until later in the day, she would have to proceed without the dog's spirit-sensing assistance. She brewed up a pot of dark roast, filled a thermos, then headed to Arno's house.

She got there at quarter after seven, to find Arno leaning against the side of his Lexus SUV scanning his phone.

"Running a little late," he said as she climbed out of the Forester.

"Arno, I was up until one o'clock."

"So was I," he countered.

"Fine, you win the early bird contest."

Ann described her plan to look elsewhere for Hal.

"Sounds good. I have a meeting I need to get to, but if you wanted to check out other areas of the airport this morning, Gwen isn't there—Russo told me she was running down to Wilmington to check out a plane for a friend. I can take you to the Scanridge offices this afternoon, if you think that's a possibility, although honestly if Hal's ghost is haunting an office building, I'm going to be disappointed in him. I'll talk to the owner about getting you onto the quarry property. But how do you plan to get access to his house? Gwen's not likely to invite you in."

Ann shrugged. "I'll think of something after the caffeine kicks in."

She left Arno's house and headed over to Avondale, figuring there was no harm in her wandering around the airport until Arno was available. If Hal wasn't necessarily tied to the location of his death, maybe he wasn't tied to the time of his death either. Maybe he was a daytime spirit.

As early as it was, the dark asphalt of the ramp was already sending up shimmers of heat, so she headed for the relative coolness and slight shade of the hangar rows. She found Ellis in his hangar puttering around his plane.

He straightened from his work. "Any luck last night?"

"Nope, you didn't miss anything." She nodded at the Stinson. "That's a great-looking plane."

It was a handsome plane: a high-wing tailwheel, the upper half of the fuselage and wings cream-color, the bottom half a deep chocolate brown, the two halves separated by a narrow strip of gold. The empennage was decorated with a distinctive bow-and-arrow logo. The seats were chocolate brown faux leather with cream piping, the interior lined in wood. The aluminum panel housed only a few rows of instruments.

"It looks like an old car," said Ann, delighted.

"They called later models of this plane 'station wagons.' They figured all the men who had flown in World War 2 would want to come home and keep flying. Turned out most of them wanted to leave their war experience behind when they got home, I guess."

She nodded to the bottles of engine oil staged next to the plane. "Changing the oil?"

"Yup."

"Need any help?"

"Sure—it's always easier with two people."

They were draining the old oil when she heard a voice from just outside the hangar.

"Miss Kinnear?"

She turned toward the voice, allowing the brimming drain pan to tip and eliciting a squawk of remonstrance from Ellis. She turned back to her assignment, but not before she had time to take in Lincoln Abbott standing on the pavement outside the hangar. He was wearing what was evidently, based on Ann's earlier interactions with him, his usual work uniform: a blue oxford shirt with the sleeves rolled up, too-large khaki pants held up by a brown leather belt, and sneakers. In one hand he held an iPad and in the other a digital audio recorder the size of a Pez dispenser.

"Mr. Abbott, now's not the best time."

"My apologies, I don't mean to distract you from your work, but I was wondering if I might have a word when you're done."

"No."

"No?"

"No."

After a pause, he forged ahead. "Gwen Burridge, who is co-owner along with Arnold Scanlan of Avondale Airport since the death of her husband, Hal Burridge, has been making some accusations about a job Mr. Scanlan hired you for—"

"I'm fully aware of her accusations, and I have no intention of discussing them with you. If you have any other questions, please call my brother."

"He gave me pretty much the same answer, although a little more colorfully."

"Well, there you go," said Ann. "You can either get the

message less colorfully from me or more colorfully from him, but the message will be the same."

She got the nod from Ellis that her assistance was no longer needed, and she turned to Abbott. He began to raise the audio recorder, but she shook her head and he dropped his hand, disappointed.

"Lincoln," she said, deciding to try a more conciliatory tack. "I've appreciated your approach to the stories you've written about me in the past. I appreciate that you didn't seem to have a bone to pick, or that you didn't try to sensationalize it. But at this point you must know that Mike handles all my statements to the press, and you've already gotten your response from him."

"It just seems to me like you should appreciate the fact that I'm not just running with Gwen Burridge's accusations that you're preying on a man who recently lost his best friend—"

"Ellis," she said, her eyes still on Abbott, "can we lower the hangar door?"

Abbott held up his hands. "Don't go to the trouble—I'm leaving. But if you have second thoughts, here's my card." He fished in his pocket and removed a tattered business card.

Ann folded her arms and looked at him, stone-faced.

He put the card back in his pocket. "Fine. If you need my contact information, they have it in the airport office."

Abbott turned away, revealing a dark circle where perspiration had stuck his shirt to his back. He trudged across the ramp in the direction of the parking lot looking, Ann thought with some satisfaction, very much like one of Russo's students after a lesson.

After Ellis had finished the oil change, they grabbed lunch at the nearby Italian restaurant, then she met up with Arno and followed him to the Scanridge Transport offices. He showed her around the offices, cubes, break rooms, and supply closets. When introductions were required, he introduced her as a potential new employee. However, based on the furtive glances and whispers after she and Arno moved on, she guessed that, thanks to Gwen, most of the Scanridge staff knew that Ann was already in Arno's employ.

Their last stop was Hal's office, a tastefully decorated but largely characterless space with a window overlooking the parking lot and a glass wall overlooking the cube farm.

"Do you want to stay overnight?" asked Arno uncertainly. "There's nobody here at night, and I could get someone to set up a cot."

Ann looked around the office. "Not for now. You're right—it doesn't really seem like the kind of space that would draw a person back. How are you doing with getting permission from the quarry owner for us to go there?"

"Haven't been able to get in touch with him yet, but I'll keep trying."

"Maybe tomorrow."

"Yeah." He ran a finger along the edge of Hal's desk and looked morosely at the fuzz of dust it picked up. "What are you going to be doing between now and then?"

"Maybe I'll take a swing past Hal's house."

"It's Gwen's house now."

"If we're lucky, its former resident is still there."

38

A t nine o'clock, Ann climbed out of her Forester a block away from the Burridge home into air that was warm and heavy even at this late hour. The house was set in a wooded area of widely spaced houses, which minimized any worry about nosy neighbors. However, the nearest neighbors weren't so far away that they wouldn't hear an enthusiastically barking dog. Scott had returned from Baltimore with Ursula that afternoon—in fact, it was Ursula's "I'm home!" bark that had awoken Ann from the doze she had just fallen into— and she would have welcomed the dog's spirit-sensing prowess. However, she had left Ursula at the townhouse since she hoped to keep her visit quiet, literally as well as figuratively.

In fact, she had originally planned not to tell Mike and Scott about her surreptitious trip to Gwen Burridge's home until she realized, with some embarrassment, that there was no realistic excuse she could give for why she was heading out late in the evening without them. She really needed to expand her social circle in West Chester.

She had no intention of trying to get into the house, and she knew it was more likely that Hal Burridge would haunt his house than his yard, but she figured it couldn't hurt to check it out.

Arno had assured her that, as far as he knew, there was no security system, even for the house itself: "Her hangar is surveilled like Fort Knox, but evidently they didn't much care what happened to the house."

She had expected to have to sneak around the yard under cover of darkness, hoping that she wasn't caught out by an ill-timed glance out the window by the home's occupant. However, she had driven by the airport on her way to the house and been rewarded with the sight of Gwen's Corvette parked next to her hangar and a light on inside. The only other vehicle in evidence was an unfamiliar SUV of an unfortunate khaki color in the parking lot. She'd surely hear the growl of the Corvette's engine in plenty of time to slip away into the woods that surrounded the house.

It was an unusual house for this part of southern Chester County. Mid-century modern was not Ann's thing: too unrelentingly geometric, with what seemed like an unnecessary skimping on windows. The front of the Burridge house certainly fit this mold: rectangular stone forming an imposing wall pierced only by a row of windows placed far too high for someone to actually look out of and one inexplicable opening at eye level, like the aperture in a castle through which archers could shoot at their enemies. On the right side of the house was a space originally intended as a carport, but which had been repurposed with era-appropriate furniture as an outdoor sitting area. Further to the right, slightly detached from the house and cleverly masked by plantings, was a multi-bay garage built in the same style as the house, with a stone path connecting it to the front door.

Keeping to the shadows at the edge of the yard, and scanning the area for any sign of Hal Burridge, she made her way toward the backyard.

The back of the house was more to her liking. The windows here were framed in red cedar, which made a nice contrast to the dark gray siding and the rectangular stone blocks that formed the lower level. Outdoor lighting illuminated a large stone patio.

Even better for Ann's purposes, a combination sitting and dining area, housed in another rectangular construction projecting from the main part of the house, was lined almost entirely with windows and was lit by a few dimmed mid-century lamps. She peered into the room, looking for some sign of Hal, but the room appeared to be spirit-free. However, if someone, living or dead, did come into the room, Ann would be able to see them while staying hidden in the darkness of the backyard.

Ann scanned the yard and saw the vague shape of two chairs arranged picturesquely under a tree and well out of the pool of light cast by the lights from the house. She could sit there and keep an eye out for Hal. The chairs were near another path that led from the detached garage to the back door, but if Gwen came home, Ann could retire to the woods and then return to her observation post once Gwen was inside. She didn't relish the idea of spying on Gwen Burridge, but perhaps it would provide her with some hint as to whether Hal was inside the house: a telltale flicker following Gwen, or maybe something more obvious.

As she neared the tree, she saw that the chairs were Acapulco chairs—oval frames strung with rope to form a human-sized basket. She lowered herself gingerly into one of them. With the exposed metal and spiderweb netting, it looked like a chair more intended for visual effect than for utility, but it was very comfortable—like settling into a hammock. She relaxed into the netting.

The warm, moist air cocooned her, a slight breeze rustled

the trees that surrounded the house. She heard the distant call of a screech owl. Somewhere behind her a chorus of peepers set up their rocking thrum.

Through the sound of the peepers, she thought she heard an engine approaching. She was reluctantly readying herself to leave the comfort of the chair for the cover of the trees, but the sound was definitely not a Corvette. It paused somewhere nearby, then moved off again.

"What the hell??"

Ann shot forward in the chair, a blinding light in her eyes, barely avoiding going sprawling onto the lawn. She held her arm up to shield her face from the beam.

She heard Gwen's voice again from behind the light, tight with anger. "What are you doing in my yard?"

"Can you get that light out of my eyes?"

The light moved off her face and, as her eyes adjusted, Ann could see Gwen standing on the path between the garage and the back door, one fist on her hip, her expression stormy.

"I repeat, what are you doing in my yard?"

Ann considered her options but decided that making up a story would no doubt be worse than 'fessing up to the truth. "Still looking for Hal."

"I can't believe you have the balls to trespass on my property."

"It's not like I'm creating a disturbance. How did you even notice me?"

"You were snoring." Gwen examined her, her expression shifting from angry to calculating. After a moment, she said, "I tried to overlook the fact that you're bilking Arno out of his money, but I can't overlook the fact that you're on my property without my permission." She turned toward the house and started for the back door.

Ann climbed out of the chair. "What are you doing?"

"I'm calling the police." Gwen got her keys out of a messenger bag slung over her shoulder and unlocked the door.

"Are you kidding me? The police?"

Gwen turned back to her. "I expressed my concern about you taking advantage of Arno and you came to my hangar and told me to fuck off. Then you show up in the dead of night on my property without permission. I think I have every justification to call the police."

"I was sitting in your lawn chair!"

"You fell asleep—who knows what you might have done if you had caught me unawares rather than the other way around."

"Falling asleep in a lawn chair isn't exactly the sign of a hardened criminal."

"No, it's the sign of an incompetent one." Gwen opened the door and stepped inside.

Ann stepped up to the door and Gwen blocked her way. "I wouldn't recommend trying to come into the house, that will just make it worse for you."

"I don't want to come into the house. But I do want to say that two can play your game. There's only your word that I told you I was here to look for Hal. If you call the police, I'll tell them that I felt bad about telling you to fuck off, I came by to apologize, and I fell asleep in your lawn chair while waiting for you to get home. Doesn't paint a very threatening picture, does it? What does it say about Gwen Burridge, the Peregrine Falcon, the woman with nerves of steel, if she panics at the appearance of an unannounced visitor here to make an apology?"

Gwen stood in the doorway glaring at Ann, her lips pressed together. Finally she said, "Fine. I don't need to deal with the bureaucratic red tape of a formal report, but if I see you on my property again, I will call the police."

Without a word, Ann turned and stalked down the walkway.

"If I see Hal," Gwen called after her, "I'll tell him you were looking for him."

39

When Ann got back to the Forester, she debated the merits of just curling up in the back seat and taking a nap, but with her luck, Gwen Burridge would call the cops with a report of a vagrant sleeping in a vehicle. She climbed into the driver's seat and leaned her head against the steering wheel. She couldn't believe she had fallen asleep in Gwen Burridge's lawn chair—she hoped that Gwen didn't feed that tidbit to Lincoln Abbott. At least it appeared that Gwen hadn't snapped a photo or taken a video.

She pulled out her phone and sent a text to Arno.

No sign of Hal at house.

He replied a moment later.

I got the key to the quarry. We can go there tomorrow morning. Meet me at my house at 8.

She tapped out her response.

OK. Talk to me before you talk to Gwen.

He sent back a question mark, but she tossed the phone onto the passenger seat without replying.

She stopped at Wawa, got a large dark roast coffee—slightly bitter at that time of night—and a roll of Tums, then turned the

Forester toward West Chester. As she approached the townhouse, her phone buzzed in the seat next to her. She glanced at the screen and saw that it was a text from Mike. She'd wait to find out what he wanted in person.

When she reached the townhouse, the space on the street where she usually parked was occupied by another vehicle. Occupied, in fact, by an SUV of an unfortunate khaki color. Unless there were two drivers with the same bad taste in car colors, this was the same SUV she had seen at the airport.

As she trudged up the steps to the front door of the townhouse, she could hear male voices and laughter. She was so jittery from caffeine that it took her two attempts to get her key into the lock.

Mike, Scott, and Corey Duff sat in the living room, wine glasses in hand, an open bottle of something red on the coffee table.

"What are you doing here?" Ann directed her question to Corey. "Kind of late for a social call, isn't it?"

The three men stood up.

"I tried texting you that Corey was here," said Mike.

"It's too bad you have to keep going out in the middle of the night," said Scott. "I know you're not naturally a night owl. Sit down, I'll get another glass." He disappeared into the kitchen.

Mike and Corey resumed their seats, and, after a moment, Ann dropped into a chair.

"Sorry about the late-night visit," said Corey, "but I was in the area. I drove by and saw the lights were on and thought I'd stop by and see if you had thought any more about the documentary."

She opened her mouth to tell him she had seen his rental SUV at the airport, but Mike spoke up.

"Have you gotten an answer from Garrick yet?"

"No, he's still playing his cards close to the vest." Corey

grinned. "But I'm guessing that if I told him that we were going ahead without him, he might decide he wants in the game after all."

Scott returned with the glass and poured for Ann.

"Corey, you should absolutely go ahead with just Ann," Mike continued. "Masser's already so full of himself that being the subject of another documentary would just make him even more insufferable than he already is." He took a sip of wine. "Hard as that is to imagine."

Corey laughed. "I recall you two never really hit it off. "

"We shouldn't be drinking on empty stomachs. Sweetie," Scott said to Mike, "can you fix us a snack?"

"I don't have an empty stomach," said Mike "We had a big dinner a couple of hours ago."

"Corey might want a snack. Come out to the kitchen with me and make a snack for Ann and Corey."

Mike rolled his eyes and stood up. "Obviously Scott feels that I'm not helping the cause. We'll be back shortly with a snack." He followed Scott into the kitchen.

Ann took a sip of wine and realized it wouldn't aid her efforts to avoid falling asleep in the chair. Maybe Mike would fix her a coffee drink, although her stomach sent up a protest at the idea of more coffee.

"I understand from Masser that he's sending you some business," said Corey.

"Recently?" asked Ann, surprised.

"He didn't say when it was."

She considered. "He did send me a referral a couple of months ago. Another midnight engagement, of course." She took another swallow of wine. "How come I can't get hired to talk to someone who died in the middle of the afternoon? I'm tired of being a night owl."

Corey sat forward. "Of course, I'm not going to wait around

for Garrick if he keeps stalling, but it would be great to have both of you. People want to see you together. You're like Beauty and the Beast. Esmerelda and Quasimodo."

"Katniss Everdeen and Haymitch Abernathy."

He grinned, "The Night Owl and the Vulture."

She laughed tiredly. "Garrick does look like a vulture." The wine had begun to mellow her out a bit. "I saw an SUV just like the one outside at the airport. Were you looking for me?"

He sat back and took a sip of wine. "I stopped by to talk with Gwen Burridge, I'm working up a proposal for a project focused on her. The experience of being a woman in areas as dominated by men as aerobatics and air racing, how Hal Burridge helped her realize her dream but then how she found a way to support that dream on her own ... " He stopped when he noticed Ann's expression. "What?"

"Does she know you're trying to talk me into doing a documentary as well?"

"Well, yes, I did mention it—I had to explain what I was doing in Chester County. It's not my usual stomping ground."

"And what did she say?"

"Not much, as I recall. She said that she knows you."

Ann gave a harsh laugh. "Oh, she knows me, all right."

"Is she your client?"

"No, Corey, she's not my client. She's someone who is spreading the word to everyone at the airport—and beyond— that I'm a fraud, despite the fact—" She stopped herself.

"Despite the fact ...?"

"Never mind."

When Gwen had escalated her smear campaign from the airport to the *Philadelphia Chronicle*, Ann thought that was as bad as it would get. But what additional damage could Gwen do with a documentary, produced by an obviously smitten filmmaker, as her platform. To what public relations purpose would Gwen put her story of Ann Kinnear-as-stalker ... a stalker so inept as to fall asleep in her target's backyard?

She put her glass down with a thunk.

"Did you drive Gwen home from the airport?"

"Yes, her Corvette wouldn't start. How did you know?"

Ann groaned and dropped her head back against the chair.

Corey set aside his own glass. "Ann, if there's some problem with me working with Gwen, I'd like to know what it is. I think she would be a great subject, but I'd be willing to reconsider if I understood what was going on."

"No, go ahead. Do the documentary with Gwen Burridge." She picked up her glass and swallowed the last of her wine. "I'm sure the Peregrine Falcon will make a much more exciting subject than a night owl like me."

40

The next morning, Ann sat in the passenger seat of Arno's Lexus SUV, one hand holding a large cup of Wawa iced coffee, the other holding Ursula's collar. The dog was perched on her lap, front paws braced against the arm rest, nose out the open window. With no need for stealth on this trip, Ann had decided to avail herself of the dog's spirit-sensing abilities—anything that might enable her to close out this engagement and get a few good nights' sleep before the next engagement.

"So you fell asleep in her lawn chair?" Arno asked, his voice hovering between annoyance and amusement.

"It's been a week since I've gotten a good night's sleep."

"And no sign of Hal while you were there?"

"No. Not that that's definitive proof he's not there, but we should exhaust our other options before trying the Burridge house again."

"You'd go back?"

"Arno, I'm always committed to discharging my clients' engagements successfully, but Gwen has pretty much guaranteed that I won't give up on this until I find that contract for you."

They reached the padlocked gate that gave access to the dirt road and the field she had seen from the air.

"I'll get the gate," said Ann, wanting to save Arno from having to wrestle his crutches out of the back of the SUV. "Can you hold Ursula for a minute?"

"Yeah, sure."

Ann deposited the dog in Arno's lap. She climbed out and opened the gate, then closed it again after Arno had pulled through. She climbed back into the SUV and resumed custody of the dog.

When they got to the field, Ann saw that the two small structures she had seen from the air were, in fact, benches, although they looked more like upended crates than what one might find lining the paths of a park. One was an appropriate size and height for a man to sit on comfortably, the other one smaller.

She climbed out of the vehicle and set Ursula on the ground, then strolled over to the benches as Arno got his crutches out of the back of the Lexus. The smaller bench was topped with a piece of weathered and torn blanket. Ursula jumped onto it and began her usual procedure when on any padded surface: attempting to fluff it up with her front claws. The fabric was so ratty that she threatened to claw it right off. Ann picked her up and replaced her on the ground.

"Who was the smaller bench for?" she asked Arno.

"His dog, Rosie. She died earlier this year."

That would explain Ursula's interest in the bench—it not only gave her a higher vantage point, but also constituted territory claimed from a competitor. Ann wondered if Rosie's spirit was haunting the quarry.

"It had been quite a year for Hal," she said.

Arno heaved a sigh. "Yeah, it had been."

She turned to survey the scene. The sun and heat had baked the field grass to a yellow-brown stubble, but the contrast to the brilliantly blue sky was striking and she could imagine it would be quite pretty in less ferocious temperatures. The field sloped gently down to where Ann knew the quarry pit lay, although from this angle, the scar in the ground provided merely a pleasing visual break between the stretch of grass and a copse of trees on its far side.

"Why don't we hang out here for a little while," she said, "and if I don't see him, I'll wander around a bit."

"Sounds good."

They turned back to the benches. Arno headed for the smaller one, but Ann said, "Let me take that one. The higher bench will be easier with your leg."

"Thanks, I appreciate it," said Arno. He lowered himself onto the bench and rubbed his knee. "It is giving me some problems."

Ann was too tired to make small talk, and Arno seemed content to occupy himself with his phone. She got a Tums out of a roll in her knapsack and popped it in her mouth. She had to stop drinking so much coffee but with the sun having warmed the bench and the soporific hum of machinery from the other side of the quarry, she needed all the help she could get to stay awake. Ursula, under no such constraints, jumped into her lap, curled up, and immediately fell asleep.

However, it quickly became clear that even copious amounts of coffee were not going to be enough to keep her awake if she continued sitting on the bench. She put Ursula on the ground and stood.

"I'm going to walk around a little bit."

Arno nodded and began to push himself off the bench, but Ann waved her hand.

"You should still be resting your leg," she said. "I can look around on my own."

"Sounds good," he said, lowering himself back down.

She struck out across the field, Ursula trotting behind her on the end of her leash. Ann had looked up the quarry on Google. There were two pits, the one near the benches inactive, the dusty paths traced into the ground around it fainter in comparison to those leading to and from the second pit. The tree coverage across most of the remainder of the quarry property hid any ground features, but she had been able to orient herself in terms of the relation of the field to the airport, and that was the direction she headed.

When she reached the woods that surrounded the field, she saw it was just a tangle of opportunistic trees and shrubs that had taken over what might have been farmland before the quarry was established. She walked along its border for a short distance before she came to a break in the undergrowth--what appeared to be a long disused path. She hadn't ventured more than a dozen feet from its opening when Ursula's leash snagged in one of the small branches that blocked the path. Ann got the leash untangled and continued on for another dozen feet carrying the dog, but that made clearing the way for herself awkward.

She made her way back to the field and walked back to the benches.

"That was quick," said Arno, looking up from his phone.

"It's going to be too much trouble with Ursula," said Ann. "Can you keep an eye on her?"

"Sure." Arno took the leash and looped it around his wrist, then returned his attention to his phone.

Ann went back to the path and made her way along it, earning some scratches on her arms and legs and a watering eye when a branch broke free of her grip and smacked her in the face. The central part of the wooded area was denser—and blessedly cooler—than its perimeter, but in a minute or two, more light began filtering through the branches and then she stepped into a small clearing, bounded on its far side by the chain link fence that marked the border between the quarry property and the airport. She could see the windsock, turning toward the slight breeze, and most of the runway, but the airport buildings and the parking lot were hidden behind a slight rise in the ground.

Her initial plan had been to get as close as she could to the airport and then follow the fence along the shared border, but on either side of the clearing, bushes and brambles grew right up to the fence, and in some cases through it, blocking her way.

She picked her way across the rocky ground toward the fence, curious if she would see more of the airport from a different vantage point, when she noticed a strip of lighter stones against the darker soil. As she approached, they resolved themselves into letters as tall as her arm: *H + G*

The same letters Gwen had drawn in the air with the smoke from her Extra on the day of her wedding to Hal.

Had Gwen come to this out-of-the-way place to create some sort of memorial for her dead husband? Ann tried to imagine Gwen collecting the stones, arranging them carefully on the ground, orienting them toward a path no one other than she was likely to walk. It wasn't a scene that jibed with the Gwen Burridge she knew.

But it did jibe with her impression of Hal Burridge—the man who had cried tears of joy at his wedding, the man who had looked so forlorn at being shunned by his young wife at a friend's funeral. If Ann hadn't yet found Hal Burridge, she suspected that she had found his handiwork.

She cast her gaze around the clearing, looking for any sign of Hal, but as far as she could tell, she was alone.

As she looked back at the letters, another shape a short distance away caught her eye. This one was far less clear than the letters, the stones forming the shape barely visible above the surrounding soil, but it was unmistakably the shape of a heart.

She looked up and tried to judge whether the letters or the heart would be visible from anywhere else. She thought not. The trees surrounding the clearing would probably block the line of sight from almost any location a plane was likely to be, and the slight rise in the ground between the clearing and the airport buildings meant they were unlikely to be seen from the ground.

If Hal was the constructor of the letters, why would he put them here ... and when had he done it?

Had Hal constructed the letters when he was alive? Had he brought his dog, Rosie, here and occupied himself with this project, planning to bring his wife to this strange rendezvous point? Based on the video Mike had found of Gwen and Hal's wedding, it had obviously taken place in the summer—had Hal been planning an anniversary surprise for Gwen?

Or had Hal constructed the letters after he died? If a person without Ann's ability had been in the clearing, would they have seen the stones moving through the air then settling into their designated spots? Even with her ability, would Ann have seen the man moving the stones? She could see some of the dead, but not all of them.

But if Hal was still interacting with the world of the living, she felt that she should be able to perceive him. She shaded her eyes against the bright morning sun and looked around the clearing again. If he was only dimly manifested, she might not be able to see him.

However, if he didn't want to be seen, she was sure he could keep his presence hidden from her.

Suddenly, the clearing, dominated by those stone-etched letters, didn't feel so benign. She jerked her head toward a movement in the trees but could see nothing other than the breeze flipping the leaves: dark side to light side to dark side. There was a rustle from behind her. She whirled around and squinted against the sun.

"Hal?" she called. "Hal Burridge?"

The breeze stilled, the leaves hung motionless, the rustling in the undergrowth silenced.

Most likely a squirrel or groundhog, she reassured herself.

Most likely.

She made herself count to a hundred, turning slowly so that she wouldn't be caught unawares by someone or something coming up behind her, then hurried toward the path leading back to the field and the benches.

However, after a dozen yards, she realized that she wasn't on a path—or at least not the same path she had used to reach the clearing. She considered backtracking to the clearing and finding the original path, then discarded that idea as silly. It wasn't as if she was in the middle of a wilderness—she was on a fence-bound property of a few dozen acres. Any path that headed in general away from the airport would bring her to the field eventually, and she could use the sound of planes departing and landing to orient herself as needed.

Much to her irritation, the ground quickly became more densely wooded, and she was extricating her shirt from a bramble that had snagged it when she noticed the light from an open area ahead of her. She tore her shirt free and pushed on through the undergrowth.

She broke out of the woods at the bottom of the field that sloped down from the benches, only a few feet from the pit. Arno was still seated on the larger bench, one hand holding his phone, which still occupied his attention, the other absently stroking Ursula, who was curled up on his lap.

Ann turned back to the pit. Curious, she inched toward the edge, expecting with each step to see the bottom, but the sides continued to stretch down into the earth. It wasn't until she was almost at the rim, tendrils of her hair blown back by a whirl of breeze skipping over the edge, that she could see the shocking aqua-colored water at the bottom.

She heard a sharp bark, then Arno's voice.

"Ann!"

She jumped back, startled, and looked up the slope to see Arno, now standing, and Ursula, straining at the end of her leash.

"Be careful," he called, "the edge may not be stable."

She backed quickly away from the pit, then made her way up the slope.

"Any luck?" he asked as she reached him.

"I saw—" she began, then stopped. Suddenly it felt wrong to share with Arno what she had seen—she felt a little guilty having seen it herself. Assuming Hal had created the letters and the heart, it was obviously meant only for Gwen. She wondered briefly if Arno would see the letters if she took him to the clearing, or would the work of a dead man be visible only to her?

"I saw all the way to the bottom of the pit," she said. "Quite a drop." She took Ursula's leash from him.

"Yeah, you don't want to lose your footing at the edge." He pulled a handkerchief out of his pocket and patted droplets of sweat off his forehead. "How much longer do you think we should wait?"

"I think we've given it enough time this morning," said Ann. "I'll come back tonight."

They got into the Lexus and Arno started down the dirt road toward the gate.

"Flying lesson today?" he asked.

"No, I decided to put the lessons on temporary hold—I'm not getting enough sleep to feel good about going up."

"Wise move. When do you want to meet up for the trip back to the quarry?"

"Let me try one time on my own, and if I strike out, you can come the next time." She figured that Arno on his phone was not the motivation Hal Burridge would need to make an appearance.

"Okay. Let me know how it goes." He handed over the key to the gate. "If you have something to report—or even if you don't —don't worry about waking me up."

"Will do."

He glanced at his watch. "What are you going to do between now and then?"

"Try to take a nap," she said.

41

A t nine that evening, Ann headed back to the quarry.

She had left Ursula back at the townhouse. She had explained to Scott that, if she needed to return to the clearing, she wouldn't have someone else with her to wrangle the dog. However, the other reason was that the more she thought back to that frisson she had experienced in the clearing at the quarry—that sense of being watched—the more certain she felt that if there was a spirit there, it was one that she'd prefer to deal with on her own.

She unlocked the quarry gate and looped the padlock into the chain links but left it unlocked. If she happened to misplace the key, she didn't want to be stuck inside.

She trundled down the dirt road to the field and climbed out of the Forester. She scanned the field, which was lit by a quarter-moon.

"Hal Burridge?" she called into the darkness. She waited a minute, then called again. "Hal?"

There was no response.

She wondered if she would have to go back to the clearing to find him. She wasn't looking forward to making her way through the woods in the dark. She'd leave that as the last place she explored. She scanned the area. Where else might he have spent time at the quarry?

She spent some minutes walking the perimeter of the field, giving the pit a wide berth, and several more tracing a giant X through its middle, with no luck. She briefly considered if walking some sort of grid pattern would be productive, but it hardly made sense. It wasn't as if she was searching for a body— she was looking for a person who could make himself known to her if he was here, assuming he wanted to be found.

"Hal Burridge!" she called again and was unsurprised when she received no response.

Where should she wait? She looked toward the benches but was hesitant to sit down—she was pretty sure that if she did, she'd fall asleep.

Then she thought of that pool of aqua-blue water she had seen at the bottom of the pit. It was an arresting sight. Maybe Hal had enjoyed looking down on it. Was he a risk-taker? She gave a sardonic smile. He had married the Peregrine Falcon, hadn't he?

She pulled an LED flashlight out of her knapsack and walked down the slope toward the pit. When she got to the area where a few boulders poked up through the soil, she edged forward even more cautiously, playing the flashlight over the ground in front of her. The rounded rocks there might have provided a pleasant vantage point from which to enjoy the view during the day, but she had no intention of approaching closer to the edge of the pit in the dark.

She switched off the flashlight and stood still, the breeze whispering out of the pit ruffling her hair. Without the noise of the machinery humming across the quarry property from the active pits, it was even more peaceful than it had been during the day.

She tried to find a comfortable stance for an extended vigil, but quickly decided that it wasn't realistic to expect to spend the entire night standing or walking. She flicked on her flashlight and shone it around her, examining the few rocks poking up through the sandy soil. Even with the padding of a blanket from the Forester, they should make a sufficiently uncomfortable seat that she wouldn't be likely to nod off. She'd sit by the quarry pit for an hour. If Hal hadn't made an appearance, she'd move to the benches for an hour and then, if there was still no contact, she'd try the clearing. She turned to make her way up the slope to retrieve the blanket from the Forester.

She almost walked into a man.

She let out a squawk and stumbled backwards. Her heel caught on something and she went sprawling. She scrambled to her feet.

"My apologies," said the man. "I didn't mean to startle you."

As with Bryan, he glowed faintly, but his appearance was more substantial than Bryan's had been, even on Ann's first visit. His thick hair was shot with gray, his frame thinner, and his face more drawn than in the videos she had watched, but it was clearly the man she had been looking for.

"Hal Burridge," she said breathlessly.

"Yes. Ann Kinnear, I presume."

Ann gulped air, trying to quiet the thumping of her heart. "How do you know me?"

"You're one of Russo's students, correct?"

"Yes."

"And obviously what they say about you is true, since you can see and hear me."

Ann shuffled sideways so that she no longer had her back to the pit. "I've been looking for you. How long have you been here?"

"Oh, for ever so long."

"I mean tonight—did you hear me calling you? Were you watching me?"

"Yes."

She shuffled further from the pit. "How about earlier today?"

"When you were here with Arno? Yes."

"Why didn't you let us know you were here?"

"I'm not in the mood to speak with Arno."

"Oh?"

He gazed at her, silent.

She brushed her hands on the seat of her pants. "Can we sit down?" she asked, nodding up the slope toward the benches.

After a brief pause, he said, "I suppose so."

She climbed the slope, and although he moved silently, she could sense him behind her. She fought the urge to glance back. When she reached the benches, she stepped toward the smaller one.

"Not there!" he snapped. "That's for Rosie." He pointed to the larger bench. "You sit there."

"Okay." She sat on the larger bench and Hal sat on the smaller one.

"So, you saw me with Arno," she prompted.

"Yes."

She waited for more, but he was silent. She debated about what approach she should take. Should she jump right to asking him about the location of the contract, or should she spend some time building some rapport with him—and satisfying her own curiosity? She opted for the latter.

"Have you been to the airport?" she asked.

"I can't seem to leave the quarry."

"Why do you think you're here?"

"I was happy here." He again lapsed into silence.

"I saw the letters you made in the ground," she said. "I also saw a video of your wedding, of Gwen skywriting the letters. It's romantic that you've recreated that."

Hal sat forward. "Has Gwen seen the letters?"

Ann hesitated. "Not that she's mentioned to me."

"How is she doing?"

Ann chose her words carefully. "She's obviously in mourning for you, but she's getting on as best she can."

This time it was Hal who waited for more, while Ann stayed silent. She didn't want to risk saying something that would cause Hal to disappear, or that would make him angry.

After a moment, he said, "You could bring her to the quarry, show her the letters in the clearing. You could help me talk to her."

Ann hesitated. "I don't think I'm in a position to be bringing your wife anywhere. And she's not likely to comply even if I tried."

"Why?"

"I went to your house last night, thinking I might find you there. She didn't know I was going to be there—I was afraid she would tell me to stay away if I asked her—so she wasn't too happy when she found me there. On top of that, she's telling everyone that I'm a fake. It wouldn't support her story if she started visiting your old stomping ground with me to have a chat with you."

He nodded slowly. "She's a practical woman—I can imagine it would be hard for her to imagine that this is possible, but if you bring her here, I'll tell her something to prove that it's me."

"We tried that once already. It didn't keep her from claiming I'm a fraud."

He laughed softly. "As I said, she's a practical woman. But not an ice queen, like some people think. Russo told me that she practiced skywriting those letters over and over again so that it would be perfect on our wedding day—everything she did had to be perfect—but she flew an hour west to practice so that I wouldn't see it and have the wedding surprise spoiled." He turned in the direction of the airport. "I loved watching her fly. From the clearing, I can see the planes take off. I can see Gwen take off. I can still see her fly."

Ann felt as if she was letting the conversation get away from her, just as she had with the conversation between Gwen and Bryan. She couldn't risk postponing what she needed to ask him any longer. "Arno hired me to find out where you put the contract that you signed."

His attention snapped back to her, his expression hardening. "I'm surprised you're willing to help him with that."

"What do you mean?"

He shrugged. "I guess there's not much loyalty in the world these days."

"I don't know what you're talking about. Arno hired me, he's my client, I'm trying to execute on the job he hired me to do."

"You have to make your own decision, I guess, but I don't have to go along with it." He leaned forward. "Arno talked me into doing something I would never have done if I had thought things through with a clearer head—if I had talked with Gwen about it beforehand." He looked away. "Just like Bryan talked Gwen into doing something she never would have done if I had been there for her. Too bad you can't talk to him about his role in this whole mess."

She hesitated. "I have. I originally went to the crash site to look for you. Bryan is there."

He looked back at her, his eyes narrowing. "Bryan is at the crash site?"

"Yes."

"That bastard. He killed me."

"I know. He told me."

"He told you?"

"Why not? What does he have to lose?"

His hands balled into fists. "I remember Bryan swinging a jack leg at me in the hangar, and the next thing I knew, I was in his Cessna headed for Clinton County."

"You woke up in the plane?"

"Yes."

She hesitated. "'Woke up' in the sense of ... really waking up?"

"If you're asking me if I recovered consciousness in the plane before I died, then yes."

"What happened then?" she asked, almost not wanting to know.

"Calvert clubbed me with a flashlight until I died."

She felt the blood drain from her face. "Jesus," she breathed.

Hal gave a harsh laugh. "I guess he didn't tell you that part."

"No."

He glared at her. She hoped that his anger was still directed at Bryan, and not at her for having broached the topic.

"And then you brought the plane down," she said.

"I was justified, don't you think? He ended my life." He paused. "In more ways than one."

Ann drew a shaky breath. "I guess I can't blame you."

Hal dropped his head into his hands, then looked out toward the pit. "Gwen must have been so worried. We'd had an argument, I stormed out of the house, and then I end up in a pile of plane wreckage hundreds of miles from home."

Ann tried to sort through what she had learned. She had finally found Hal Burridge, not hundreds of miles from home in Clinton County, but right here in his virtual backyard. And now the conversation looked like it was going to devolve into an argument over who wronged whom worst in the Hal-Gwen-Bryan triangle. If she could just get Hal to tell her where the contract was, to accept the fact that he shouldn't be in a position to keep a legal agreement from being executed, she could extract herself from this sordid mess.

"But you did sign the contract, correct?" she asked.

"I did, but if I had known what would happen as a result, I would never have done it. I haven't destroyed it in case circumstances change and it would be helpful to have it, but I don't believe those are the current circumstances."

"In what circumstances would it be helpful to have it?"

"I'd have to talk with Gwen about that. I need you to bring her here."

"Hal, as I said, I don't think—"

He stood. "If you won't bring Gwen here and help me talk with her, our business is done."

There was a flicker, like moonlight bouncing off breeze-blown leaves, and the spot where Hal Burridge had been visible a moment before was empty.

42

Ann stood by the side of the road at a spot from which she could just see the clearing with *H + G* etched in the ground. She could also see the airport—the buildings and hangars shimmering in the heat. It was only mid-morning, but the thermometer had already been showing nearly eighty degrees when she left the townhouse. At least the sun was somewhat obscured by a high layer of haze, so the rays felt a little less brutal than they had the previous day.

She glanced at her watch, then raised a pair of binoculars to her eyes and scanned the quarry fence. Nothing. She lowered the binoculars and rubbed her arms. She had been watching and waiting for almost an hour.

She had called Russo that morning on the pretense of having a question about her homework and had worked the topic around to Gwen Burridge. She heard exactly the news she had hoped to hear—Gwen was going to be away from Avondale for the day, flying to Virginia for a meeting with an airshow organizer, expected back that evening. Gwen should be taking off any minute now. Ann raised the binoculars to her eyes again and thought back to her encounter with Hal Burridge the previous night.

So Hal had not only not died in the crash in Clinton County, but had not died in Bryan's hangar either. He had died in the air after regaining consciousness during the flight. She smiled mirthlessly. That must have been quite a surprise for Bryan. And there was no way he could spin it that made it self-defense. Bryan had clubbed Hal to death with a flashlight because he couldn't afford for Hal to be alive when he landed. No wonder Bryan had left out that part of the story.

As she thought back through her encounter with Hal, her attention kept getting drawn back to one seemingly minor moment: Hal's reaction when she had almost sat on Rosie's bench. She thought, too, of Ursula clawing at the tattered blanket, which Ann had chalked up to just another instance of the dog's evident belief that any fluffy surface could always be made just a little fluffier.

She had dropped the binoculars again to give her arms a rest when she heard the sound she had been waiting for—a roar from the direction of the hangars that could only be the Lancair firing up. A few minutes later, the plane taxied out from behind the main hangar row and headed toward the runway.

She scanned the fence line again. She couldn't see any sign of Hal, but she wasn't sure whether that was because he wasn't there, or because binoculars wouldn't enable her to see him even if he was.

But if this didn't draw Hal Burridge away from the benches, nothing would.

She stuffed the binoculars into their case and climbed into the Forester as Gwen's plane shot into the sky.

∾

WHEN ANN GOT to the quarry, she could see no sign of Hal at the benches, or on the grassy slope that led down to the quarry pit.

Gwen's plane had disappeared to the south, and Ann could no longer hear even its receding buzz. If Hal had gone to the clearing, she wasn't sure whether or not he would wait there for Gwen to return. She approached the benches.

To cover all her bases, she checked the larger one first. It was too heavy for her to move, but when she peered underneath it, she saw nothing more interesting than gravel and dead grass.

She switched her attention to the smaller bench. The base of this one was fully enclosed, but the bench was lighter, and she was able to tip it onto its side to check under it, and to examine the underside of the top. Nothing of interest. She tipped the bench back onto its base and examined the top. Unlike Hal's bench, Rosie's was padded, with the blanket tacked to the edges with upholstery nails.

But the nails on one side had been pulled out.

She slipped her hand into the opening and her fingers touched plastic.

She pulled out a large Ziploc bag, inside of which was a gray folder with silver stripes. Her heart thumping, she opened the plastic bag, pulled out the folder, and flipped it open. Arno had said that Hal had used the folders for everything, and she didn't want to risk bringing Arno a folder that contained nothing more interesting than some dirty magazines or Rosie's pedigree papers.

It was definitely a contract: the blocky spacing, the tightly printed text. She flipped through it until she found the signature page.

Acceptance by Seller - The foregoing offer to purchase real estate is hereby accepted in accordance with the terms and conditions specified above.

Harold Burridge (SELLER)

Arnold Scanlan (SELLER)

It was signed by both Hal and Arno.

She was shuffling the papers square when a paragraph on the first page caught her eye.

Turriff Brothers Development Corporation (herein "Purchaser") hereby offers to purchase from the owner, Scanridge Enterprises (herein "Seller"), the real estate which comprises the Avondale Airport located in Avondale Township, Chester County, Commonwealth of Pennsylvania ...

She felt a virtual thump in her gut. She closed the folder, lowered herself onto the dog bench, and looked out across the field.

So the contract didn't concern Scanridge Transport, as Arno had told her. It concerned Avondale Airport and its sale to a developer that was known throughout Chester County for their large, glitzy, and shoddily made houses.

That's what Hal had meant when he questioned her loyalty.

Her association with Avondale hadn't been long, but she did feel a loyalty to it, and to the people who would suffer if the airport closed: Russo, Dottie, even Ellis. She liked the small size, the slightly tatty FBO, the bumpy runway that Russo assured her would make her landings on any other runway seem like skating on ice. If Avondale closed, she could take lessons at Chester County or Brandywine, but it wouldn't be the same.

She heard the thrum of an engine and turned to see the flight school Warrior climbing away from the runway. She knew what Russo would be saying: *If you lose your engine now, where will you land? You can't get back to the runway—they call it the impossible turn for a reason.* This engagement had certainly taken an impossible turn, she thought bitterly.

She could slip the folder back into the plastic bag and tuck it under the torn blanket or carry the folder to the edge of the pit and let the pages flutter away into that shocking aqua water. Arno Scanlan had hired her on false pretenses; did she still owe him an honest conclusion to the engagement? She sighed. She could hardly maintain her righteous indignation at Gwen Burridge's accusations of fraud if she failed to execute on the engagement.

That didn't mean she couldn't take legitimate steps to stop the sale of the airport once she had discharged her responsibility to Arno.

She glanced around, part of her hoping that Hal would appear, would do something that would prevent her from having to let Arno know that she had found the contract, but the field appeared uninhabited save for herself, the only sound the buzz of the Warrior as it followed the pattern, no doubt for a series of touch-and-go landings.

She pushed herself to her feet and slipped the folder back under the tattered blanket. She had done enough jobs that involved finding missing items for her clients that she knew they liked to pull the treasure out of the ground themselves, not have it pulled out for them. She'd bring Arno back to the quarry and show him where the contract was.

And then she'd try to convince him to throw it away.

43

A nn entered the Avondale FBO and stepped up to the counter. The scarred wooden countertop that had annoyed her in the past now struck her as charming. Dottie looked up from her desk behind the counter, then glanced at her computer monitor. "Do you have a lesson today?"

"Not today. I'm looking for Arno."

Dottie stood. "You know, Hal's death hit Arno hard. He hasn't been himself since Hal died."

Ann sighed. The FBO's charm was going to wear thin pretty quickly if she had to deal with the effects of Gwen's smear campaign every time she entered. "It must be hard for him, running the airport and the trucking company all by himself," she said. She didn't add, *Lucky for him—and unlucky for you—he's planning to be running only one of them soon.*

Dottie ran a fingernail along one of the scars in the counter-top. "He might sometimes wish he could talk over the business with his late partner, run some ideas by him." She gave a tight smile. "But that would be silly. Wouldn't it."

"I don't know," said Ann, sorely tempted to explain to Dottie just how *silly* Arno's business with Hal was, "I guess that depends on what kind of person Arno is. And what kind of person Hal was. Do you know where Arno is now?"

Dottie appeared ready to launch another volley in her defense of Arno, then sighed and waved her hand in the general direction of the hangars. "Out there somewhere."

"Thanks."

There were only a few hangar rows at Avondale, so it didn't take her long to check them out. As she came to Ellis's hangar, at the end of the last row, she found Ellis and Russo fiddling with something in the Stinson's engine compartment.

She stepped up to the door. "Hey, Ellis. Hey, Russo."

"Hey, Ann, what's up?" said Ellis.

"I'm looking for Arno. Have you seen him?"

"Not me," said Ellis. He glanced at Russo.

"He was here earlier, but I think he had to run over to Scanridge for something," said Russo. He removed a pristine white handkerchief from his pocket and wiped his fingers. "Want us to let him know you're looking for him when we see him? Although you probably have his cell number if you're doing a job for him ..." He trailed off.

"I'm close to wrapping up my current job," said Ann.

"Did you get in touch with Hal?" asked Ellis.

"I found what I needed to find."

"Is it something to do with the airport?" asked Russo.

Ann raised her eyebrows. "Why do you ask?"

Russo shrugged. "I've been hearing a rumor that Arno wants to sell. Is it true?"

"Arno's my client, I can't comment one way or the other."

His expression fell. "That's a comment in itself."

"No, it's not," Ann shot back. "Don't read anything into the fact that I'm not participating in the rumor mill."

"It's not just me I'm worried about," he said, more sad than angry. "I don't know that Gwen could stand much more bad news."

"What do you mean?"

"Her husband's dead. Her mechanic's dead. Some say he was more than that, but either way, he was a member of her team. One of her biggest supporters is dead. To have the airport sold out from under her, or for her to have to fight to keep it from being sold, would cap off a pretty sucky year."

"Who's her supporter?"

"Preston Gilman. Didn't you know him?"

"It doesn't ring a bell."

He finished wiping his fingers, folded the handkerchief so that the greasy part was on the inside, and tucked it back into his pocket. "Now that I think about it, he probably died before you started coming to Avondale." He brightened. "Not that that would keep you from—"

She glared at him.

He raised his hands. "Okay, okay, no more kidding around."

"What happened to him?"

"Plane crash. Loose fuel line. He had gone down to Ocean City, New Jersey, for lunch. Must not have noticed that he was losing fuel until the engine started to cut out. He tried an off-airport landing but hit some power lines."

"And he was friends with Gwen?"

"Yeah. He went to all her performances, sometimes even went out to Octoraro Lake to watch her practice, socialized with her and Hal. He was friends with a lot of the pilots at Avondale —did their flight medicals for them. A good guy."

"Where did the crash occur?"

"Near Union Lake, outside Millville."

"When did it happen?"

"Just about a year ago."

"What time of day?"

"Mid-afternoon? I don't recall exactly. Why?"

Ann shrugged. "No reason. Other than that I'm becoming a student of crash investigations."

"It's good to study crashes—lots of lessons about the things not to do." Russo looked at his watch. "Speaking of which, I've got to go, lesson in a couple of minutes. Nice plane, Ellis."

"Thanks," said Ellis, blushing with pleasure.

Russo headed off toward the FBO.

"Have you heard anything about Preston Gilman's accident?" she asked Ellis.

"Nope. But I haven't been around long enough to hear all the airport stories," he said, closing the cowling and locking it in place. "Why?"

"It seems weird that there's yet another crash tied to Avondale."

"But Bryan's crash was an accident, right? Pilot loss of control, disorientation at night."

"That's the claim."

"And that was a pilot issue, whereas it sounds like Preston Gilman's crash was a mechanical issue."

She pulled out her phone and tapped *millville nj union lake* into her GPS app. "Crap."

"What's the matter?"

"I was thinking of running out there, but it would take too long."

"The reason to have a plane is so you don't have to sit in traffic." Ellis got out his own phone and tapped. "Union Lake isn't far from the Millville airport. I'll fly you. Unless you care whether Gwen knows you're going there."

"I don't much care what Gwen knows at this point."

He dropped his phone in his pocket. "Why do you want to go?"

She gave a grim smile. "Morbid curiosity."

SHE WAS grateful that they didn't run into Arno before they took off. She still planned to tell him about the contract, but she wanted to see if she could talk to Preston Gilman first. If she had a better idea of Gwen Burridge's role in all this, it might make doing the right thing by Arno easier. The folder had been hidden at the quarry for weeks, another couple of hours wouldn't make a difference.

As the Stinson gained altitude, she wondered momentarily if Gwen did have Ellis's plane programmed into the FlightAware tracking app. Even if she did, Gwen should be well on her way to Virginia by now, and a scheduled meeting with an airshow organizer suggested that it wouldn't be easy for her to cancel the trip. Even if Gwen did turn around to follow them to Millville—even if she tailed them to the site of Preston Gilman's crash—there wasn't much she could do to prevent Ann from speaking to another of her associates who had died in an unfortunate accident.

She heard Ellis say something over the headset.

"What?" she yelled. "I can't hear you—this plane is incredibly loud!"

"I know," he yelled back over the headset, "but talking isn't the main attraction. Look, you can open the window." He slid the window open and the noise in the cockpit grew even louder.

Ann laughed delightedly and slid her own window open. "That's great! It is like being in a station wagon."

He stuck his hand out the window and let the wind buffet his fingers. "Slow and low, that's the way to go."

"As long as you're not in a hurry."

"You should never be in a hurry in these planes."

Before they left Avondale, Ann had called to arrange a rental car, while Ellis had called a buddy at the NTSB to find out the general location of the crash. When they arrived in Millville, she picked up the rental car keys while Ellis got the Stinson settled in the tie-down area, then they headed for the crash site, Ann driving while Ellis navigated.

The land was flat, as she had anticipated from the arrow-straight roads that she had seen from the air, converging on Millville like the radial threads of a spiderweb. They left the jumble of buildings around the airport and drove through neighborhoods of single-story homes fronted by sunbaked yards. As they neared Union Lake, the land gradually became more wooded until they reached what Ellis's map identified as the Union Lake Wildlife Management Area on their right, the houses on their left now more widely spaced and interspersed with farm fields.

"Where did the guy at the NTSB say the crash was?" asked Ann, glancing around for any signs of a plane crash.

"He just said it was near Carmel Road," said Ellis. He looked at the map. "Carmel Road is pretty long."

"Maybe you could call him back and see if you can get more specific information about the location ... or we could ask that guy."

Ahead of them, standing by the side of the road, was a chubby man of about sixty, curly white hair blowing in the breeze. He was waving half-heartedly.

Ellis looked around. "What guy?"

"That guy," said Ann, pointing, "the one who's waving."

The man's waving became more frantic as they pulled abreast of him.

Ellis looked in the direction Ann was pointing. "I don't see anybody."

As they continued on, Ann looked into her side view mirror. The man was running down the road after them, now waving both arms.

She hit the brakes. "I think we found Preston Gilman."

44

"I thought you were going to drive past without stopping," the man gasped as Ann and Ellis climbed out of the car. "You're the first person who's seen me."

"You still don't see him?" Ann asked Ellis.

Ellis scanned the area. "Nope."

So evidently it was possible for the dead to get breathless—or maybe just over-excited.

"Preston Gilman?" Ann asked as the man reached them.

"Yes! Yes, I'm Preston Gilman."

"Pleased to meet you—I'm Ann Kinnear and this is Ellis Tapscott."

"The dead guy is here?" asked Ellis, his voice spiking. "Cool!"

"Ellis, could you go back to—"

"Absolutely not," said Ellis. "I took you to the crash site in Clinton County—*twice*—I flew you here, you scared the crap out of me at Bryan's hangar. I am *not* going to be left out anymore."

She realized that the visit to Preston Gilman was not exactly part of her engagement for Arno Scanlan, so, she reasoned, she wasn't bound by the confidentiality of her contract with Arno.

Plus, it might be handy to have a witness who would not be likely to lie about the experience afterwards.

"Okay, fine," she said.

A car approached and slowed. Ann gave them a thumbs up and a wave, and the occupants waved back and accelerated away.

"I don't feel like having to wave off every Good Samaritan who stops to see if we have car trouble," she said to Preston. "Can we talk in the car?"

"Sure," said Preston. "Just don't drive away. I don't know what would happen if I tried to go any further than this, but I don't think it would be good."

"Ellis, you get in the front seat and Preston and I will get in back."

Ann and Ellis climbed into the car, Preston materializing in the seat beside Ann.

"Ellis, I don't suppose you have earbuds you'd be willing to put in and play some loud music?" said Ann, anticipating the response.

"Nope."

Ann wasn't sure if the *nope* was in response to whether or not Ellis had earbuds or his willingness to put them in and play loud music, but it was clear from his tone that it didn't much matter. She sighed and turned to Preston. "You certainly made it easy to find you," she said. "It's not always like that."

"I've been trying to flag someone down for the past year."

"That must have been boring."

"Not boring—although it seems like it should have been—but very frustrating."

"Why were you trying to flag someone down?"

"I have a message I need to get out. My plane crashed in that field over there about a year ago—"

"We know. We came here specifically to ask you about your crash."

He sat forward, excited. "Really? Why? Are there suspicions about the cause?"

"Not officially. The official explanation was that it was an accident caused by fuel exhaustion due to a loose fuel line."

Preston nodded. "Yes, I concur with the loose fuel line explanation, but not with the *accident* part. I believe my plane was sabotaged. I believe someone loosened the line on purpose."

"And who do you think did that?" asked Ann, her heartbeat accelerating.

"Gwen Burridge. She's a pilot at Avondale Airport."

"Oh, I know who—" She stopped herself. She realized that with Ellis sitting in the front seat, she had to choose her words with care. "I know that person," she said.

"So you already suspected her?"

"I suspected something odd was going on."

"What? What's he saying?" asked Ellis from the front seat.

"I'll give you the recap later," replied Ann. She turned back to Preston. "What makes you think that person did what you think they did?"

Preston glanced toward Ellis. "You don't want the young man to know what we're talking about?"

"That's the goal."

He nodded. "I'll try to give you the whole story so you don't have to ask questions that would tip him off." He smiled sadly. "If you know who Gwen Burridge is, I'll assume he does, too, and has no doubt already fallen under the spell of the Peregrine Falcon. Am I right?" Before Ann could reply, he held up his hand. "No need to answer. I can imagine." He sat back in his seat. "I myself was smitten from the first. Such talent as a pilot, and such a beautiful woman. I wanted to do what I could to support her career—I did do what I could. Before she got her pilot's license, I would take her up in my Mooney, let her fly it once we were in the air. After she got her license, I would let her use the plane when I didn't need it. When she and Hal became an item and he got her the Extra, I went to all her performances, cheered her on, along with all her other fans. Although there was one thing I could do to support her endeavors that no other fan could." He looked down at his hands. "She achieved so much so quickly." He turned his gaze out the window. "I knew she could be single-minded in her pursuit of her goals, but I never imagined how single-minded."

He seemed lost in memory. After a moment, Ann prompted, "How singled-minded was that?"

He roused himself. "Single-minded enough to do whatever she felt needed to be done to protect those goals." He wrung his hands and turned to Ann. "As I was taking off from Ocean City, I saw her Corvette heading away from the airport. Hard to mistake that car, even from two hundred feet. She would have no reason to be there, except if she wanted to make sure that flight would be my last."

"Let's say that person did do what you think they did. The outcome wasn't guaranteed—you might have been able to make a successful emergency landing."

"And I would have, if it hadn't been for the damn power lines. But if the emergency didn't kill me, no harm, no foul. The report would have reflected a mechanical failure, and even if I had expressed my suspicions, why should anyone believe me?"

"I know that feeling," said Ann. "But what you're accusing that person of ... it's pretty extreme. Why would they do it?"

He looked down at his hands again. "I can't tell you that. Suffice it to say she thought I was going to make her life difficult and that was enough for her to decide she had to get rid of me." He looked back at Ann. "That's why I was so glad when you saw me. I need to get the word out. Even if the authorities can't do anything, someone needs to be keeping an eye on Gwen. If you could let Hal know—"

"Hal's dead."

Preston's eyes widened. "Dead? Did he die in a plane crash?"

"Yes, but—"

He sat forward. "It was her! I don't know why she would have wanted to kill Hal, but once she had committed one murder, it would make a second one easier to justify."

"It wouldn't have been just one more murder, it would have been two. Bryan Calvert was in the plane as well."

Preston fell back against the seat. "Calvert too?"

"Yes."

He turned and gazed out the window again. Ellis started to say something, but Ann shushed him with a gesture. He gave a theatrical sigh.

After a minute, Preston said, "I wish I didn't have reason to think it was her. Gwen was like a daughter to me at one time. But another crash of another plane based at Avondale Airport." He turned back to Ann. "You have to find out if Hal or Bryan did something that was going to make her life difficult."

"The NTSB said the crash that killed Hal and Bryan was an accident: loss of control in flight."

"Did they examine the plane carefully for signs of sabotage?"

"They couldn't," said Ann slowly. "It was largely destroyed in a post-crash fire."

Preston bounced forward again. "You see—she could have done the same thing she did to me, and no one would know."

"The report—and Ellis, who was at the site—said there was a strong smell of fuel, which suggests it wasn't fuel exhaustion."

"So maybe not a loosened fuel line, but something else." He nodded, warming to his theory. "It wouldn't be smart to use the same technique twice—too likely to raise suspicions."

"It would help me understand your theory if you would tell

me what you were going to do to make that person's life difficult."

Preston scowled at her. "So you can decide if I'm jumping to conclusions."

"Well ... yes."

"I can't tell you that. I don't know what Bryan Calvert might have done to make Gwen's life difficult, but Hal knew her secrets. Maybe she didn't want them revealed."

Ann rubbed her forehead. "But according to the first person you mentioned, the person we're talking about wouldn't have known that the second person you mentioned would have been on the plane." She glanced into the rearview mirror. Ellis glared back at her. She turned back to Preston. "What secrets were they keeping?"

"That's all I'm going to say," he said firmly. "But I am relying on you to alert the appropriate people to ensure that she can't hurt anyone else."

Ann threw up her hands in exasperation. "Who am I supposed to tell, and what am I supposed to tell them, if I don't know why this person was sabotaging planes to try to get rid of their occupants?"

"You seem like an intelligent young woman, I'm sure you'll think of a way."

Ann clamped her lips together, hoping Preston would say more, but he just returned her gaze, his hands folded in his lap. She sighed. "I'll do what I can. I'll come back and tell you what happens."

"No need, dear," said Preston, looking relieved. "I've been waiting here in the hopes that someone like you would come along and I could tell my side of the story. I don't think I'll be here if you come back."

∾

"OKAY, HE'S GONE NOW," she said to Ellis.

Ellis spun around in his seat. "Preston thinks Arno messed with his plane?"

"Ellis—"

"And that he messed with Bryan's plane? We have to get back to Avondale—Gwen might be in danger!"

"No, Ellis—"

"I know you don't like her," he continued, "but this is some serious shit—"

"Ellis, just stop. It's not Arno."

"Then who ..." His eyes widened. "Gwen?"

Ann climbed out of the back seat and resumed her place in the driver's seat. "There's no proof anyone did anything wrong."

"But he's saying Gwen sabotaged his plane? And Bryan's?"

"Ellis, I know you're curious, but I really don't want you involved in—"

"I'm already involved up to my eyeballs! Is Preston saying Gwen sabotaged his plane and Bryan's?"

"Well ... yes, but—"

"Why would she do that?"

She rubbed her temples. "Ellis, I have a headache."

"Ann," he said, sounding as menacing as it was possible for him to sound.

She puffed out an exasperated breath. "Okay, fine. Preston wouldn't tell me why he thinks she would sabotage his plane, and he didn't know why she would sabotage Bryan's, except that Hal was on the plane and that he 'knew her secrets.'"

"What secrets?"

"He wouldn't say."

"He doesn't sound very reliable."

She laughed drily. "Dead people are no more reliable than live ones in my experience."

"What are we going to do now?"

"I have to think about what to do with what he told me, if anything. But right now, I need to wrap up this engagement with Arno." She pulled her phone out of her pocket and tapped an entry on her contact list. In a moment, she spoke. "Arno, it's Ann. I have something to show you. Can you meet me at Avondale this evening?"

45

The Stinson descended toward Avondale just as the sun touched the western horizon, sending an ominous orange glow across the Chester County landscape. The wind was picking up, high clouds scudding above them foretelling stormy weather, but Ellis managed the gusting cross-wind nicely with some expert rudder work.

They had just pushed the plane into the hangar when Arno's Lexus SUV pulled up and Arno climbed out.

"You've got something for me?" he asked Ann.

"Yes. At the quarry."

"I'll drive us over," he said, turning back to the Lexus.

"I'm coming, too," said Ellis.

Arno glanced over at Ann, who shrugged. The engagement was almost over, and she was tired of trying to keep Ellis in the dark. "Can't see the harm. He has been very helpful, and you can decide whether or not to tell him what I've found once you've seen it." She didn't add that Ellis, along with the rest of the Avondale community, would find out what she had found soon enough, unless she was able to talk Arno out of acting on the contract.

Arno mirrored her shrug. "Suit yourself," he said to Ellis.

As Ellis climbed into the back of the Lexus, Ann heard the sounds of an approaching plane. She looked over at Arno.

"Gwen?" she asked.

"Sounds like it," he said. "Let's get a move on."

Arno climbed into the driver's seat and Ann took the passenger seat. Gwen's arrival was actually a turn of luck, since it meant that Hal was likely to be back at the fence, watching her land. Ann hoped so—she was too tired to mediate an argument between Hal and Arno.

Arno sped across the ramp, passing a surprised-looking Dottie, who was bringing the *Learn to Fly Here!* flag inside the FBO for the night. Arno turned the Lexus toward the quarry's back gate.

When they reached the gate, Ann got out and unlocked the padlock and pulled open the gate, then pulled it shut after the Lexus had passed. Leaving the padlock looped through the chain links but unlocked, as she had on her previous visit, she climbed back into the vehicle. As they rolled down the dirt road, she lowered her window, admitting not only a bit of breeze but also the thrum of cicadas emanating from the woods on either side.

When they got to the gravel-and-dirt parking area, Ann said, "Park so that the headlights are pointed at the benches."

Arno brought the Lexus to a stop on the slight slope, the light casting stark shadows in the deepening dusk. Ann glanced around. She didn't see any sign of Hal.

"Stay in the car, okay, Ellis?" said Ann.

Ellis threw up his hands. "Are you kidding?"

"Just wait here, Tapscott," said Arno. "We won't be long." He turned to Ann. "Okay, show me what you found." He climbed out of the driver's seat and, leaving his crutches in the back seat, hobbled to the front of the car. He stopped, waiting for Ann to get out.

"Sorry, Ellis," she said. "As Arno said back in Clinton County, it's his dime and he gets to call the shots."

Ellis crossed his arms and glowered at her. She suppressed a laugh—he looked like an angry grade schooler.

"I promise I'll update you as much as I can when this is all over," she said.

He looked out the side window. "Fine."

Ann climbed out and closed the car door, then crossed to where Arno stood.

"It's hidden in the dog bench," she said.

She led Arno to the benches, then pointed at the missing tacks on the side of the blanket on top of the smaller bench. "In there."

Arno reached in and pulled out the plastic-wrapped bundle. He extracted the folder, tucking the plastic bag into his pocket, and flipped it open. He grinned. "Excellent. Excellent work." He tapped the pages back into alignment and tucked the folder under his arm. "Your bonus check will be in the mail tomorrow." He turned toward the Lexus.

"It's not about Scanridge. It's about Avondale," she said.

He turned back to her. His expression was more somber, but not all the good cheer had left. "You read it?"

"I wanted to make sure it was what you were looking for before I brought you out here."

He examined her for a moment, his face impassive, then he shrugged. "I thought you might not take the job if you knew what the contract was really about."

"I wouldn't have."

"Well ... I appreciate you showing me where it was despite your personal reservations."

"Arno, do you really want to see the airport get plowed under to be replaced with a bunch of crappy homes in a development they'll call 'The Reserve at Avondale' or some such nonsense?"

He grimaced. "No, of course I don't want that, but I also don't want to keep trying to juggle the airport with Scanridge. The future is in Scanridge—not some out-of-the way GA airport with a dodgy runway. I can't take the time to sweet-talk all the people who feel like they have a say in the running of this airport, and I don't have much incentive for shelling out a million bucks for the runway project."

"You may not care what one flight school student thinks about the sale of the airport—you might not care what it will mean for Russo and Dottie and Ellis and everyone else who works there or who keeps a plane there, and I know you don't care what Gwen thinks about it—but you should care what Hal thinks. He told me he would never have signed the contract if he had thought things through with a clearer head. If you act on that contract, you'll be taking advantage of a man who was not thinking straight."

Even in the stark illumination of the SUV's headlights, Ann could see that Arno's face was getting red. "For every person who's going to care what happens to Avondale, there are two—probably more—who care what happens to Scanridge. I could repave the runway next year or I could give jobs to a dozen more truckers. I could spend my time trying to negotiate with the stuffed shirts on the township board about noise ordinances or I could spend my time trying to figure out what would make a better delivery experience for our customers. You might not agree, but I know which one I'd pick." He limped back to the car and jerked the door open, the ceiling light illuminating the surprised face of Ellis in the back seat. Arno climbed in and slammed the door.

Ann followed him to the open driver's window. "Arno, hear me out—"

The vehicle's engine fired up. "Kinnear, get in the car or walk back. Your choice." He glanced into the rearview mirror and let out a groan. "Oh, for God's sake."

Ann turned to see Gwen Burridge picking her way down the dirt road toward them behind the pool of light from a flashlight.

46

Arno leaned his head out the open window. "What the hell are you doing here?" he called as Gwen approached them.

"I might ask you the same thing," she said.

"How did you even know we were here?"

"Dottie said she saw the three of you going like a bat out of hell in the direction of the quarry, and I'm always interested when you're in a big hurry to go somewhere associated with Hal."

She reached the vehicle and stepped up to the open passenger-side window.

"Gwen—" began Ellis, opening his door.

"Close the door, Tapscott," Arno growled.

Ellis reluctantly pulled the door shut.

"I see you found it," Gwen said, nodding toward where the folder lay in Arno's lap.

"Kinnear found it. If you hadn't been so convinced that she was a fraud—or hadn't felt the need to paint her as one—you might have been the one to find it. And I'm pretty sure it never would have seen the light of day."

"Would you two please stop talking about me like I'm not here?" said Ann.

Gwen ignored her. "Hal didn't know what he was doing when he signed that contract."

"He knew exactly what he was doing," retorted Arno. "He said he wanted to get away from Avondale. He said he wanted to start fresh with you somewhere new."

"Why would he want to get away from Avondale?" asked Gwen, her voice rising.

"You tell me."

"I already told Arno that Hal regrets having signed the contract," said Ann.

Gwen shot her a look. "How do you know?"

"I spoke to him."

"Where?"

"Here."

Gwen looked around. "He's here?"

"Not at the moment, but he was."

"Hal?" Gwen called into the darkness.

"Oh, now she believes," muttered Arno.

"Hal!" Gwen stepped back from the car, scanning the area.

"Kinnear," said Arno, "I'm leaving. Get in or walk back. Last chance."

"Hal," said Gwen softly.

Ann looked toward Gwen. Next to her stood Hal Burridge, glimmering in the darkness.

Ann could barely hear Gwen's breathless, "I can see him."

"Who? What?" said Arno, squinting through the windshield.

In the back seat, Ellis was shifting back and forth, trying to see around the passenger seat headrest.

"Hello, Gwen," said Hal. "I asked Ann to bring you here. This isn't exactly what I had in mind, but I'm so glad you're here."

Gwen didn't reply, staring open-mouthed at Hal.

"I thought you'd want to get away," he continued. "Away from Avondale, away from everything that happened here. And away from what happened in Bryan's hangar." He turned to Ann. "Did you tell her what Bryan did to me in the hangar?"

Ann shook her head.

"Tell her now."

"Gwen, can you hear what Hal is saying?" Ann asked.

"No."

Ann glanced into the Lexus. Arno and Ellis were both following the parts of the conversation they could hear, looks of confusion on their faces.

"Arno," said Ann, "put the windows up and turn on the radio. There's something confidential I want to say to Gwen."

"Listen, this is my—" he began.

"Arno, just do it," she said in a tone that was evidently sufficiently convincing. Arno rolled up the windows and in a moment she could hear the sounds of a talk radio program emanating from the vehicle.

She turned back to Gwen. "Hal says he thought you'd want to get away after everything that happened here." She glanced at Hal.

"Tell her about what Bryan did," he said, his voice urgent.

Turning again to Gwen, she said, "Bryan attacked Hal in the hangar. He tried to revive him but couldn't. He didn't want to go to jail, so he loaded the body in the plane and planned to bury it in Clinton County." She hoped Hal wouldn't insist that she convey the news of the mid-flight murder to his widow. She hurried ahead before Hal could offer her more prompting. "Hal says he thinks you'd want to leave Avondale now that you know what Bryan did to him at the hangar."

"What Bryan did to him at the hangar? That's what he said?"

"Yes."

"But I was there, too," Gwen blurted out.

So that was the part of the story of that night at Bryan's hangar that Bryan had left out. He hadn't loaded Hal Burridge's body into the Cessna by himself. He hadn't tidied up the evidence of their altercation alone. Gwen must have known that Hal's truck was at the quarry because she had driven it there herself. Gwen and Bryan's conversation at the crash site had sounded like they were talking in code because that's exactly what they were doing: updating the other on what had happened that night, and afterwards.

Ann looked toward Hal. His expression hadn't changed—he was still gazing adoringly at his wife.

"Can you hear what she's saying?" Ann asked.

"No. What's she saying?"

"She says she's glad to be here, too."

Gwen looked at Ann, then back at Hal, her eyes wide. "Did he hear what I said? Does he know I was there?"

Ann gave a quick shake of her head. "He wanted to take you away from Avondale. That's why he signed the contract."

Gwen turned toward her husband. "Hal, some hard things happened at Avondale, but to me the airport is where I grew up, where I met you, where we got married, where we built a life. I don't want to lose it."

Before Ann had a chance to convey what she had said, Hal spoke.

"I wanted to take you away from the airport." He laughed mirthlessly. "As it turned out, it would have had the added benefit of taking you away from Bryan Calvert, although I didn't know that at the time." He took a step toward her. "If I had known you would still feel this way about the airport after the initial shock of me giving you the news about the Turriff Brothers deal, if I had known that Ann had found the contract in Rosie's bench, I would have taken care of it before now. I blame myself for that, Gwen. What had I become? Certainly not the man you married. I could forgive you for anything, sweetheart. I hope I've proven that."

"She doesn't want to lose the airport," said Ann.

He nodded. "I understand. I'll take care of it, Gwen."

Ann heard the thunk of the SUV doors' locks. The radio went silent.

"What—" said Arno and tugged experimentally at the door's inner handle.

"Hal ...?" Gwen's voice was tinged with fear.

"You told me once that I think of everything," Hal said, his eyes on Gwen. "I didn't think of everything this time—I made a mess of this—but I'll fix it. I'll take care of everything."

"He says he'll take care of everything."

"No ..." said Gwen.

"I brought down Calvert's plane," said Hal. "A car should be child's play."

"Arno, Ellis, get out of the car," said Ann, her voice taut.

Arno grabbed the handle and pulled. "I can't," he said, his voice muffled by the raised window. He jabbed at the controls on the door's armrest. "I can't unlock it."

Ann grabbed the outside handle and pulled. The door stayed shut. "Climb out the window!"

Arno and Ellis began stabbing at the window controls, but the windows stayed up.

"I'll take care of it, Gwen—don't worry," said Hal.

The car began to trundle forward.

"Hal, stop it!" Gwen yelled.

Ann stepped after the slowly moving vehicle, still pulling at the driver's door handle. "He says he'll take care of it and not to worry," she yelled across the vehicle to Gwen.

Gwen also started after the vehicle. She grabbed the handle of the back door, next to where Ellis sat, and pulled. "Hal, I said stop it! You're making the same mistake all over again."

"She says to stop it and you're making the same mistake," Ann gasped, her steps quickening as the car began to roll faster.

Arno was trying to turn the wheel, but it was locked in place. "Ellis," he yelled, "give me a hand."

Ellis leaned forward between the front seats and grabbed the wheel, but the car continued its roll straight for the pit.

Ann heard Hal's voice in her ear, her neck tickled by a movement of air that felt like breath. "The car will go over the edge with Arno and the contract in it. There might be a fire, then no more contract. If there's not a fire, I'll take care of it. No contract, no sale. Gwen won't say what happened—I know she can keep a secret. So there's only you to say what happened here, and who will believe you? Tell Gwen."

Ann broke into a jog as the car accelerated. She could hear Gwen's footfalls on the other side of the car, next to Ellis's door. Although she couldn't see the quarry pit in the darkness, she could visualize it gaping ahead of them. She was running now, praying that she didn't stumble and fall under the wheels.

"Tell her," Hal whispered in her ear. "Tell her the airport will be saved."

She opened her mouth to relay the message but was too breathless from adrenaline and fear to speak. Now she didn't need to visualize the pit, she could sense its empty expanse yawning in front of them, like the Kraken opening its mouth to swallow a tiny boat.

Suddenly the vehicle jolted—Ann realized they had reached the scattering of boulders just before the drop-off—and she heard a scream from the other side of the vehicle.

Then the Lexus swerved to the left and Ann lost her hold of the handle and fell. She reached out her arms, trying to break the fall, but a bright bolt of pain exploded across her face. She rolled away from her best approximation of the vehicle's path and came up on her hands and knees.

She looked up to see the vehicle trundling along the edge of the quarry pit. She tried to suck in air to call out—what, she wasn't sure—and sucked in blood instead. She staggered to her feet.

Arno had managed to steer the Lexus away just in time, and the vehicle was beginning to slow. However, just as Ann was about to breathe a sigh of relief, the left front tire hit a low boulder embedded in the ground. It rolled up the boulder and the SUV began to list to the right. The left side rose ... and rose ... and then, as if in slow motion, the vehicle toppled onto its right side with a crunch of metal and glass. The engine died, and with it the illumination from the headlights. In the light from the waning crescent moon, Ann could see the mechanics of the undercarriage, like the innards of a dissected frog.

She stumbled toward the vehicle, her hand to her nose. She could feel blood coursing across her mouth and down her chin. As she approached the Lexus, she saw a dim glow moving through the darkness in the direction from where Ann had heard Gwen scream—a glow that must be Hal Burridge. Gwen's scream must have distracted his attention from the vehicle long enough to allow Arno to steer away from the pit.

Ann reached the vehicle. It was balanced on the unstable ground at the brink of the pit—in fact, the front of the vehicle dangled over the drop. She tried to find an angle from which she could look into the vehicle, but she couldn't get close enough to the edge of the pit. She briefly considered climbing onto the driver's side—now the top of the vehicle—to open the doors, but the vehicle was perched so precariously on the edge of the pit that she was afraid of dislodging it.

"Ann? Gwen? Hello?" she heard Ellis's tremulous call from inside the vehicle.

"I'm here," she called back. "Are you okay?"

"Yes, I'm okay, but Arno is hurt. I'm going to see if I can get into the front seat to help him."

The vehicle shifted slightly, and a pebble went bouncing into the pit.

"Ellis, don't move!" she yelled. "Stay still—I'll be back."

She wiped her sleeve across her face to clear the blood and yelped at a jolt of pain. She staggered toward where she could see Hal Burridge's glowing form.

He was kneeling next to Gwen, who was rolled in a ball, gripping her upper arm.

"Sweetheart, what's wrong?" he cried. He turned to Ann. "Ask her what's wrong."

"What's wrong, Gwen?" said Ann, sounding like she had the world's worst cold.

"I hit a rock when I tripped. I think my shoulder's dislocated," Gwen hissed through gritted teeth.

"Dislocated shoulder," honked Ann.

"What can I do to help?" asked Hal, frantic.

Gwen tried to push herself into a sitting position. "Did the Lexus ... are they ...?"

"It stopped before it went over the edge." She glanced at Hal. His eyes, bright with concern, were fixed on Gwen. "It's on its side, next to the pit. It's not stable. If the edge gives way, if Arno or Ellis starts to move around, it's going to go over."

Hal fixed hard eyes on her. "With Arno and the contract in it. Tell her."

"And Ellis," she shot back. "You can't possibly think it's right that he dies because he stumbled into this screwed-up situation."

"What's he saying?" asked Gwen.

Ann ignored her.

"It will save the airport," said Hal, turning his attention back to Gwen.

"It might save the airport in the short term," said Ann, "but what will it do to Gwen's reputation?"

"What—" began Gwen, but Ann silenced her with a cut of her hand.

"What happens when they find Arno's truck at the bottom of the quarry pit?" she continued. "What happens when they find out the Peregrine Falcon was at the quarry when it went over? Or what if she has to hide the fact that she was here when it happened, like she hid—" She stopped.

"Hid what?" asked Hal, turning from Gwen to Ann.

Like she hid the truth of what happened in the hangar was what she had intended to say. But as far as she could tell, Hal didn't know Gwen had been at the hangar that night. If Gwen had shown up after Bryan knocked him unconscious, and if Bryan didn't mention her presence at the hangar after Hal regained consciousness in the plane, he couldn't know.

"Like she evidently hid from you how she really felt about the airport," she said. She battled the urge to turn away from Hal to check on the SUV. "What are her fans going to think? How long will they keep being her fans when they find out she was mixed up with such a suspicious accident? How long will Jura Bernois and Gwen's other sponsors keep up their sponsorships, and what will happen to her planes—and her career—when that stops? There *is* such a thing as bad publicity, and this would be it."

Hal Burridge's expression was stricken. He looked back down at Gwen, who was still trying to sit up. "You need to help her," he said, his words directed at Ann. "Help her sit up. I can't help her like that anymore. There's only so much I can do for her now."

"Hal," said Ann, as gently as she could, "don't do it. Ellis and Arno. Don't let it happen."

She held her breath, forcing herself to keep her eyes on Hal.

The field was silent—the wind had died, the cicadas were quiet. Then Ann heard a groan of metal from the direction of the pit. Her heart in her throat, she twisted to look back at the Lexus. As if pulled by an invisible wrecker, the vehicle teetered for a moment, then tilted to the left and slammed to the ground on its wheels.

Ann turned back to where Gwen lay. She was still fighting to sit up.

But now she was alone.

47

After helping Gwen to sit up, Ann made her way to the Lexus. As she approached, the back door opened, and Ellis almost tumbled out.

"Are you okay?" she asked.

"I'm okay, just a little rattled up, but Arno's unconscious. I think he hit his head when we rolled over. Jeez," he said, his eyes widening as she reached him, "are *you* okay?"

"I think I broke my nose, but I'm fine otherwise. Can you call 911?"

"Sure. I'll meet the ambulance at the gate."

"Sounds good. Thanks, Ellis."

Ann climbed into the front passenger seat of the Lexus. Arno sat, awkwardly twisted, in the driver's seat, blood dripping from a gash on his forehead. He stirred and Ann put a hand on his arm. "Stay still, Arno."

"What the hell ..."

"You got banged up, but an ambulance is coming."

He nodded blearily, then winced.

"Will you be okay for a minute? I'm going to go check on Gwen."

"Gwen ..."

"I think her shoulder is dislocated."

Ann began to climb out of the car but stopped at Arno's voice.

"She ... she was trying to open Ellis's door."

"Yes."

He was silent for a moment. "I'll be damned."

Ann made her way back to Gwen, who was hunched forward and cradling her arm.

"The ambulance is on its way."

"Are Ellis and Arno okay?" asked Gwen, her eyes down, her voice thready with pain.

"Ellis is fine. Arno's a little banged up but I think he'll be fine as well."

"Is Hal still here?"

Ann looked around. "I don't see him."

"Is he going to come back? Are they safe?"

"They'll be fine," Ann said, with more conviction than she felt. She lowered herself onto the ground next to Gwen and blotted at her nose with the neck of her shirt. The bleeding had mostly stopped. She tried to scrub the blood off her lips and chin, but she'd need a washcloth and a basin of warm water for that.

"I spoke with Preston Gilman this afternoon," she said.

Gwen glanced up an her, then back down. "Did you."

"He saw your Corvette as he took off."

"How observant of him."

"He says you killed him because he was going to make life difficult for you."

Gwen shifted, evidently trying to find a more comfortable position. "I'll bet the prosecutor is going to be thrilled to take that evidence to court."

"Was it to save your career?"

Gwen glared at her. "My career is dead. It was dead the minute Arno decided to get you involved in this whole fiasco." She grimaced in pain, then continued, her voice gravelly. "It was over the minute Preston's plane hit those power lines. I've just been living through its death throes for the last year."

"Then why did you sabotage his plane?"

"I didn't sabotage his plane." Now Gwen's voice was weary.

Ann raised a disbelieving eyebrow. "If it wasn't you, who was it?"

Gwen closed her eyes. "Find out yourself, Nancy Drew."

A FEW MINUTES LATER, Ann heard the wail of sirens and could see lights strobing through the trees that lined the dirt road. An ambulance emerged into the field and started down the slope toward them, followed a moment later by a rescue truck. Their headlights illuminated the scene.

One uniformed man emerged with Ellis from the front of the ambulance, another emerged from the back.

"Where's the head injury?" Ann heard the first man ask Ellis.

"In the car," said Ellis. "The other two are over there," he said, waving toward Ann and Gwen.

"Calvin," the man called, "check them out."

"Will do, Don." Calvin knelt beside Ann. "I'm Calvin. I'm a paramedic. What's your name?"

"Ann Kinnear."

"Good to know you, Ann. Looks like you took one to the nose. Let me take a look." He tilted her head back and pressed gently on either side of her nose.

"Ow," said Ann. She waved toward Gwen. "I think her shoulder is dislocated."

"Mario will check her out." Calvin pressed some gauze to Ann's nose, eliciting another aggrieved *ow*.

"Gwen Burridge, dislocated shoulder," called Mario from where he knelt by Gwen.

Calvin lowered a cold pack gently onto Ann's nose. "Can you hold that in place, Ann? We'll get you to the hospital to get that checked out."

"Don't think I need to go to the hospital," she said.

"It's a good idea for them to take a quick x-ray just to make sure it's nothing serious," said Calvin.

Mario eased a sling under Gwen's arm. "We can't do much for the shoulder in the field," he said, "but we'll get you some pain meds."

"Tylenol," said Gwen.

"We can do better than that," he said with a smile.

"Tylenol."

Don, who seemed to be in charge, jogged over from the Lexus, followed more slowly by Ellis. "What have we got?"

"Gwen Burridge, dislocated shoulder. Ann Kinnear, broken nose," said Calvin.

"Okay. We're taking the gentleman in the Lexus in the ambulance. Put in a call for another ambulance for Ms. Burridge. Can you take Ms. Kinnear in the truck?"

"Sure thing, Don."

Don jogged back to the Lexus, where another paramedic was easing a collar around Arno's neck.

Ellis reached the group at the top of the slope, cradling one hand in the other.

"You hurt your hand?" asked Calvin.

"Just my pinky." Ellis held his hand out for inspection.

Calvin examined Ellis's hand. "We'll put a splint on that, and you'll be good to go. You have a way to get home?"

"Yeah, I live right over there," said Ellis, gesturing with his good hand toward the airport. "I can walk back."

"How come he doesn't have to go to the hospital?" asked Ann in an aggrieved honk.

"Because it's a finger, not a face," said Calvin sternly.

Ann turned back to where the paramedics had staged the stretcher next to the Lexus's driver's door. As they maneuvered Arno out of the seat onto the stretcher, the silver-and-gray folder slipped off his lap and onto the ground.

Just then, a breeze whistled across the field, flipping the folder open. One by one, sheets peeled off the top as if being dealt by an invisible dealer at a poker table.

Don's partner, holding the stretcher steady, looked after the papers as they danced toward the rim of the pit.

"Crap. Sorry about that," he said.

"What?" asked Arno groggily.

"It's nothing, sir," said Don, shooting a dirty look at his partner.

Ann glanced back to the group behind her. Mario had helped Gwen to her feet and was trying to turn her toward the ambulance, but Gwen's eyes were fixed on the scene at the rim of the pit, a thin smile on her lips.

Ann turned back. She could just make out a dimly flickering figure, the height and width of a gaunt man, standing at the edge of the pit. The sheets skipped past him, disappearing into the pit, and when the last one had disappeared, the figure did, too.

48

Ann pulled the Forester into the now-familiar Clinton County highway pull-off and climbed out. As she opened the back door to retrieve the backpack that Ellis had assembled for her back in Chester County, she caught a glimpse of herself in the window. In the three days since the events at the quarry, the swelling around her nose had diminished somewhat and the rings around her eyes had faded from angry pinks and purples to morose brownish-reds and yellows. The ER doctor had confirmed she had no other injuries than the broken nose and had taped it up and sent her home.

Arno had fared the worst: he had spent a couple of days in the hospital while they monitored his head injury. He had also re-injured his leg and was looking at more physical therapy and possible surgery.

The ER doctor had popped Gwen's arm back into place and fitted her with a sling. She declined the offer of an overnight stay and Dottie had arrived to give her a ride home.

Ellis was fine, although Ann had heard from Russo that the young man was having some difficulty working on the Stinson with a splint on his finger.

Ann had spent most of the intervening days trying to catch up on her sleep.

She shouldered her backpack and scanned the trees for the first yellow ribbon that marked the path to where Hal Burridge had forced down Bryan Calvert's plane. She spotted it and set off through the woods.

She hadn't told Mike or Scott her true destination. Avoiding their involvement as accessories-after-the-fact still seemed like a good idea, and she didn't want to have to deter one or both of them from accompanying her to the crash site. As far as they knew, she was making a drive up to the Adirondacks to pick up some things from the cabin.

When she reached the campsite, she did her best to duplicate Ellis's setup, then headed for the crash site. It was still hours until the time of the crash, but if Hal could appear wherever and whenever fate decreed for him, perhaps the same would be true for Bryan Calvert. Plus, perhaps the crash site would provide some respite from the continuing heat wave, as it had on her earlier visits. She was disappointed to find there was little discernible difference—the temperature was sweltering no matter the location.

Bryan seemed tied to both the location and the time of his death and, as on her earlier trips, it was near midnight when she finally saw him, although if she hadn't been looking for him, she might have missed him. The light he cast was far dimmer.

"I didn't expect to see you here again," he said.

She had to strain to pick out his words.

"I wasn't sure if you'd still be here," she replied.

"I thought I would have gone by now. I hoped I would." He squinted at her. "What happened to your face?"

"Broken nose."

"Does the broken nose have anything to do with why you're here?" His tone was resigned.

"Yes. It's been ... an interesting time."

She examined him. Here she was with the man who, if Hal Burridge was to be trusted, had clubbed a defenseless man to death. She was miles from anywhere, and hours from help, even if anyone had known where she was. She had expected that she would be afraid if she found him still at the site.

But Bryan Calvert looked so morose, so beaten down, so ... *like death warmed over*, she thought, that she couldn't summon much concern beyond a kind of tired sympathy.

She gestured toward the charred log. "Can we talk?"

After a moment, he nodded and lowered himself onto the log.

"Yeah," she said, marshaling her thoughts. "An interesting time."

She told him what had happened since her last visit: about continuing her search for Hal in Chester County, about contacting Hal and finding the contract, about locating Preston Gilman and learning of his belief that Gwen caused his crash. She told him about the nearly fatal events at the quarry, and about the injuries to Arno, Gwen, and Ellis.

He watched her, expressionless, until she was done.

"Did the cops look into what happened at the quarry?" he asked.

"Arno and Gwen managed to convince them the SUV started rolling on its own and Arno couldn't stop it because of his leg injury. Ellis agreed to play along."

Bryan raised an eyebrow. "And the authorities bought it?"

Ann shrugged. "No one who was there was accusing anyone of any wrongdoing. It's hard to know what crime the police could have investigated."

"Well, I guess that ties things up nicely for everyone."

"Not quite. I still can't figure out why Gwen would want to bring Preston Gilman's plane down." She leaned forward. "I'm asking you to tell me what happened. Arno isn't my client anymore—I'm here to satisfy my own curiosity. Nothing you tell me can do Gwen any harm—the authorities won't pay attention to anything I say. And it obviously can't do you any harm."

He looked at her speculatively. "I don't know that satisfying your curiosity should be any of my concern."

She nodded and turned her gaze to the star-dappled sky for a moment, then turned back to him. "You said you thought you would be gone by now. That you hoped you'd be gone." She paused, but he was silent. "Why do you think you're still here?"

"You're the expert. You tell me."

"Unfinished business?"

"Things feel pretty finished for me," he said, his voice tired.

"You were more present the first time I saw you here," she said, "slightly less so on my second visit. I think that every time you shared a piece of the truth about what happened—the fact that there had been an altercation between you and Hal at the hangar, then the fact that he had actually died in the plane—it ..." She searched for the right words. "... let this life loosen its grip on you a little."

He gave a sad smile. "Letting life loosen its grip sounds like it should be frightening, but it doesn't sound frightening. It sounds like it would be a good thing."

"I think if you still have a secret to tell and have a willing—and discreet—audience to listen to it, it could let you move on."

"To what?"

"I don't know."

He hesitated. "You say Gwen hurt her arm?"

"Dislocated it."

"Can't fly, I assume."

"Not at the moment."

"Does she plan to fly again?"

"I don't know."

"She shouldn't."

"Why not?"

"That's the secret."

PRESTON GILMAN PASSED under the banner strung across the airport drive that read *Welcome to the 19th Annual Avondale Airport Community Day*. He made his way toward the hangars with the rest of the crowd that had congregated for an opportunity to watch an aerobatic performance by Avondale's most famous pilot: Gwen Burridge, the Peregrine Falcon.

A pilot himself, he could still appreciate the military precision of her snap rolls, the seemingly uncontrolled tumble of a Lomcovak and the breath-taking recovery, the elegance of the arc as she brought the Extra past the crowds in a beauty pass, her signature hunting dive. But he had never regained that pure joy he experienced the first time he had watched Gwen Burridge fly—before she became his patient.

Before he had seen her practice over Octoraro Lake the day before.

He made his way to her hangar and rapped on the door, then stepped in without waiting for an answer.

Although the interior of the hangar was dim, he was unsurprised to see that she was wearing her usual extra-dark round sunglasses.

She turned when she heard the door open. "Hello, Preston. I can't talk for long, I have a performance in a few minutes."

He closed the door behind him.

"I was at Octoraro Lake yesterday," he said. "I heard you were going to be practicing for today's show and I went out to watch. I saw what happened."

Her mouth tightened. "Nothing happened."

"Gwen, nobody does an outside half Cuban 8 that low to the ground."

"It was a practice, Preston. That's what practices are for—to test the envelope. I'd never do that in a show."

"Not intentionally."

"What does it matter? It all worked out fine."

"This time."

"Every time." She glanced at her watch. Even from where he stood, Preston could see the glint of the diamonds studding the four compass points of the watch. Jura Bernois, no doubt. "Preston, I have to go."

He stepped between her and the door. "I can't do it anymore, Gwen. I can't keep covering for you. What if there's an accident?"

"If there's an accident, there will only be me to blame, and I'll make sure no one else is endangered."

"Maybe you don't care what would happen to you, but there would be an investigation. They would review my records. You have to stop performing."

She crossed her arms. "Or what?"

"Or ... I'll have to tell them what's what."

"And who's 'them'?"

"The air bosses. The FAA."

She laughed bitterly. "The FAA. 'We're not happy until you're not happy.'"

"It's not a joke, Gwen."

"It's my career, Preston. It's my life. I'm fully aware that it's not a joke."

"What's not a joke?" came a voice behind Preston.

He turned to see Hal Burridge standing next to the hangar door. Preston turned back to Gwen. "Maybe I should tell Hal about my concerns."

"You don't think he already knows?" she snapped. She grabbed her helmet off the workbench. "Think carefully about what you plan to do, Preston. I can make your life as unpleasant as you can make mine."

She stepped around him and strode to the hangar door. Before she opened it, she paused, and although she had her back to him, Preston knew that the Peregrine Falcon was putting on her game face. She straightened to her full, considerable height. She pulled her shoulders back. Then she stepped through the door, and he could hear the crowd's applause before the door closed behind her.

Preston looked up at Hal. "So ... you know?"

"I know."

"What will we do?"

Hal laid a hand on Preston's shoulder. "I'll take care of it," he said. "I'll take care of everything."

"WHAT WAS THE ISSUE?" Ann asked Bryan.

"Gwen has macular degeneration. Stargardt disease. A blind spot in the center of her vision that's getting progressively worse. She hides it pretty well, but if you know what to look for, you can tell. She always wears sunglasses, even when it isn't that bright out, because she's sensitive to light. She has trouble seeing if it's dark—that's why she rides her bike if she has to go out at night, and why I was worried about her when she drove Hal's truck from the hangar to the quarry."

"I did notice her tripping when she was moving around the campsite after it got dark."

"And did you ever notice how, when she talks to you, she won't have her face turned right toward you? It's because her central vision is affected, so she has to use her peripheral vision to see you."

"And she was flying in airshows in this condition?"

"Airshows. The White Lake Air Races." He shrugged. "She had gotten away with it for a while, and as far as I know, no one suspected anything was wrong."

"How do you know all this? Did she tell you?"

"Not until later, after Gilman's plane crash."

"And Gilman knew? How?"

"He was not only her Number One Fan," Bryan said with a grim smile. "He was also her Aviation Medical Examiner. He figured out what the problem was when she went to him for her medical, but he signed her off anyway."

"And she tampered with Preston's plane to try to keep him from revealing her secret—either to kill him or to scare him quiet."

"She didn't tamper with Gilman's plane. Hal did."

Ann sat forward. "Hal?"

"Yeah. He told me what he had done a couple of weeks after Gilman's crash, when he had started down the road of drowning his guilt in whiskey."

"But Preston said he saw Gwen's car near the airport when he took off on his last flight—the flight when his plane crashed."

"She told me she followed Hal out there. She was worried about what he would do. She was trying to keep him from doing something stupid, but she got there too late."

"Hal killed Gilman because he was going to keep Gwen from flying?"

"Yeah." Bryan sighed. "It was a stupid thing for him to do. At most it only bought Gwen the time until her next medical. She wasn't likely to find another doctor who would cover for her. Even she realized there was only so long she could keep it going before she had to ground herself."

They were silent as Ann digested the news. Finally, she said, "It must have been a disappointment for Gwen to watch her husband fall apart."

"She wasn't disappointed," said Bryan, an edge in his voice. "She was devastated. She loved him—even after Preston, even after the two of us got involved. She might have hated what Hal had done, but she still loved him." He was silent for a moment, then gave a sardonic smile. "Hal lived to make Gwen happy and he died because she wasn't happy. He fell apart after Preston's crash—that's when he started drinking. If it wasn't for his drinking, Gwen would have never screwed around with me, and if she hadn't done that, Hal would have never shown up at my hangar that night."

"And you wouldn't have killed him."

After a pause, he said, his eyes on the ground, "That's right. I wouldn't have killed him."

She leaned forward. "Are there any other secrets, Bryan?"

He looked up at her, his eyes bright. "No. No more secrets."

SHE STAYED at the campsite through the following day, reviewing her homework for her next flying lesson, eating fruit and trail mix, taking occasional nips of Slow & Low from the flask she had brought along, but mainly enjoying one glorious nap after the other.

A little before midnight, she went to the crash site and waited there for two hours, but there was no sign of Bryan Calvert.

The following morning, she made her way back to the road, removing the yellow plastic ribbons from the trees as she went.

49

Ann pulled into the parking lot of Avondale for her lesson. It was a perfect day for flying—the heat wave had finally broken, there was not a cloud in the sky, and the light breeze was right down the runway.

When she got to the FBO, she found a harried-looking Dottie.

"Didn't you get my voicemail?" Dottie asked. "Russo's out with a student who's on his first cross-country and he's been looking for Summit Airport for half an hour. Russo radioed in to say he didn't think they'd be back to Avondale any time soon and asked if you could move your lesson to tomorrow."

As if on cue, Russo's voice crackled over the FBO's radio.

"Avondale, the Warrior reporting in. We've completed our second scenic circuit of central New Castle County. If we go any further east, I'm going to be sorry that I didn't bring lifejackets aboard."

Ann laughed. "That poor guy. He'll never find Summit with Russo razzing him like that."

"You guys got to Summit and back okay," said Dottie.

"Yeah, thank God. But I'll bet Russo found something to complain about."

"He said you did a good job with the navigation," said Dottie, busying herself with a stack of paperclipped receipts.

"Really?" said Ann, a little glow of pride igniting in her chest.

"He said you bounced on the landing."

Ann groaned. "He's relentless."

"You're scheduled to solo next week, right?"

Ann's stomach gave a little flip. "Yup."

"Getting it in just under the wire. If we can just get the township board moving, the runway project should start any week now."

"I've gotten so used to landing on the runway as it is now, a smooth one might throw me off my game."

Dottie had just gotten Ann slotted into a lesson the next morning when the FBO phone rang. Dottie picked up the receiver, giving Ann a goodbye wave. "Avondale Airport, Falcon Flight Services."

Ann started back toward the parking lot, then stopped and shaded her eyes with her hand to examine the heavy equipment staged in the field on the far side of the runway.

"Hey, Ann!"

She turned to find Ellis standing beside her, an *Avondale Airport* baseball cap shading his eyes. She had caught glimpses of him when she was at Avondale for her lessons—helping out at the A&P shop, where a mechanic from a nearby airport now worked a few days a week, zipping around in the fuel truck, sweeping out hangars—but hadn't had a chance to talk to him much. "Hey, Ellis. How's the job going?"

"I'm having a blast—I love it here. I even got a real place to live—a studio apartment in Cochranville."

"What about school in the fall?"

"I'm going to take a year off to help with the runway project."

She turned back toward the equipment. "So Arno agreed to invest some money in Avondale after all."

"It's not Arno, it's Gwen. Didn't you hear? Gwen bought out Arno, she owns the airport now."

Ann turned back to Ellis, her eyebrows raised. "No kidding?"

"Nope. She's smoothing things over with the township board about the approvals for the runway project." He dropped his voice. "Sounds like Arno had ruffled some feathers."

Ann laughed. "Imagine that." After a beat, she continued. "Ellis, I feel like I owe you some information—"

Ellis held up his hand. "I don't want to know."

She paused, surprised. "You don't?"

"I know you and Gwen didn't see eye to eye, but now I'm working for her and I don't want to hear anything against her."

"I wasn't going to say anything against her. In fact, whatever impressions you got about what was going on based on our trips to Clinton County and to Preston Gilman's crash site, it's not what I thought. Gwen's in the clear in terms of the plane crashes."

Ellis's shoulders relaxed. "I've got to say I'm glad to hear that. I like working here. I like working for her ... but I like it even better knowing that she hasn't been running around sabotaging planes."

"That's for sure." She looked back toward the line of repaving equipment. "I'll have to congratulate her."

"She's usually in her office in the FBO these days, but she wasn't there when I stopped in a little while ago." His phone buzzed and he glanced at it. "Got to go. Nice seeing you, Ann." He turned to go, then turned back. "Hey, I hear you're soloing soon."

"Jeez, are there no secrets around here?"

"Be sure to wear a shirt with a tail!" he called gaily, and with that cryptic comment, he headed back toward the FBO.

WHEN ANN PULLED out of the Avondale parking lot, rather than heading toward West Chester, she turned instead onto the road that led to the back gate of the quarry. When she got there, the gate was closed but the padlock on the chain was unlocked. Ann slid the gate open and drove through.

She thought of the last time she had been there and shivered. She had gotten the okay from Russo to overfly the quarry a few times and wasn't surprised to see no evidence of Hal Burridge from the air. He had told her that he couldn't leave the quarry, and she had warned both Ellis and Arno not to make a return trip there, but the idea of Hal haunting the quarry—especially after what he had done with Arno's SUV—had been keeping her up at night. Would Hal pose a danger to anyone else—a quarry supervisor walking the perimeter of the property on a security check? Someone who got a key to the gate so they could let their dogs off-leash for a run? Randy teenagers looking for a lover's lane? She knew from experience that people were rarely more dangerous when they were dead than they had been when alive, but they were rarely less dangerous.

She had been postponing her return to the quarry, although she knew it was a thread she had to tie up. If Gwen was at the quarry, this was the best time for Ann to tie up that loose thread —when there was someone else there who appeared to still have some power over Hal.

Gwen's Corvette was parked next to the benches, although Gwen herself was not in evidence.

Ann scanned the field. There had been rain the night before and the grass, previously baked to a crackling brown, was already recovering some of its green. Blue chicory flowers and delicate Queen Anne's lace prettily dotted the field's perimeter.

The sun was bright, and it would be easy to mistake the flicker of a spirit for sunlight bouncing off blades of grass.

She thought about waiting for Gwen in the Forester, and then flashed back to the crunch of the Lexus's tires on the gravel of the parking area as it began to roll toward the pit. She hopped out of the vehicle and, with another scan of the field, settled herself on the smaller bench.

Half an hour later, Gwen emerged from the path that led to the clearing where Ann had seen the stone-created letters and heart. Her arm was in a sling. She pulled up at the sight of Ann, then continued on to the benches and sat down on the larger one.

"That's quite a pair of shiners you've got there," she said.

"I look a little less like a Mardi Gras mask than I did a few days ago. How's your arm?"

Gwen shrugged her uninjured shoulder. "It will heal."

Ann nodded toward the woods. "You visited the clearing?"

"Yes."

"Did you see the letters?"

"I did."

"It's romantic that he drew the same letters in stone that you drew in skywriting at your wedding. I saw the video," she added.

Gwen raised an eyebrow. "What do you mean?"

"It says *H + G*."

Gwen stared back at her, expressionless.

"The letters you spelled out at your wedding." Ann paused. "What do *you* mean?"

"It doesn't say *H + G*. It says *Goodbye*."

Ann felt a weight fall from her shoulders. "Ah."

After a pause, Gwen said, "That means he's not coming back, doesn't it?"

Ann drew a deep breath. "Yes, I think that's what it means.

Maybe he finally saw that he was doing you more harm than good."

Gwen turned her gaze toward the quarry pit. "He only ever wanted what was best for me. He was just confused about what that was."

"Bryan's gone from the crash site as well," said Ann.

Gwen snapped her eyes back to Ann. "You went back *again*?"

"Yes. I thought there was still something he wasn't telling me. I was right. I know about your eye condition."

Gwen examined Ann, her expression unchanged.

"And I know that's why Hal killed Preston," Ann continued. "To keep the secret. Is that what sent Hal into a—"

"A tailspin?" Gwen laughed mirthlessly. "You're more right than you know." The hand of her unslung arm gripped her leg. "He started downhill before Preston's crash. I was practicing out by Octoraro Lake. Bryan was there to video and Hal was keeping him company. I lost sight of the ground. I got lower than I intended. A *lot* lower." She drew in a deep breath. "Hal wanted to know what had happened, and I told him about the Stargardt's and about the fact that Preston was covering for me. Then Preston had second thoughts, and Hal ... took care of it."

"What happened to the video of the maneuver?"

"I found the memory card in Hal's office at home. He had hidden it with an ophthalmology magazine he got to read up on Stargardt disease—he didn't want to do any research online. I destroyed them both." She turned to Ann. "And if you tell anyone that, I'll deny it."

"I'm sure you would," said Ann, "but as I'm sure you've decided already, I don't have any reason to tell anyone. Hal's dead. Bryan's dead. I'm guessing Arno's happy to leave everything to do with the airport behind. What good would it do? I'll keep your secret ... as long as you stop flying."

"I couldn't fly aerobatics or races with my shoulder like this."

"But your shoulder will get better. You might be tempted to get back in the game, be tempted to change your plans ..."

Gwen smiled grimly. "I never change my plans." Then her smile turned amused. "Speaking of changing plans, I understand from Corey that you've agreed to do the documentary."

"Yeah. I decided I like the idea of being able to control my own message. It will be a good resource to have—" She looked pointedly at Gwen. "—to combat the disbelievers."

Gwen nodded. "Yes." After a pause, she continued. "And maybe even to win them over."

Ann smiled, surprised. "Maybe." She looked out across the flower-flecked field. "Once I said I was willing, Garrick Masser signed on." She laughed. "Corey said he was going to call it *The Vulture and the Owl*, but Garrick threatened to withdraw. I suspect that this entire project is going to be punctuated by episodes of Garrick threatening to withdraw." She looked over at Gwen. "Corey talked about doing a documentary on the Peregrine Falcon ..."

"I turned him down. I don't want to give anyone an excuse to go digging into my past, or Hal's."

They sat in silence for a few moments, then Ann roused herself. "By the way, I heard you own Avondale now. Congratulations."

"Yes. Arno bought out my half of Scanridge, I bought out his half of Avondale. He was happy to get the airport off his portfolio. Although," she said, more cheerfully, "he got a fraction of what he would have if the deal with Turriff Brothers had gone through."

"And you got enough from the deal to repave the runway as well."

"Well, no. I had to raise additional funds to do that."

"Your sponsors?"

"No. They dropped me. Having an airport manager as a

spokesperson wasn't really the image they wanted to project." Her hand drifted to her bare wrist.

"Did you sell your watch?"

Gwen laughed ruefully. "I did, but that will hardly cover the bill. I'm going to raise the money by selling the Extra and the Lancair."

Ann raised her eyebrows. "No kidding."

"I would never kid about my planes." Gwen turned toward the grassy slope leading to the pit. "I can raise a million dollars from the planes. Plus, I won't have to worry about shelling out for their care and feeding."

"So no more trips to White Lake."

"No."

"Under other circumstances," said Ann, "I would have liked to have seen you race."

"I would have liked that, too."

They were both silent for a moment, then Gwen nodded, as if to herself. "I'll announce my retirement once the sling is off. Nobody wants to see the Peregrine Falcon with a clipped wing."

"Are you going to be happy with running the airport?"

Gwen was silent for a moment, and Ann thought she wasn't going to answer. Then she spoke.

"I paid for flying lessons by working the desk at the Avondale FBO, and I soloed on my seventeenth birthday in an Avondale flight school plane. My instructor was a man with the look of a southern gentleman and a mouth like a sailor. When I landed, he cut the tail off the shirt I had worn for the occasion and wrote my name and the date on it in black marker. I still carry that piece of cloth in my flight bag." She looked at Ann. "Russo will be doing that for you soon."

Ann's stomach flipped. "Sometimes I feel like I'm ready, but sometimes I feel like I'll never be ready."

"He won't send you up by yourself until you are."

"Spoken like the true caretaker of Avondale Airport. Not quite as glamorous as the airshow circuit."

Gwen turned to Ann, the trademark Peregrine Falcon smile on her face. "Speak for yourself. I'm going to make Avondale Airport the envy of every general aviation airport in the country."

Ann smiled back. "I don't doubt it."

THE END

NEXT IN THE ANN KINNEAR SUSPENSE SERIES ...

Book 4: A Furnace for Your Foe

They say that dead men tell no tales. But when good intentions are twisted to evil ends, and the perpetrators don't care who gets burned in the process, the truth must come out, and it will take Ann Kinnear's particular skill to uncover it.

Can Ann learn why arson experts are coming to grief on the trails of Mount Desert Island before becoming a victim herself?

Spirit senser Ann Kinnear is back on Mount Desert Island, Maine, to take part in a documentary with her colleague and competitor, Garrick Masser. The topic? The recent death of Leo Dorn, head of the Stata Mater research lab, who fell from a cliff-side trail on his wife's estate.

Ann has barely unpacked before Dorn's hiking partner and fellow researcher Shelby Kim disappears, and now Ann wonders if Leo's fall really was an accident. But when Ann finally locates Shelby, the young woman isn't talking.

Then a warehouse on the Manset waterfront burns to the ground and Ann knows she's getting close to the truth.

Will Ann overcome hell and high water to plumb the depths

of Mount Desert Island's secrets, or will this be her fall from grace?

Find out in Book 4 of the Ann Kinnear Suspense Novels, *A Furnace for Your Foe*!

> Heat not a furnace for your foe so hot
>> That it do singe yourself.
>> — William Shakespeare, "Henry VIII"

Join Matty Dalrymple's occasional email newsletter (mattydalrymple.com > About & Contact) and receive an Ann Kinnear Suspense Short and notifications of book launches and author events!

ALSO BY MATTY DALRYMPLE

The Lizzy Ballard Thrillers

Rock Paper Scissors (Book 1)

Snakes and Ladders (Book 2)

The Iron Ring (Book 3)

The Lizzy Ballard Thrillers Ebook Box Set

The Ann Kinnear Suspense Novels

The Sense of Death (Book 1)

The Sense of Reckoning (Book 2)

The Falcon and the Owl (Book 3)

A Furnace for Your Foe (Book 4)

The Ann Kinnear Suspense Novels Ebook Box Set - Books 1-3

The Ann Kinnear Suspense Shorts

All Deaths Endure

Close These Eyes

May Violets Spring

Sea of Troubles

Write in Water

Non-Fiction

Taking the Short Tack: Creating Income and Connecting with Readers Using Short Fiction (with Mark Leslie Lefebvre)

The Indy Author's Guide to Podcasting for Authors: Creating Connections, Community, and Income

ABOUT THE AUTHOR

Matty Dalrymple is the author of the Ann Kinnear Suspense Novels *The Sense of Death*, *The Sense of Reckoning*, *The Falcon and the Owl* and *A Furnace for Your Foe*; the Ann Kinnear Suspense Shorts, including *Close These Eyes* and *Sea of Troubles*; and the Lizzy Ballard Thrillers *Rock Paper Scissors, Snakes and Ladders*, and *The Iron Ring*. Matty and her husband, Wade Walton, live in Chester County, Pennsylvania, and enjoy vacationing on Mt. Desert Island, Maine, and in Sedona, Arizona, locations that serve as settings for Matty's stories.

Matty is a member of Mystery Writers of America, Sisters in Crime, and the Brandywine Valley Writers Group.

Go to www.mattydalrymple.com > About & Contact for more information and to sign up for Matty's occasional email newsletter.

facebook.com/matty.dalrymple

twitter.com/mattydalrymple

instagram.com/matty.dalrymple

ACKNOWLEDGMENTS

Many people helped me bring this book to fruition. My deep thanks to ...

Vicky Benzing and Matt Chapman, for generously sharing their experiences as air race and aerobatic pilots.

Tim LeBaron and Craig Hatch, for offering insight into plane crash investigations.

Bill Lokes, for his unflagging patience in answering my many questions about the potential of A&P equipment to be used as a weapon.

Jonathan Martin, Aviation Director of New Garden Airport in Toughkenamon, PA, for offering insight on the management of a general aviation airport.

Chris Grall and Gayle Weber, for providing input on all things camping.

Sergeant Rodger Ollis of the Coatesville Police Department and Ken Fritz, FF/EMT-P, for advising me on police and first responder procedures (as they have done for many of my previous books).

Jane Kelly and Lisa Regan, for plot brainstorming and emotional support brunches.

And, as always, special thanks to my favorite general aviation pilot, Wade Walton—who just happens to fly the same plane as Walt Federman—for offering both his expertise and his unflagging support.

Any deviations from fact—intentional or unintentional—are solely the responsibility of the author.

Cover design: Lance Buckley

ISBN-13: 978-1-7344799-2-8 (Paperback edition)

ISBN-13: 978-1-7344799-3-5 (Large print edition)

Made in the USA
Monee, IL
15 July 2023

39353701R00193